BLIND TRUST

BLIND TRUST

A NOVEL

BARBARA BOXER

with Mary-Rose Hayes

CHRONICLE BOOKS
SAN FRANCISCO

This is a work of fiction. Names, places, characters, and incidents are products
of the author's imagination or are used fictionally. Any resemblance to actual people,
places, or events is entirely coincidental.

Library of Congress Cataloging-in-Publication Data available.

ISBN: 978-0-8118-6427-5

Manufactured in Canada.

Designed by Suzanne LaGasa
Typeset by DC Type and Janis Reed
This book was typset in Perpetua and Trade Gothic

10 9 8 7 6 5 4 3 2 1

Chronicle Books LLC
680 Second Street
San Francisco, CA 94107

www.chroniclebooks.com

Dedicated to my grandchildren:

Zachary
Zain
Sawyer
Reyna Sofia

CHAPTER ONE

January 1

TUESDAY

Ellen Fischer Lind lay on her right side gazing sleepily out the window into a dark dawn.

Ben stood beside the door in his navy bathrobe, hand on the thermostat. "It's freezing in here."

Ellen rolled over into the warm indentation left by his body. "It's healthy to sleep in a cool room."

"Spoken like a true Californian!" Ben was a big man, his black hair frosted with gray, eyebrows a bristling bar over dark eyes that could glow with warmth or stab hard and sharp as steel. Right now he was smiling as he crossed the room, pulled her into a sitting position, took her head between both hands, and planted an enthusiastic kiss on her lips. "Happy New Year's—and it'll be a good one. I promise you that!"

"Knock on wood! It's only seven hours old."

"Superstitious baloney, but at least I'll touch wood for you. Okay—I'll even stroke it!" Ben trailed his index finger down the carved headboard of the bed, then curved his hand gently into the hollow of her shoulder. "Where's your robe?"

Ellen looked vaguely about the room. "Bathroom? Laundry?"

"Take this." Ben grabbed the closest garment at hand, his favorite old sport jacket, which he'd flung over the back of his chair last night; it was sand-colored, worn soft over the years and threadbare at the elbows. Though admittedly tight on him these days, it was engulfing on Ellen. He folded it around her waist, rolled the sleeves above her wrists, then scooped her tangle of reddish hair inside the turned-up collar. "There." He leaned back and studied her critically. "You look like a mouse in a cave."

"I've never been called a mouse before!" With a wry smile, recalling her political opponents and their sycophantic media outlets, she added, "A rat, maybe."

"A rat, hell! What do they know? More like a fox in its hole! Excuse me—a vixen. A cunning little vixen!"

"Much better. I like that! Plus, we saw *Cunning Little Vixen*—my first opera—our second date. Loved it."

Ben prompted, "And the company? Did that measure up?"

"They were terrific, too."

"I wasn't talking about the chorus at the Metropolitan. I was talking about your seat partner."

"You mean the woman with the big hair and the important pearls?"

"No, my love, the person on your other side."

"Oh, him!" The corners of her mouth tucked into an impish smile. "Sure, I remember him. He was okay."

"Just okay?"

"You want me to spell it out for you—again?"

"Always!" He grinned and patted her on her baggy tweed shoulder. "Stay warm, now—I'll be back."

Ellen wrapped her arms around her drawn-up knees as she contentedly watched her husband's retreating back view. Tomorrow she would return to her life as U.S. Senator Ellen Fischer, California Democrat, *earnest conscience of the nation,* as Ben was inclined to tease, but for right now she was content to be Mrs. Benjamin Lind, not yet four years married.

She listened to the sounds of Ben's progress through the apartment: the soft slap of his leather slippers on the hardwood floor, the silences as he crossed each Persian rug with its warm crimson-and-rust medallions, then faintly, in the kitchen, the creak of cabinet hinges, the clink of mugs, and the faint rush of water as he filled the coffeepot.

Ellen enjoyed her kitchen with its cool, pale green walls, stainless-steel appliances, and counters of dark green granite, ordered in the United States, quarried in Brazil, cut in Carrara, Italy, and shipped back to Washington, D.C., to this light-filled apartment Ben had bought overlooking Pennsylvania Avenue.

At first, moving in, she'd felt uncomfortable here.

The apartment wasn't right for her, it didn't fit. It seemed like a palace, and Ellen didn't live in palaces.

With Joshua Fischer, whom she still mourned in her heart, whose young, intense face still glowed across her private office in the Senate Hart Building, her lifestyle had been far more modest.

Josh had had little interest in money or the things it could buy.

His vision had been one of *living* one's talk, of raising up the poor and the beleaguered middle class, not rising high above them. Ellen and Josh had lived in Oakland in an old brown-shingled house strewn with books and papers, with a shaggy yard out front where the aged oak tree would have provided a fine place to hang a swing.

When Josh died in a car crash and Ellen, against all odds, won the hotly contested Senate seat he had been seeking, she found herself haunted by what was lost and what could never be. She had moved across the city to a convenient downtown condo in Jack London Square, where she never really unpacked, and in D.C., for years she rented a basement apartment from a colleague.

But then, suddenly, there was Ben.

She never thought she'd fall in love again, but she did.

She never thought she would marry again—it seemed a betrayal of Josh—but she had.

She never thought she'd be rich, but she was. Ben Lind, her new husband, from a Southwestern family of style and substance, had exposed her to a whole new level of sophistication, and Ellen now mingled with leaders of society and the arts as well as politics.

She no longer shopped for vintage designer clothes in thrift shops, but in high-end boutiques. She gave smart dinner parties.

At times she felt uncomfortable living, if not on the first tier of luxury, then on what must certainly be the next level down—and enjoying it.

But what was she supposed to do? Not marry Ben because he was rich? Insist that he give away his money and join her in a life-style below that to which he was accustomed, just on principle? And, to be realistic, she was not only a lot older, but her life had drastically changed from the seventies when she and Josh were first married.

These were also less innocent times, and more nerve-racking. Physical and mental stress came with the job descriptions of Senator—and of Congressman, as Ben had been for twelve years until just yesterday. They were under constant, sometimes hostile, scrutiny, and they both needed the security of drivers, doormen, and the surveillance cameras in the lobby of their building.

Aware that serenity should be generated from within, Ellen had once considered taking yoga classes. She had friends who extolled the merits, both mental and physical, of meditation, or tai chi—but that took discipline and time.

Ellen had never been noted for her patience, and as for time, forget it.

Instead, to counter the tensions of her daily life, she found it far more effective to sink into a fragrant tub in her marble bath-room and listen to Bach on the stereo, and sometimes Ben would massage her neck and shoulders while she soaked.

★ ★ ★

Now Ben was opening the front door onto the small hallway with its clanging, old-fashioned, brass-caged elevator, and the two other front doors, painted glossy black like their own: Admiral and Mrs. Bernard Kramm to the left, Signor Giuseppe Fratelli of the Italian embassy to the right.

The Kramms got the *Washington Post* and *USA Today*.

Signor Fratelli got the *Wall Street Journal* and *Corriere della Sera*—though his doorway would be empty this morning since he was home in Rome for the holidays.

Ellen and Ben got the *Post*, the *New York Times*, the *Wall Street Journal,* and the right-wing *D.C. Times* to keep up with what Ellen termed "the opposition"—which brought her to the final and most important of her life changes. She would never have believed in a million years she'd *marry* the opposition, and not only a Republican but an Arizona Congressman.

Now, however, Ben was a civilian.

He'd cleared every trace of his twelve-year tenure from his office, and yesterday had officially turned over the office keys to his successor, Phelps Lavalle.

Both men would have been civil, making all the right moves, smiling and wishing each other good luck, but beneath his urbane smile Ellen knew Ben would have been seething. He neither liked Phelps Lavalle nor approved of the far right and, to Ben's mind, the dangerous direction in which Lavalle was helping to take the party for which Ben had worked so hard and so long.

Ellen still thought that Ben could have defeated Lavalle, and hated that Ben relinquished his seat without a fight even before the primary. Ben was a natural-born fighter. He had a fighter's body—those big shoulders, that bear-like stance. He might be cultured and highly intelligent but he was also tough. Ben would never have passed up a fight on his own account, but he had done it because of her, even over her strong objections and, finally, her outright pleading. "Maybe I could win the battle," Ben had said, "but not the war."

"Meaning?"

"My Congressional seat is the battle, but your Senate seat is the war. You're the one they're really after, and it's not worth it to me to have them drag us both down."

He'd protected her then, as he protected her still. Although he would no longer be bound by House ethics rules when applied to his financial affairs, Ben was keeping his investments in a blind trust to avoid any possible accusations of conflict of interest for her. "We can't run any risks," he'd said.

Ellen knew Ben would sorely miss his old life, but it wasn't all bad.

When one door closed, another invariably opened. Ben was now on the verge of accepting a partnership with the eminent Washington law firm of Hirsch & Kellerman, and expected to be once again practicing corporate law, in which he excelled.

The day after tomorrow, in fact, on January 3, Ben's sixtieth birthday, Joel and Anita Hirsch were coming to dinner. The two couples had much in common. Ben and Joel were both Jewish and Republican, while Ellen and Anita, of mixed Jewish and Catholic heritage, were diehard Democrats.

Ellen liked them both: Joel, big, bald, and jovial; Anita, small, plump, and sparkly. They were the perfect dinner companions. It would be a stimulating evening of good conversation, good food, and congratulations to Ben on achieving the big 6-0, culminating in a toast to his new career with Hirsch & Kellerman—soon to be Hirsch, Kellerman & Lind.

Ellen looked forward to it.

★ ★ ★

Ben would be stooping for the papers now, and Ellen heard, in her mind, his reflexive grunt as his lower back twinged, his snort— more of a *hunh!*—as he reacted to the headlines with amusement or disgust.

This morning, however, he was unnaturally silent, which Ellen ascribed to a holiday deficiency of scandal or horror.

She heard the soft *whoosh* as the heavy refrigerator door opened and closed again, and knew Ben would now be leaning over the counter, the *Washington Post* spread out in front of him. He was a fast reader—with his trained eye and keen lawyer's brain, he could extract and digest the meat from each column in record time before meticulously refolding the papers and presenting them to her. He was always considerate that way. Lazy in bed as she waited for her coffee, wrapped in Ben's jacket, which still comfortably harbored the warm personal essence of his body, Ellen thought with pleasure of the day ahead.

After the coffee and newspapers they'd enjoy a leisurely breakfast—toasted bagels and fresh-squeezed OJ in the kitchen—then a chat with family and friends on the phone. Perhaps they'd brave the cold for a short, brisk walk. After the Rose Bowl on TV they'd enjoy a cocktail in front of the fire, then dinner—something easy, perhaps grilled steak and a tossed green salad.

It would be their last opportunity to spend time alone together for quite a while.

Ben would be working long hours in his new position.

Ellen's workload would be even tougher.

With a new Senate term about to begin, and a Democratic majority in both houses, she would not only be taking over as Chair of the Energy and Environment Committee, but also of the Subcommittee on Constitutional Rights and Homeland Security.

Denis Rogan, the previous Secretary of Homeland Security, had resigned unexpectedly in September, officially citing health issues, which Ellen understood as the code words for heart problems or cancer.

The first order of business for her subcommittee would be the nomination hearings, starting Monday, for Rogan's replacement, ex–California Senator Carl Satcher, and, as usual, Ellen's stomach clenched at the thought of going head-to-head with Satcher, her old adversary.

They had been enemies from the day she defeated him, the incumbent, to win her first Senate term.

She would never forget that sudden encounter on the icy steps of the Capitol, eight years ago almost to the day.

Had he been able to get away with it, Ellen sensed he would have gleefully smashed her to the ground and kicked her, for good measure, with the metal-tipped cowboy boots he habitually wore. Instead, towering over her in his black overcoat, teeth bared in what might, from a distance, have seemed a congratulatory smile, he'd grated, "You know, you only got elected because that son of a bitch husband of yours died at just the right time!"

Nothing had changed since then.

Carl Satcher was still ruthlessly ambitious, self-seeking, and treacherous, he still hated her—and now the President, a Republican, had nominated him to be Secretary of Homeland Security, one of the most powerful jobs in the country.

She couldn't bear to think of it.

Ellen leaned back against the pillows—where was Ben? Surely the coffee was ready by now—her hands linked behind her head as she focused on the weeks ahead.

Under her gavel, the hearings would go far beyond Carl Satcher's nomination—they'd include his close political ally the Vice President, who had become the administration's point person on national security, or as some called it, "the fear detail."

Vice President Craig Fulton was an increasingly controversial man who, in her view, had pushed his authority to extremes, had trampled on individual liberties and jeopardized the Bill of Rights. His speeches, the executive orders he crafted, and the policies he advocated authorized wiretapping, surveillance, and, in certain circumstances, torture, although he called it "enhanced interrogation." Anyone who disagreed, he claimed, was not merely unpatriotic but a supporter of terrorism and an enemy of the people.

The Vice President and his policies had begun to come under fire by members of the liberal press who were comparing his tactics with the Communist panic of the fifties and the McCarthy-era witch hunts. The administration's policies had been attacked in both the Senate and the House, with Ellen and Ben part of the vocal objectors. However, with the Democrats in the minority at that time, all attempts to contain the Vice President had faltered and died.

Now, however, with this new Congress, the gavels and the votes would be changing sides.

With the support of party leaders, Ellen planned to expand the scope of the hearings to include not only Carl Satcher's confirmation but a close examination of the goals, purposes, and policies of Homeland Security—and of Craig Fulton himself, whose hand was firmly behind the wheel at Homeland.

These were adversarial times.

"Witch hunt" and "fishing expedition," the conservative media cried, while the liberal media pointed to the constitutionally mandated "advise and consent" of the Senate on nominations, and the "checks and balances" the Congress was meant to exert on the executive branch.

Some on the left saw the hearings as a precursor to Fulton's impeachment.

Others saw Vice President Fulton, with just two more years to serve in his second term, as moving inevitably toward his party's nomination for President. No other potential candidate had Fulton's experience, recognition, or vision, they believed. "The Democrats are just playing politics," Fulton had charged in response to the subcommittee's expanded hearing agenda. "I don't play politics with our country's security, and neither does Carl Satcher, with whom I look forward to working after he is confirmed as Secretary of the Department of Homeland Security."

But he's not Secretary yet, Ellen thought. He has to deal with me first! She knew it would be ugly, and that Satcher would put up a fierce struggle, but that was why she was a Senator—to fight for what she believed in.

Which meant doing her utmost to make sure Satcher was not confirmed. It wasn't about her old battle with him; that was settled. It was about giving such a crucial job—running the Department of Homeland Security—to a political hack!

★ ★ ★

"Hey!" Ellen cried as Ben entered the room and placed the tray in the middle of the bed. "Coffee smells good!"

"That's about all that does." Ben's voice was tight, his expression uncharacteristically grim.

She looked up at once, wary. "What is it? What's wrong?"

"Take a look." Ben dropped the papers in her lap, the *D.C. Times* on top. "It's not in the others yet, but it will be by tomorrow."

"HYPOCRITICAL" SENATOR MAKES FORTUNE ON ENERGY STOCKS!
ADVANCES CAREER BY ATTACKING ENERGY COMPANIES

The headlines were accompanied by the most unflattering picture of herself Ellen had yet seen. In the front-page photo she scowled over her reading glasses, her mouth a hard line, every wrinkle showing in fulsome detail.

She looked like a bully. She looked mean. She looked old.

"What *is* this all about?" Ellen demanded. "Is the story as bad as the picture?"

She skimmed the paragraphs beneath. It was.

> While Senator Fischer was attacking the oil and energy companies, a source close to the principals of her family trust reveals, she was reaping the profits from the same companies she vilified . . . may also have been driving investment to "alternative energy" companies that were part of the portfolio. . . . This gross misconduct goes beyond blatant hypocrisy. It raises questions as to what extent she knowingly misrepresented her position and misled the American people, and whether Senator Fischer engaged in stock manipulation, insider trading, and other violations of securities laws and rules of the Senate. It calls into question her ability to serve in the Senate and certainly raises doubts about her ability to sit in judgment of others at confirmation hearings. . . . This squalid misconduct is simply unacceptable.

Ellen stared at Ben in dismay. "But nobody knows what's in your blind trust except our trustee, who would *never* breathe a word of it, even at gunpoint. You don't know, I don't know, and we never knew."

"There were no energy stocks in my portfolio when the trust was first created," Ben said, "but obviously buys were made later, and now somebody has leaked the details. Look at that, 'a source close to the principals.'"

"How many people have access to your portfolio?" she asked.

"Who knows for sure? But not many."

"Then I hope the leak isn't too hard to trace. My God," Ellen sighed, "why did there have to be energy stocks?"

"We'll have to do some quick damage control," Ben said. "Until we determine who leaked the information and why, we won't know the extent of the damage or what else may be compromised." He sat down heavily on the bed, the front page of the *D.C. Times* balled in his fist.

Ellen waited to hear what ideas might be forthcoming. Ben was known, after all, for his acute insights and problem-solving, but for the first time since she had known him, he seemed at a total loss.

A moment of heavy silence fell between them. Ellen thought how, just a few minutes ago, life had seemed so good; how quickly things could change. But that *was* life: change and challenge.

She laid her hand gently over his. "Don't worry. We may have taken a hit, but we can roll with the punches, right?" She thrust back the bedclothes and swung her feet resolutely to the floor. "We'll work through this. We'll find a way. *Trust me.*"

CHAPTER TWO

Vice President Craig Fulton's day began well.

Brianna had arrived home safely at 2:30 A.M.

Trailed, to her intense annoyance, by a unit of the Secret Service, the Vice President's daughter had attended a New Year's Eve party in a section of town that made her father blanch with dismay, though apparently, perhaps by virtue of its very squalor, it seemed to have become a hot neighborhood for the young and hip. Fulton knew there would be unwholesome people at the party, not to mention liquor and drugs; he'd imagined the tabloid headlines with dread—VEEP'S DAUGHTER IN DRUG BUST—and a picture of a disheveled Brianna staring sullenly through the rear window of a police car.

However, he'd woken from a fitful sleep to hear her soft footsteps on the stairs and the closing of her bedroom door.

Thank God!

He'd checked on her half an hour later, unable to help himself, and there she was, fast asleep, face wiped clean of the dark, sticky makeup she now favored, no longer the angry, hardened teen she'd become of late but once again his gentle, beloved little daughter, and he'd smiled as he softly closed her door.

Returning to bed, either in consolation for his infinite fatherly patience or as a reward for vigilance, Fulton had sunk at once into a deep sleep and his favorite dream, where, a child again, he was taking part in the annual family visit to Koczanski Ford in order to trade in last year's model, because in those days even a man such as his father, just an average Joe, accepted the idea of a new car each year as an undisputed right.

Those magnificent monsters of the fifties and early sixties still symbolized for Fulton the power, the might, and the buoyant *cockiness* of America, and when he woke again at six A.M., an hour later than usual, and crept to the bathroom so as not to disturb Grace, he was still seeing in his mind's eye those majestic Fords, Chevys, and Chryslers with their bright, tail-finned bodies of steel and chrome and their fine American engineering under the hood. His father had presented him with a T-Bird, gift-wrapped with a huge red bow on the roof, when, the first member of the Fulton family to go to college, he'd left for Penn State. It had been midnight blue with gold upholstery.

God, how he loved those cars!

He thought, Nowhere but in America!

★ ★ ★

The Vice President scraped the last of the foam from his firm jawline—for convenience when traveling, he packed an electric razor, but far preferred the sweep of a blade and the sensation afterward of scoured cleanliness—and gazed appraisingly at his reflection. A good-looking face, everyone agreed, with that chiseled jaw and nose, firm lips, the ice-blue eyes under well-defined dark brows. Although fifty-two years old, with his full head of thick sandy hair, he was regularly described in the press as boyish looking.

Fulton leaned forward, fingers braced on the vanity top, and stretched his lips into a smile, the better to inspect his perfectly aligned, whitened teeth.

Though he despised this national preoccupation with personal perfection and beauty, television cameras were merciless and television ruled the world.

Television would help get him elected President—provided he stayed the course, which he must because the country needed him.

This beleaguered but still *wonderful* country!

Where else but in the United States of America could he, Craig Fulton, son of a small-time building contractor, grandson of a humble bricklayer immigrant from Leeds, England, aspire to the highest post in the land?

He felt almost humble as he counted his blessings: Good health and good looks. A fine education. Enough money.

A clever, beautiful wife from an old New England family with property on Boston's swank North Shore, and an even cleverer daughter, a political science major at the University of California, Berkeley—though Brianna, at this time, was less of a blessing than a perpetual thorn in the flesh.

His sweet, sunny, golden-haired daughter now dyed her hair tarry black with, on occasion, an alarming strand of magenta flopping over her face. She had multiple piercings in each earlobe and habitually dressed in funereal black. It was only by the most forceful execution of his will that she wore something respectable for official family appearances and the annual Christmas card.

"It's just a phase," Grace had assured him. "It could be worse. Don't worry."

Fulton had tried to give Brianna a car when she went to Berkeley but she'd emphatically refused his gift—*A car? For God's sake, Dad, they poison the environment!*—and for transportation insisted on an ancient and rickety bicycle.

But now was not the time to worry about Brianna—for the moment, she was safe at home in her own bed.

Think positive, Fulton ordered himself, dashing astringent lotion onto his face, and from counting his blessings, he turned to a summary of his personal achievements, which were many:

Development of his father's small business into a thriving corporation.

Businessman of the Year; a prominent position in local government; four terms in Congress, adopting for his campaign colors—an appreciated human tidbit—the midnight blue and gold of his college T-Bird.

Finally, six successful, though increasingly controversial, years as Vice President.

Fulton allowed himself, once again, to relive the triumphs of those heady earlier times when, through the implementation of his own policies—the extensive placement and vigilant monitoring of surveillance cameras in highly populated and vulnerable locations, the rigorous training of first responders, the firm and unwavering government support for action—the country had been saved from disaster not once, not twice, but over and over again.

What did it matter, Fulton demanded of himself, if tele-communications companies tagged the phones of those with potentially suspicious-sounding names, occupations, or political agendas if, by so doing, just one innocent person was saved from a gruesome and bloody death?

With deep satisfaction Fulton recalled the thwarted Times Square subway suicide bomber; the foiled Big Game bombings, with explosive devices found beneath the sky boxes of college football stadiums across the country; the exposed truck bomb plot at Midway Airport in Chicago—all of them halted hours, or even moments, from execution. Countless other disasters had also been averted earlier in their planning, because he, Craig Fulton, Vice President, Founder and Executive Director of the Office for Strategic Operations (OSO)—the new and all-powerful agency that cut away the bullshit—*had gotten the job done!*

Oh yes, those had been good years, when he'd been courted and feted, and appeared on all the news broadcasts to lay out his plans for the future protection of America—and the country had listened.

Fulton had been a hero then; had he been running for President two years ago, instead of continuing in his support position as Veep, he might have won. Perhaps even by a landslide, because once his strong hand had grasped the helm of the nation's defenses, there'd been no successful terror incident on American soil.

Not one . . .

★ ★ ★

The Vice President dressed in thermal underwear topped by navy sweatpants and matching warm-up jacket, and a woolen cap with pull-down earflaps. He peered into the bedroom, where Grace's curled body formed an inert lump under the white duvet, then padded quietly down the stairs to the kitchen, where he drank half a glass of Gatorade, switched on the coffeemaker to be ready for his return, and left by the side door.

It was still pitch dark, bitterly cold, and Fulton gasped as the air seared his lungs. He pulled the cap lower on his head and trotted over the grass to the roadside, his feet crunching in the frost rime, to where the two black SUVs idled in readiness.

Inside each vehicle, he knew, the heaters would be roaring. People were soft, he thought with mild contempt. Well, when he was President, he'd change all that.

The driver's window of the first car lowered at his approach to release a cloud of steamy air. "Ready when you are, sir."

"Right! Fall in!" ordered the Vice President, who had been too young for Vietnam and too old for the Gulf War. He started down the driveway toward the main gates, where armed Navy guards stood vigilant 24/7, and the second SUV followed closely behind him.

Fulton's eyes stung with tears and his nose began to leak, but mere cold never stopped him, nor did rain or burning heat— only fog, in which unseen enemies might lurk—and each day he ran four miles on the streets and pathways of Rock Creek Park before returning to his home gym, where he did forty minutes of crunches and bench pressing.

Consequently, he was in better shape than most people on the Hill, young or old. The President himself was growing soft and was inclined to sleep in on Sundays and holidays, more so now that his tenure was entering its final phase, and these days he even allowed himself a drink or two before dinner.

When he reached the gates, Fulton jogged in place while the steel barriers were moved aside. The first of his guard vehicles passed through, he followed, the second SUV pulled out behind him, and the small procession set off in the dark.

Minutes ticked by.

Fulton opened up his stride, watching his feet pound along the pavement—one two, one two, one two—panting softly, his breath streaming.

A quick check of the pedometer revealed one mile covered, three more to go, and now, suddenly, the dark, the cold, and the stillness closed in on him, ravaging his mind with the sheer injustice of his life.

Although he had done so much for the country he loved, now, in the absence of clear and present danger, people had ceased to believe any danger still existed. Had they such short memories? Did no one possess any common sense? Any gratitude?

In some quarters he was derided, if not despised—even, these days, by his own daughter.

Of course, he shouldn't be surprised, since Brianna attended Berkeley, that renegade cesspool of liberalism that relished dragging his country down to its knees. Fulton had wanted her to go to Georgetown, or to his own alma mater, Penn State, but she'd insisted on Berkeley, where in her words *it all happened,* thus moving as far from home as possible while still remaining in the same country.

Now she barely spoke to him.

He was a reactionary old fart, she insisted. He embarrassed her in front of her friends. He was a fascist.

It was pointless to reason with her, because she refused to listen.

In fact, a growing number of people had stopped listening, and fewer seemed to care.

The whole country had turned soft and needed to be saved from itself, an obligation the Vice President had long ago decided was his destiny, though how could he accomplish such a destiny if he was denied the chance at the top job?

Fulton thought of Grace, who would be in bed for at least another hour, and forced back a sudden impulse to turn and flag down the slowly pursuing SUV, pound on the window, and demand to be let in and driven home. With sudden longing, he imagined himself flinging open his bedroom door, diving beneath the warm covers, and allowing sleep to carry him blissfully back to Koczanski's Ford dealership in northwestern Pennsylvania in 1962 when life was so simple.

But no. He wouldn't give in. Vice President Craig Fulton never gave in.

★ ★ ★

Toward the end of his run, with the endorphins finally kicking in, Fulton's depression lifted as quickly as it had fallen upon him.

He reminded himself that plans had been set in motion, and that this troublesome patch would soon be behind him, with all obstacles removed, his pride intact, and his policies vindicated.

He would be a hero once again, respected and even revered.

With the weakening, if not actual removal, of Senator Ellen Fischer from the scene, Carl Satcher would be confirmed as Secretary of Homeland Security.

With Satcher's organization and money behind him, he, Craig Fulton, would begin building his campaign for the presidential nomination and then, under his leadership as Commander in Chief, the country would not only find its feet but return to its glory days.

Look at the big picture! Satcher had commanded—and he, Craig Fulton, would do just that.

CHAPTER THREE

Coffee mug in hand, Ellen paced between the table and the window that faced the back of the building and a jumbled cityscape of rooftops. Normally she enjoyed the view. The tower and dome of St. Ignatius Church lent a romantic, European flavor, which reminded her of Tuscany, though she'd never been to Italy. She'd love to go there sometime with Ben. This morning, however, the view seemed menacing rather than romantic, the rooftops dank, the light from the office windows sourly jaundiced.

Ellen flicked on the TV and surfed the channels. None of the news was good.

Hollywood's most glamorous couple was announcing a breakup.

The Midwest was crippled by a severe ice storm.

Two ferryboats had collided off the coast of Sweden; the death toll was 850 and rising.

Nothing yet about her and Ben.

The phone rang, the private line. Ellen reached for it. Caller ID was blocked, and Ben laid his hand over hers. "Careful."

"It'll only be my mother. Or Ruthie."

"Do they get the *D.C. Times*?"

"Maybe they're just calling to wish us a happy New Year's."

Ellen waited through the fourth ring, when the message clicked in: *We're not available right now. Please leave your name and number, the time you called, and a brief—*

The caller hung up.

Her mother, or her sister, or any friend would have left a message.

"Wrong number," Ellen said. "Or a salesperson."

"So early on New Year's Day? On the private line? I don't think so."

"We'll have to change the number."

"I'm afraid this is just the beginning," said Ben. Then: "How about we check out *Slaughterhouse* on the radio."

Ellen stared at him. "Already?"

She clicked to WHAP AM, just in time to catch the Wagnerian passage that introduced the program, culminating in a dramatic drum roll.

"*It's eight A.M. on January 1 of a whole new year. Thanks for spending it in the Slaughterhouse with the king of talk-show radio, Sam Slaughter!*" Then the ingratiating and generically Southern voice of Lonnie, Slaughter's presenter and sidekick, gave way to the voice Ellen loathed but couldn't afford to ignore: that of the self-termed Slaughterman himself.

The infamous radio talk-show host was mean-spirited, inaccurate, provocative, disgusting—but he had a magical voice. Freighted with authority, holding the orotund tones of an Orson Welles or James Earl Jones, it ranged from a suggestive purr to a roaring basso profundo.

His ratings were phenomenal. When the Slaughterman spoke, people listened—as they'd be listening right now.

"*Well now, we're going to have a fine old time this morning! My goodness yes, what a great start to the year! And to get us into the mood, why don't we have a listen to this tune Lonnie here's dug up for us. . . .*"

Immediately, the kitchen resonated with a familiar song from *Fiddler on the Roof.*

If I were a rich man
All day long I'd biddy biddy bum . . .

Ellen had always enjoyed *Fiddler on the Roof.* She'd even performed in it once, in a long-ago high-school production, but now she feared the worst. She also suspected a deliberate religious slur—Slaughter wouldn't neglect an opportunity for offense.

Ben clearly felt the same, and they exchanged glances.

"Yes sirree, folks, that's the song Senator Ellen Fischer's loving spouse, lame-duck congressman Ben Lind, was probably singing when he put their money into oil and coal and other energy stocks at the same time wifey was pretending to be outraged at those same companies . . ."

"Oh, the little shit!" Ben reached for the radio.

Ellen caught his wrist. "Wait."

". . . and if you believe it was a secret, then I have a bridge to sell you—no, scratch that, BUY you. And not a bridge, either, but a condo right next door to dear Ellen, the fanciest address on the grandest street in Washington—the street where the PRESIDENT lives, for Pete's sake! But where else would they set up housekeeping? Hubby can sure afford it. No ifs and no buts, he IS a rich man!"

"And Ellen bleating on about how she's going to save the spotted tree toad and help the working person and squish the Republicans under her shoe," Lonnie broke in.

"Well," Slaughter said, *"I guess he's RICH, and SHE'S a real . . ."*

Ben took in a quick breath. His eyes were dangerous.

"Democrat!" Slaughter said.

"They're shameless," Ellen muttered.

Slaughter continued, *"Think about the mister and missus talking about the megamansion they're going to build for their retirement, when they're done sticking it to the American people. Because thanks to a real patriot out there, we've learned today of some truly squalid misconduct. We now know that all the time Ellen was running off her righteous mouth against Big Oil and the energy companies and carbon emissions and how those industries have JUST GOT TO GO regardless of the layoffs and the plant closings and the working people thrown out in the street—and let's not forget she calls herself a champion of the people—she was running to the bank with her hands full of the profits she and her husband made for themselves thanks to our so-called lousy capitalistic system."*

Again a fragment of musical commentary: *If I were a rich man . . .*

"Aw shucks, give him the benefit of the doubt," Lonnie said. *"All HE did was be rich, he couldn't help it. He inherited it. But SHE tracked it down and married it!"*

"You're so right. Hypocrite, thy name is Ellen! And the American people can't tolerate hypocrisy! Now then, folks, we'll be right back, and we'll be taking calls, right after these messages. . . ."

Ben finally and determinedly clicked off. "This crap has reached a new low," he said.

"I thought I'd become immune," Ellen said. She felt queasy, but knew she'd just have to get over it.

Years before, her old friend and mentor, Shirley Lester, twelve-term Congresswoman for California's 4th District, older, seasoned, African-American, had told her, "Honey, you can't begin to imagine the evil stuff people have said about me over the years! If I'd let it get to me, I'd have quit life itself, let alone politics. But remember three things: First, there *are* good people out there; they just don't make so much of a racket. Second, if you don't make waves, then the bad guys don't get washed overboard. And third, nobody bothers to bad-mouth you unless they're afraid of you. So think of it as kind of a compliment."

Some compliments, however, Ellen could do without.

Slaughter's voice, via radio and blog, reached millions. People listened, many believed without question—and the truth was no defense.

The phone rang again. Again no caller ID.

Another hang-up.

"Of course, it could be just some hungover clown who thinks he's calling Pizza Hut," Ben said.

"How did they get this number, anyway, whoever it is? How did *anyone* get hold of *anything?"* Ellen demanded, feeling exposed and vulnerable even in the safety of her own kitchen, fair game to be picked off at leisure while she stood helpless, not knowing from which direction the next attack would come. Ben was at least looking more like himself, no longer adrift now that he was thoroughly riled up and angry.

"We need to find out what's really going on," he said.

Ellen followed him to his desk, watched him boot up his computer, and waited as the familiar iceberg of his screen saver floated serenely into view on its dark Arctic sea, only the tip showing above the water and the rest descending toward the ocean floor in overlapping, convoluted layers like sculpted drapery. The picture was a symphony of blues, from darkest to most pale, restful on the eyes, bringing instant serenity until one thought of the message of that iceberg: that the bulk of its mass lay unseen beneath the water and was far more deadly.

The iceberg disappeared, to be replaced by the red-and-gray masthead of the *Bridger Report,* a daily right-wing news blog, blatantly partisan but generally considered responsible:

President and family attend New Year's services at St. Martin's.

Eight dead in Indiana ice storm.

Ferry disaster: Little hope of more survivors.

Senator Fischer: Blind trust misconduct.

Ben clicked on the link, and they grimly scanned the entry:

Senator Ellen Fischer, Chair of the Energy and Environment Committee, is happy to advance her career by slamming the oil and energy companies. However, according to a recent whistle-blower, it seems she's not above reaping massive profits from the stocks in those same companies held by her husband, newly ex-Congressman Ben Lind, in his blind trust. The American people can tolerate a great deal, but not hypocrisy of such caliber, and never such squalid misconduct from a person in the public's trust. . . .

Attempts to reach Senator Fischer have been unsuccessful. . . .

"That answers one of our questions," Ben said.

"But not who leaked the information about your portfolio," Ellen said.

"Whoever did that," Ben said bleakly, "had better put his running shoes on right now, because I'm going after him. I'll get him, too."

When Ben spoke in that tone of voice, so quiet and controlled, black eyes cold and hard as agate, Ellen almost felt afraid of him.

If she had been the traitor at the law firm who'd set up Ben's trust, or at the brokerage house handling the portfolio, she'd certainly be afraid. They'd never have dared do such a thing if they'd known Ben.

She sank into one of his dark green leather armchairs and listened while he called his trustee, retired judge Zachary Ray, at his home in Phoenix. Under normal circumstances, on a holiday morning, it would be far too early to call somebody two time zones earlier, particularly Judge Ray (she could still never think of the dignified old man by his first name, let alone address him as Zach, as Ben did), but as Ben pointed out, the judge was always bragging about how he was bright eyed and bushy tailed by six A.M.——and now he was being given a chance to prove it.

The judge answered at once, as if he was waiting for Ben's call. Ellen could clearly hear the crisp, authoritative voice, sounding much younger than eighty-two: "What's up, Ben? I'm assuming you're not calling so early just to wish me a happy New Year's!"

★ ★ ★

Back in the kitchen, over more coffee, the bagels long since tossed down the garbage disposal, Ben said, "That's one angry old man. Of course, he has no idea who's responsible, but one way or another, he'll find out. The problem is if it *isn't* someone at the law firm or the brokerage house."

"Who else would it be?" Ellen asked. "Some outsider with access?"

"Someone who creates his or her own access."

"You mean a computer hacker?"

"Exactly."

"That's above my pay grade," Ellen said. "Any thoughts on how we can deal with this?"

"Zach suggested we hire an investigator. He says he has somebody in mind, a guy who came up in front of him in court back in the nineties, on charges of hacking into government files. Zach knows he was more lenient than he should have been, but this guy was very young, still in his teens—awesomely talented and far better off recruited to the side of the angels rather than doing serious prison time. He makes a fortune consulting for major corporations now, but of course, he owes Zach in a major way. Zach will talk with him as soon as he can find him, and he feels so bad about all this that he'll hire him on his own nickel. He says if anyone can track down our intruder, it'll be this fellow: John something. John Brown. Or Browning. Or Brannan? Hell, I've forgotten his name already. Probably a good sign. These people who walk through firewalls make sure they don't leave shadows."

Ellen attempted a smile. "That's the most mixed metaphor I've heard in years." Though she was glad the judge planned actively to help them, the thought of a hired hacker intercepting some other shadowy individual in cyberspace not only seemed far-fetched but remarkably like bolting the stable door after the horse was gone. She wondered, "Suppose it is a freelance hacker. Who would've hired him?"

"Considering those hearings coming up, I can think of several possibilities," Ben said. "As can you."

"Right." As Ben headed to the computer in the den, Ellen recalled her euphoric mood, lying in bed thinking how great the day was going to be.

Just an hour ago. No time at all.

And now she'd been smeared, and Ben, too, for something of which they were entirely innocent.

The D.C. Times: The American people will not tolerate hypocrisy!

The Slaughterhouse: The American people can't tolerate hypocrisy!

The Bridger Report: The American people can tolerate a great deal, but not hypocrisy of such caliber. . . .

Squalid misconduct . . .

And again, Squalid misconduct . . .

As if they'd all gotten together and agreed on the language, thought Ellen, acting like an echo chamber as they always did. As if the source of the leak had actually sent out a press release.

The story would be all over the Web within minutes, on network news by nightfall, in all other print media by tomorrow at the latest.

Her supporters would be outraged. They'd demand to know why Ben hadn't been more careful (and to her shame, she found herself wondering, just for an instant, Why wasn't he?), but that was the whole point of a blind trust for someone in elected office, that you *didn't* know what investments had been made in your name.

And now, through no fault of theirs, Ellen's credibility might be shot, both at home and abroad.

There was a possibility she could be asked to resign from the Energy and Environment Committee chairmanship, despite the focus she'd finally gotten from the Senate on global warming, after all those long, hard days and nights, those lengthy phone calls around the country and around the world, and last year's trip to India to meet and confer with Asian ministers and heads of state to get them to move on the aggressive reduction of greenhouse gases.

In addition, as Chairman of the Judiciary Committee's Subcommittee on Constitutional Rights and Homeland Security, her authority at Carl Satcher's nomination hearings might also be seriously compromised. Tom Treadwell, Senate Majority Leader, would ask—if he didn't indeed demand—that she step down there as well. When she considered the next senior Democrat on the committee, Ken Stearns of Michigan, she stopped cold. That absolutely must not happen.

But how to defend herself? What to do?

This attack on her was so well timed, with the story set to break on a national holiday, when everyone who was normally there to help her was busy elsewhere. Her staff, well able to cope with crisis and with disaster when necessary, were all celebrating New Year's with family and friends, and David Makins, her communications director, with whom she would need to prepare a statement and arrange a press conference, was in Maine with his family.

One cause for relief: At least Derelle would be available.

By her own choice, Derelle Simba, Ellen's Chief of Staff, had no social life or outside interests beyond the job. She lived alone in one of the smallest of the Watergate apartments, a one-bedroom, overlooking the interior courtyard. She owned little furniture beyond the essentials. The pristine black-and-white kitchen was seldom used, and the refrigerator habitually contained nothing but bottles of mineral water and containers of leftover take-out food.

Nor would Derelle have been partying through the night.

For her, New Year's was just another date on the calendar. She would already have been up for hours, impatient for the long, empty day to be over.

She might well have already caught the *Slaughterhouse* and be waiting for an appropriate time to call Ellen.

Still wearing Ben's jacket over her nightgown, Ellen punched in Derelle's number, longing for the sound of that abrupt, rather husky voice. She'd ask, *What's our best option to make this go away? Should we try to downplay it or go on the attack? We need a strategy. We have to meet today, as soon as possible. Like right now.*

But Derelle didn't answer, neither her landline nor her cell, which was strange because Derelle always carried her cell phone. It might as well have been an extension of her body, but now: *The party you are calling is not available at this time . . .*

Perhaps she had misdialed. She checked her address book and tried again. No luck.

Ellen took a quick shower, then dressed in no-nonsense charcoal wool slacks, a white turtleneck sweater, and thick socks. She gazed down into the bare branches of the trees lining Pennsylvania Avenue, opened the window, and took several long, deep breaths, as bracing as ice water splashed on her face.

Derelle might have been out for coffee; she'd surely be home again by now.

The party you are calling . . .

Which was when Ellen belatedly remembered her Chief of Staff saying she might go to New York over the holiday.

And do what?

Ellen couldn't imagine Derelle among the cheering mob in Times Square counting down as the ball dropped, but there was no reason why, just once, she couldn't have done what most people did on New Year's Eve and go to a party.

After all, Derelle wasn't clairvoyant. She couldn't have known that the one time she decided to sleep late would be the time she was most needed.

★ ★ ★

At one o'clock, Ellen heated some soup.

The phone rang and she pounced on it despite Ben's warnings.

But it wasn't Derelle, or a member of the press; it was her mother, up in Albertson, Long Island.

Immediately following the obligatory New Year's greetings, Sarah Downey asked anxiously, "Is it true, dear? What they're saying? Esther Jacobs called me and told me such awful things! It was on that horrible man's radio show. How terrible for you. Ben shouldn't have done that!"

"He didn't know anything, Mother. He had no idea what was in his portfolio."

"Oh, surely, dear. He must have known."

Ellen tried to explain the point of a blind trust, that a public official's financial holdings weren't revealed to him, to prevent conflicts of interest, but her mother either genuinely didn't understand or was determined not to.

"You can't tell me a brilliant lawyer like Ben wouldn't have made it his business to find out," she said, "to avoid just such a situation!"

Thanks for that, Mother, Ellen thought. Such a comfort!

As soon as she hung up, her sister Ruth called, supportive as always, but Ellen could tell by the tone of her voice that she, too, had doubts.

And if two of her closest supporters in the world had doubts about her, what would the rest of the country think?

★ ★ ★

Ellen had been calling Derelle all day and again in the early evening, still with no response.

By now her emotions had traveled beyond frustration to the edges of anger. Derelle never made herself inaccessible like this. She *must* be aware by now that Ellen was trying to reach her.

Then with a sudden pang of alarm—and of shame for not having thought of it before—she wondered whether Derelle had had an accident, been mugged, or struck down by a bus. Ellen wanted to call the hospitals and check police reports, but Ben stopped her.

"You can't chase around looking for her. You don't know where to start. You're not even sure which city she's in. You'll have to wait."

"You're right," she acknowledged. Then a quite different possibility presented itself: Perhaps Derelle had indeed known Ellen was trying to reach her and why. Perhaps Derelle, disappointed and disgusted by someone she had always admired, had walked away without a word, without even giving Ellen a chance to explain.

But no, Derelle was way too levelheaded. She'd understand the purpose of this attack at once.

Certainly she'd never just up and quit.

Although, Ellen had to wonder, how well did one ever know someone else—even when you'd known them forever?

CHAPTER FOUR

January 2

WEDNESDAY

The Senate dining room was almost deserted so early in the morning, particularly the day immediately after the holiday and with the new Congress not yet sworn in. Ellen saw only the junior Senator from Delaware enjoying a solitary breakfast, half hidden behind the *New York Times,* and her own Chief of Staff seated at a secluded table in the back.

"Happy New Year's, Senator," Derelle Simba said, rising at Ellen's approach, and Ellen allowed her own hand to vanish into Derelle's much larger one. Her Chief of Staff stood almost six feet tall and towered over her diminutive boss. Physically, Derelle was imposing, with skin the color of milky coffee, close-cropped reddish hair, and the golden eyes of a lioness. She moved like a lioness, too, with long, sinuous strides. Never having known her last name, Derelle had adopted the name Simba in her teens since she heard it meant "lion" in Swahili.

"Thanks, and back to you," Ellen said wearily. "I guess it can only go up from here."

They sat. Ellen tossed her coat and scarf over the back of her chair, removed her woolen cap, and ran her hands through her hair.

"I ordered coffee and rye toast," Derelle said. "Hope that's okay?"

The coffee arrived and was poured. At least it was good and hot. Ellen needed it. She had barely slept.

Her relief last night when Derelle finally called had been so profound she'd nearly lost it.

She'd almost yelled, *Damn it, where were you, who were you with, why did you switch your phone off this one particular time I needed you so badly?*

But she hadn't. Just as well. Derelle was entitled to some well-earned downtime.

Ellen spread honey thickly on her toast to give herself the sugar rush and the energy she needed, and added more cream and sugar to her coffee, which she usually took black.

"So," she asked finally, "what's your take on this situation?"

"That somebody wants to discredit you—it seems obvious who—and they think they've found the perfect way to do it."

"Apparently."

"But taking this blind trust issue on its own," Derelle said, watching her spoon as she stirred and stirred her coffee, "let's be realistic. It looks bad, but it shouldn't be enough to sink you. Basically it's your husband's problem, not yours."

Ever since they'd gotten married, Derelle had habitually spoken of Ben as "your husband." Previously she'd referred to him as "the Congressman" or Mr. Lind. On countless occasions, he'd asked her to call him Ben, but she never had and by now he'd given up.

"It reflects badly on me," Ellen said. "People won't believe I didn't know what was in it."

"That's true. David says all kinds of stuff has come in— e-mails, calls from constituents—most of it negative. But not knowing what your husband had in a blind trust—when he didn't know himself—it's not like it's a *heinous* crime!"

Ellen thought of how the teenage Derelle, upon her rescue from Juvenile Hall in Oakland all those years before, had set herself the task of learning ten new words every day. This had probably been one of them.

"The real challenge," Derelle said, "is getting people to believe you and Mr. Lind *didn't* know. You need to make a statement ASAP. David's waiting for you back in the office."

"You guys have been working hard."

Derelle shrugged. "The way we see it, if this is all it is, people will eventually get bored, move on, and forget. What is or isn't in somebody's stock portfolio, especially when everything's legal, isn't exactly a sexy issue, you know what I mean? What worries me and David is how the attacks and the language seem so orchestrated. They've accessed your husband's files and your unlisted phone number. They're organized, which probably means there's more where this came from." Derelle raised her eyes at last. "Sorry to say this, Senator, but this trust issue could be just the tip of the iceberg."

Ellen thought at once of Ben's screen saver, of that frigid Arctic sea and sky, that small icy protrusion above the water and, beneath, the thousand-foot cliff lying in wait. She felt a touch of that cold creep down her spine as she wondered what else might be out there waiting.

★ ★ ★

Ellen and Derelle rode the elevator down to the subway, where the small electric trains smoothly and quietly connected the Capitol with the Senate and Congressional office buildings. After a short wait, they climbed aboard and sat together in the front seat. Normally Ellen enjoyed taking the train. It was clean and bright down there, and the cars, seating four to six in an open compartment, reminded her of long-ago fairground rides. Plus, it gave her a quiet opportunity to think while watching the fifty state flags—the only ornamentation on the track—slide past in order of the states' admission to the Union. Often she'd find herself noting New York, number eleven, her state of birth, and the golden bear of California, her adoptive state, number thirty-one.

This morning, however, as she attempted to marshal her turbulent thoughts, the flags flicked by unnoticed while Derelle, BlackBerry in hand, frowningly scanned her e-mails.

Ellen didn't ask for details of those e-mails; she knew she'd find out the worst soon enough.

Just a few minutes later, they were out of the train and into the elevator. After riding up to the main floor of the Senate Hart Building, they crossed the wide atrium with its two-story-high Alexander Calder sculpture *Mountains and Clouds*. Twenty-nine tons of steel had been used to create the jagged black mountains, while the clouds, suspended below the ninety-foot-high ceiling, were formed of giant sheets of black aluminum, which originally rotated but did so no longer. Ellen personally didn't care for the piece; she found its sense of mass and weight intimidating.

Today, however, her attention was not on the sculpture but on her office door, and the gauntlet of reporters she'd have to pass through to get there.

"Senator! How did you—"

"Senator, why did you—"

"Senator! ENERGY stocks?"

"Later!" Derelle held the door for Ellen and followed her into another maelstrom of sound and movement as a full roster of harried staff and interns called in for emergency duty struggled to keep up with the relentlessly ringing phones and incoming e-mails.

"Good morning, Senator," said Celia Chen, the office's receptionist. "David's waiting for you inside." Celia, invariably immaculate, but today with her lipstick already half eaten away and the white silk bow of her blouse unraveling, didn't attempt to wish them a happy New Year's, for which Ellen was grateful. "Burning up the airways," Celia said. "It's been like this all morning."

"Just remember, Celia, this, too, shall pass!" Ellen forced a smile and hoped the reassurance didn't sound as hollow as she feared.

Her inner office was mercifully quiet. Through the window, the view of the United States Supreme Court added calm and composure, and as always, the room welcomed her with its light, clear colors, its mix of antique and contemporary furniture, and the groups of photographs on the walls, formal and not so formal:

Ellen triumphant on the Capitol steps, in a sunburst yellow coat, after being sworn in for her second term as Senator.

Barefoot with a hibiscus blossom behind her ear, strolling hand in hand with Ben along an endless white beach.

The grinning, paint-splattered young artists of the Children's Alliance, posing beside their tree-of-life mural back in Oakland.

A framed poster from Josh's last campaign, her favorite picture of him, young and smiling and confident, hand raised, palm outward, with the caption "Josh Fischer for Senate: Fighting Your Battles for You!"

There were also photographs of past California Senators, all of them signed except for an unflattering shot of Carl Satcher, taken soon after his less-than-civil concession speech in 1998. Ellen kept it on her wall as a reminder that even the mighty and seemingly indestructible could also be vulnerable.

She found David Makins, her communications director, leaning across her desk in the act of hanging up the phone.

David was a tall, bearded man, heavily built, bald save for a horseshoe of ginger fluff around the back of his head. He looked rumpled and tired, as if he'd already put in a long, hard day. "That was the *Washington Post*—they need to hear from you. As does everybody else. We have to get something in the works."

"Of course," Ellen said. "We're in the middle of one big, stirred-up hornet's nest." She hung her coat on a hook beside her bathroom door, her woolen cap above it, and shook her head as if to clear the thoughts inside.

David pulled two more chairs up to the oval table in the center of the room, which Ellen preferred for staff meetings, so she didn't have to preside like a baron at her antique partner's desk— a huge piece designed for two large men to share rather than for one diminutive woman working alone. From the first, David had referred to it as her "doublewide."

David had brewed a pot of coffee many hours before, and now Derelle poured herself and Ellen cups the color and consistency of crankcase oil.

Ellen grimaced. "We're taking our caffeine in solid form today, right?"

"As long as it does the job."

"I'll never sleep again—but who has time for that, anyway?"

David sat down behind a sheaf of e-mail printouts from constituents, lists of media calls, and press clips, the *D.C. Times* on top of the pile. "Hell of a way to start the year," he said. "I got here as soon as I could."

"I know you did," Ellen said. "And I appreciate it more than I can say."

As she knew by now, David's efforts to return to the capital after the holidays had been heroic.

Upon first hearing the news, he'd left his wife and teenaged daughters up in Kittery Point and driven through the afternoon to Boston as fast as he dared on the icy roads. Because all flights into and out of Logan Airport had been canceled, he'd taken the train to New York City and the last Metroliner to D.C., where, exhausted, he'd grabbed a couple of hours' sleep and made it to the office by five A.M.

Ellen felt both grateful and humble. David, Derelle, Celia—each and every one of her staff was doing their best for her, down to the newest intern.

She sipped her overbrewed coffee, set it down, and reached for David's pile of newsprint and correspondence. "Okay, let's take a look at all this."

It wasn't good.

FISCHER MUTE ON CHARGES OF HYPOCRISY
PROFITS FROM ENERGY COMPANIES FUEL SENATOR'S WEALTH

To her chagrin, even the friendliest paper, the *Oakland Tribune,* trumpeted:

RICH ON ENERGY; POOR ON ETHICS?

"The story is exploding in the print media, radio, television, and the blogs," David said, "and the phones are ringing off the hook—you'll have noticed that. And there're hundreds of messages from yesterday, too."

"So much for relaxing and enjoying their New Year's," Der-elle said.

"For some people, bashing me *is* relaxation and enjoyment," Ellen said.

"Voice mail's jammed," David went on. "And there's a ton of e-mail. . . ."

She checked some of them out:

Senator, you lost my vote.

I thought you were different!

I've stuck with you through good times and bad times but this is the end!

How could you sell us out like this?

Those were the most restrained. Others were vitriolic. A few were obscene.

Ellen thrust the pile away from her, drew a long, deep breath, and thought sadly of her most loyal supporters across the country and what they must be thinking of her this morning.

Who was the driving force behind all this?

She closed her eyes and there, once again, was Carl Satcher, in that black overcoat and cowboy boots, his hatred spewing in waves.

Ellen massaged her aching temples, rolled her shoulders, and wished she had taken up yoga after all, so she'd know how to tap into that core of peace everyone was supposed to have deep inside.

"Right," she declared, "this isn't going away, and obviously I need to hold a press conference as soon as it can be arranged. Where do you think, David? Here or in California?"

"No time to get yourself to California," David said, "and any-way, the weather's lousy clear across the country. You might not make it till tomorrow and you need to address this issue right now. It can't wait. The online editions are already running the story."

"So what do you suggest?"

"A major press conference this afternoon in the Senate Press Gallery, with a special press avail afterward for the California papers, who're waiting on their big stories till they hear from you personally." He checked them off on his fingers: *"L.A. Times, Chronicle, Mercury-News, Bee, Union-Tribune*—all of them." Casting a wary eye over Ellen's tailored emerald jacket and calf-length pin-striped skirt, he said, "And maybe you should wear something less bright and designer looking. You look expensive, and that isn't a connection you want people making right now. Perhaps a sweater." He thought for a moment. "Beige?"

Ellen responded at once. "Forget it! This is how I dress. I wear colors. Everyone knows that. People will think I'm a phony, and they'd be right. And I *hate* beige!" she added.

"If you're sure."

"I'm sure. David, you're not my fashion consultant."

He gave up without a struggle—Ellen guessed he'd known he wouldn't win that one, but his PR instincts had required him to at least try.

"Okay, stay bright, stay the real *you*," he said. "And now let's work on what you'll say."

"We don't need to work on anything. I'm telling the truth, and I'm speaking without notes. The truth doesn't *need* notes— I had no idea what was in the blind trust and neither did Ben. I'll remind them again how a blind trust operates, and why. Then I'll answer questions."

Derelle asked, "Should Mr. Lind have a statement for Ellen to hand out?"

David shook his head. "We're not bringing him into it right now. We don't want Ellen perceived as the little woman who doesn't understand money."

"But Ben *wants* to do something!" Ellen said. "He feels responsible for this whole mess. He shouldn't feel that way, but he can't help it."

"He could hold his own press conference tomorrow or the day after," David said, "at some venue off the Hill since he's no longer an elected official. Or he could do a press conference call. But my instinct still says to keep Ben out of it."

"I guess you're right," Ellen agreed.

"A situation like this, there is no 'right.' Instinct's all we have to go on, and just try to stay one step ahead." David drummed his fingers thoughtfully on the pile of newsprint. "The story's perfect for the gutter press, you know—I'm not surprised they're jumping all over it: A liberal Democrat married to a rich Republican—"

"A *moderate* Republican," Ellen put in.

"A *rich* moderate Republican—which makes you a rich liberal Democrat, something certain people find hard to reconcile or forgive. Then this blind trust business hits the fan, which smells kind of rank, and *whammo!*—it's open season! Everyone wants to rip a piece out of you! Don't forget, the rich don't need sympathy. People will reason that if you *did* know about those stocks, then you deserve all you get, and if you *didn't* know, then you must be either dumb or lying."

"That's not the way it works."

"Doesn't matter. They won't believe you—or they'll choose not to."

Ellen reflected that even her own mother and sister hadn't believed her.

David met her eyes. "They'll also assume, and please don't take offense, that you're mad as hell at Ben for putting you in this position. It's possible there'll be rumors of a marital spat. Separation. Even divorce—hey, anything to boost circulation. And this story has extra legs because of your past attacks on big energy."

Ellen sighed. David was right, the tabloids would be salivating over this. She thought of that hideous picture of herself in the *D.C. Times,* which by now must gleefully be slathered coast to coast, possibly paired with an equally unflattering and snarly picture of Ben, dredged up from old files. "So what can we do?" she asked.

"Obviously, you and Ben must be seen around together, acting normal and confident, as if this is just a bump in the road—a small one at that. And looking happy," David added.

"We're not going around all smiles making a showpiece of our marriage! How phony is that?!"

Derelle put in, "You're throwing a party tomorrow, isn't that right? For your—for Mr. Lind's birthday?"

With sudden intense irritation—her nerves must be tight as a violin string—Ellen thought: *Why* can she never bring herself to call him Ben? But she said calmly enough, "It's not a party, just dinner with Mr. and Mrs. Hirsch." She reminded David, "Joel Hirsch is Ben's new law partner—but you knew that."

"Is this partnership confirmed?" he asked.

"The dinner is to celebrate that as well," Ellen said.

"I'll be glad when the agreement is signed," David said.

"Ben will be, too."

"Are you planning to eat at home or go out?"

"At home."

"Does the building have good security?"

"Better than most."

"That's still not saying a whole lot. The hyenas will have had another full day to get out there and start yipping or howling at your heels, or whatever it is hyenas do."

"They laugh," Ellen said.

"And their laughter is chilling. . . ." Thoughtfully, David picked up the remote, clicked to station WHAP, and raised the volume just in time to hear Sam Slaughter declare in his rich baritone, *"My thought exactly, Lonnie. As our favorite environazi hypocrite would say, screw the little guy—and the great bald eagle himself for that matter—I've got mine!"*

"That man's evil. He's like a disease," Derelle said.

"And unfortunately, a lot of the country's infected," David said. He thought for a moment. "Maybe we should bring in the Capitol police tomorrow night."

Ellen shook her head. "Ben can hire a private security firm if he thinks we need it."

"Don't take any chances," David said. "They're playing hardball and you better not forget it. Where's Ben right now?"

"At home, talking with his trustee on the phone. They're tracing leads, finding who had access to his portfolio and could have leaked the information in the first place. If they have to look outside the organization, the judge knows some kind of high-tech investigator he thinks can help them out."

"His trustee's a judge?"

"Retired. Lives out in Phoenix."

"What kind of a guy is he, this judge?"

"Salt of the earth. And tough."

"What's his name?"

"Zachary Ray."

David's tired face cracked a smile for the first time that morning. "Sounds like a white-hat lawman straight from a Zane Grey novel, like he shoots himself a rattler every morning and barbecues it for breakfast!"

"He went to Harvard Law," Ellen said, "not the OK Corral. But like I said, he's tough."

"Good presence?" David asked.

"Craggy, distinguished, lots of white hair; makes you feel everybody should be eighty-two. Right now he's fit to be tied that something like this should happen on his watch."

"Would he fly in if Ben does decide to hold a press conference?"

"In a New York minute."

"On the other hand, we could hook up a remote feed from Phoenix, inject some local color and background." David made a note on his pad. "But that can wait. Your press conference has priority. Today, soon as possible."

"Make it midafternoon," Ellen said. "I'm meeting with Tom Treadwell right after lunch and it could run late."

They all fell silent, thinking of the possible outcome of Ellen's meeting with the Senate Majority Leader.

"Will that give you enough time to prepare?" David asked.

"Like I said, I don't need to prepare. Telling it straight from the shoulder doesn't need prep time."

There was a pause, broken by Derelle. "You realize all we're doing so far is damage control?"

"So?" David had pushed back his chair and half risen; he sat down again. "Any useful suggestions?"

Derelle glanced at Ellen and then back at David. "We were talking at breakfast about the timing of this whole attack, how it hit the headlines and the *Slaughterhouse* and the blogs all at once, and the identical language used. It seemed like there was definite coordination."

"Organized by who?" David wondered.

"Satcher's the most likely," Ellen said. "With the Vice President's full cooperation." She added, "I'm not paranoid—I know who they are and how they operate. The two of them march in lockstep."

"Craig Fulton knows Ellen plans to open up Satcher's hearing to include the surveillance and wiretap controversy," Derelle said, "and he wants her out in the worst way."

"So if this demonstration of my so-called hypocrisy isn't enough to force me to back down," Ellen said, "they're sure to have a second hit. We need to be prepared."

"What do you see them throwing at us next?" David asked Derelle.

"Don't know. Right now I can't think of anything else they could hold over Ellen, but they're not likely to give up, and they have a powerful organization behind them."

There was another thoughtful pause.

"Could the President be involved?" Ellen wondered.

"That's a hard one to call. I doubt it, though," David said. "He's not a detail man, and he's leaving more and more of the actual decision making to Fulton these days."

"I think we can safely assume he's not," Ellen said.

"Whether he is or isn't," Derelle said, "he can't let himself be seen as distancing himself too much from Fulton."

"Not unless it's absolutely necessary," David said. "Though I agree with Ellen that he's probably not involved. It's important to the President how he's perceived in the future compared with Eisenhower and Reagan, and he already has a book deal. He wants to leave office on a high note, with his hands clean."

"If Fulton ever gets to be President," Derelle said, "I'd hate to think of what his hands will look like even *before* he takes office."

CHAPTER FIVE

In the foyer of the Vice President's residence, at one P.M., Craig Fulton said, "It's good of you to come," shaking the hand of Douglas Brewer, Director of the FBI. Brewer was a tall, lean man, his dark eyes deep-set under heavy brows, pronounced grooves bracketing his mouth from nostril to chin. He shook Fulton's hand with economic brevity and followed him into the den, a room carefully designed for informality though clearly intended to impress, with its dark paneling and coffered ceiling, shelves of leatherbound books, massive mahogany desk, and leather armchairs grouped around an ornate stone fireplace. On the walls hung laudatory citations and autographed photographs of the Vice President in the company of important people: at the President's side on the White House lawn or in the Oval Office; joking with Jacques Chirac at a state banquet; shaking the hand of Carl Satcher at the last Republican convention.

Years before, when Fulton had chaired that first meeting of the Office of Strategic Operations, which had included the heads of all intelligence agencies, he'd noted Brewer's swift, covert scan of the walls of this room and surmised that the FBI Director had been impressed by the enduring trappings of power.

Therefore, although they could have met at a downtown venue more convenient for both, Fulton had chosen to invite Brewer here to the residence, not only to remind him of that original meeting, but to emphasize exactly who had been in charge then, and who remained so today.

It was also disarmingly pleasant here, he thought, and, in its total privacy, the ideal place to address certain aspects of the imminent visit of Johnathon Ewing, Prime Minister of Great Britain.

"The Prime Minister's wife will be with him," Fulton said as both men sat down at a small table drawn up beside the cheerfully crackling fire, "which complicates matters security-wise. Mrs. Ewing is an outgoing, independent kind of woman, inclined to wander off on her own. We'll advise against it, but we can't exactly place her under house arrest."

"Naturally." Brewer spread the starchy linen napkin across his thighs and slid the toothpick from his sandwich: four triple-decker toasted triangles containing slices of roast beef (medium to well done, the way the Vice President preferred), with Swiss cheese, ham, and tomato. He took a measured bite and set his sandwich down.

Fulton knew the Director to be an abstemious eater. He approved of that, as he approved of Brewer in general: collegiate basketball player, still worked out regularly, known for his punishing squash game, watched his weight, personally and professionally untouched by scandal of any kind, still married to his high-school sweetheart. "A true Agency man," Satcher had agreed when he backed Brewer's nomination as Director of the Bureau. "Plays it all by the book and lives by the rules. Our kind of man."

"Their own country's security protocols will be in hand," Brewer said as he took a sip of mineral water, "but as guests in our country, they'll be extended every possible service. I assure you we're on top of the situation, and you have no reason for concern."

"There's always concern," Fulton said bluntly. "It's widely known—too widely known—that during their visit the Prime Minister and his wife will be guests of the President at Camp David, as will my wife and I, and the Satchers. Certain interested parties—and I need hardly mention whom I'm speaking of—might readily perceive this gathering to be a golden opportunity for mischief. Quite apart from the helicopter ride—"

"*Marine Two* will also be deployed," Brewer said of the Vice President's own official helicopter, since, according to standard operating procedure, the President and Vice President could not fly in the same aircraft. "And they both carry anti-missile devices, as you know, sir."

"—the land site is also vulnerable," Fulton concluded. "One can't rule out an attack on Camp David itself. Its security is routinely overstated!"

Brewer began, "Sir, are you seriously suggesting—"

"An infiltration of the staff, though unlikely, is always possible," Fulton said. "Or, God forbid, a suicide bomber. Or some kind of missile. They could wipe us all out in one stroke. And quite apart from the instant power vacuum and the deaths and injuries, think of the message such a disaster would send: that the President of the United States of America, the most powerful man in the world, with platoons of Secret Service and Marines at his beck and call, to say nothing of state-of-the-art surveillance systems and weaponry, was still unable to protect himself or his guests."

Brewer refilled his water glass. "Mr. Vice President, what exactly do you need from us to put you more at ease?" he asked.

"Information," Fulton said.

"As you know, the FBI regularly forwards any intel considered remotely relevant to the OSO, as do all the other agencies," Brewer pointed out.

"It's a cliché to say that to be forewarned is to be forearmed," the Vice President said, "but clichés are only self-evident truths. I need the names and contact information of every terrorism suspect within a realistic radius of Camp David, including the D.C. Metro area, southern Maryland, and Delaware, in any context, no matter how remote the connection. We must also be regularly updated on any increase or alteration in chatter—"

"There's been none reported, and the Bureau has no sense of any imminent action of any kind."

As if the FBI Director hadn't spoken, Fulton went on, "—and any report of any unusually voluble imam, teacher, or rabble-rousing individual at any mosque, school, Middle Eastern deli, or whatever, you take it from there. The bottom line," he said, "is that we want the names of anyone *at all* you might have been keeping an eye on, for whatever reason, or were even *thinking* of watching."

"Of course I'll see that's taken care of, sir," the Director said.

And he would, too. You could always count on Brewer to do the right thing. Fulton would have his much-expanded list, even though the Director would have to pull agents from other assignments and perform miracles of juggling with other key personnel. However, if that was what it took to meet Fulton's concerns, that's what he'd do. And it would happen fast. As would, upon the Director's order, the apprehension of any or all of the suspects with no questions asked.

That was what happened in the OSO.

That was precisely why the OSO was created in the first place, to be a fast-moving, independent, super-strike force, able to act quickly without all that red tape and bureaucracy, with a short, clear line of command, and quite unassailable because it was empowered by Executive Order.

"Of course, you'll be acting under my authority," Fulton reminded Brewer.

The Director inclined his head, resumed eating his next quarter sandwich, and stacked the second toothpick neatly with the first on the side of his plate. "I understand," he said. "And I'll get right on it. You'll have your list at once."

"I appreciate it," Fulton said, relieved that one more item of his inventory was covered. He had no doubts that Brewer would complete his task perfectly. He always did. He was a team player.

CHAPTER SIX

"Good afternoon, Ellen! I like the jacket; a perfect touch of spring!" Thomas Treadwell, five-term Senator from Iowa, rose from his antique rolltop desk with its many ink-stained pigeon-holes, surely a product, Ellen thought, of painstaking Midwestern craftsmanship. He clasped her hand and steered her to a high-backed armchair of maroon leather where Ellen sat, calmed as always by the atmosphere of this room, furnished so comfortably with solid, homely pieces built to last, like that desk—and like the bespectacled Senator Treadwell himself, his genial smile and folksy manner belying shrewd eyes the washed-out blue of a sailor, or of the farmer he once had been.

The paneled walls were hung with enlarged color photographs of Treadwell's home state of Iowa, which he loved and to which he repaired as often as possible: bucolic miles of green farmland; the high prairie clouds, with thunderheads looming in the distance like thirty-thousand-foot cathedrals; a younger Senator Treadwell presenting a 4-H Club trophy to a blushing, blond-braided, overall-clad teenager; and behind the desk a new addition: a country gas station with two grizzled attendants standing beneath a hand-lettered sign proclaiming !!ETHANOL SOLD HERE!!

"Get you something?" the Senator asked. "Coffee? Tea?"

"I think I've already filled my caffeine quota for the next ten years."

"Root beer? They just sent me a case from home. It's great stuff and easy on the innards. Perks you up no end."

"Nothing, thanks."

"As you like." The Iowan sank into the other chair, leaned back, and laced his fingers across his stomach. "Okay, then, Ellen—I'll come directly to the point. This blind trust situation has hit us at a real bad time."

"That's for sure," Ellen sighed.

"Our party has a lot riding on certain upcoming events, and a great deal riding on you—well, you know all about that." Treadwell drew breath as if to say more, and appeared to change his mind. He pushed back his chair and rose to his feet. "Guess I'll have a root beer after all. Sure there's nothing I can get for you?"

When Ellen again shook her head, he crossed the room to the small refrigerator set inside a zinc-lined pine cabinet, withdrew a can, popped the top, took a long pull at the contents—"Ahhhh!"—and returned with added resolution to his step.

"So here's where we stand," he said. He regarded Ellen levelly through his narrow, rectangular glasses as he returned to his chair. "I don't have to tell you what you know already, that you're an inspirational leader who can think on her feet, and that you've always had support both from the party and from so many of the American people—which, of course, has been justly earned. You've proven yourself to be honest, tough, and energetic, with the courage of your convictions. Are you blushing yet?"

"I'm not in a blushing mood today."

"Then I'll cut right to the chase—which is that the country flat out doesn't need Carl Satcher as Secretary of Homeland Security. Plain and simple, we have to block his confirmation."

"I'm planning to do just that."

"I know—and I'm pretty sure you would have."

"What am I hearing, Mr. Leader? Doubts?"

"Normally, I'd have no doubts."

"Listen to me! Please!" Ellen clenched her hands in her lap. "Believe me—neither of us knew anything about those stocks in Ben's portfolio."

"Of course I believe you—but that doesn't stop the buzz. And the fact that you always *have* been so transparent makes it that much more difficult. You've personally raised the integrity bar. People are asking themselves, if they can't trust *you,* then who *can* they trust?"

"I've certainly gotten *that* message," Ellen said. "E-mails, phone calls, you name it."

Treadwell raised an ironic eyebrow. "Look, I've been in the Senate a lot longer than you, and I've certainly caught my own share of crap. It comes with the territory—you learn to take it or you learn to duck. But back to you," he said. "The right-wing machine has swung into action big time. It's already been suggested that you should recuse yourself. First there's the baggage you carry relating to Carl Satcher; they say you can't be objective. Second, this blind trust affair is a windfall, and they plan on pasting your hide to the barn door. To them, the appearance of impropriety is just as damning as actual impropriety. Now, I don't put too much weight on anything they say, but I've also had calls from people on our side of the aisle who feel you're just too controversial right now—too hot—and should step down as Chair, at least for this hearing. And, sorry to say, I'm expecting more of them."

"No way I'm stepping down," Ellen said flatly, color rushing to her cheeks.

"And no way do I want you to, or should you. I'm merely telling you what some of your colleagues are saying. As we all know, the next senior Democrat on the subcommittee is Kenny Stearns—a quiet guy, plays it close to the vest. I happen not to trust him—but we'll get back to him in due course." Treadwell took another gulp of his root beer and set the can carefully down on the cork coaster. "In the meantime, let me put you fully in the picture. Despite Craig Fulton's drop in the polls, in certain arenas he has a strong following. He still expects to inherit the Presidency next year, and with Carl Satcher running Homeland Security, I'd say we'd then have ourselves the perfect storm for God knows what—but not an America we'd recognize."

"No argument there," Ellen said.

"Satcher, frankly, is the simpler proposition; he's merely power hungry. Craig Fulton, however, is a lot more dangerous because he's a true believer. He's genuinely convinced that the global war on terror can only be won by fighting fire with fire, *whatever* that takes. And to do him justice, for a while there, he was doing a good job."

Ellen listened, waiting to see where the Leader was headed with this. She didn't have to wait for long.

"Let's go back to the early days," Treadwell said, "to the founding of the Department of Homeland Security, and the emergence of the OSO. Do you remember their mission as originally stated?"

"Roughly, to address the current climate of fear," Ellen said. "And to show the American people that the government has put their protection above everything else."

"Close enough," Treadwell agreed. "It all began with the best of intentions, and it was comforting to see the beefed-up National Guard presence at major events like parades and football games. People welcomed the enhanced surveillance systems installed to protect airports, bridges, and chemical plants, just as they welcomed the added protection for public schools and buildings, national monuments and historic sites, and the new security systems for checking on rail and bus passenger baggage. However, it quickly became apparent that the OSO was spread too thin. There was way too much information coming in from all sides. They needed more operatives to follow up leads, and more people familiar with the languages the U.S. needs to decipher."

"Which led to Craig Fulton's decision to redefine and expand the agency, and streamline its procedures," Ellen put in.

"With the approval of the President, who delegated the authority. At the time, it seemed only sensible. However, from that time forward, the OSO developed its own identity and momentum, increased its reach, and, as now seems inevitable, began to abuse its power." Treadwell sighed. "Dennis Rogan's a good man; he was a voice of reason. It's too bad he's quit Homeland Security."

"He's sick," Ellen said.

"Maybe that's true—or maybe he regards the OSO as a cuckoo in the nest, intent on devouring the parent bird, and wanted to get out in time."

"I hadn't thought of that. You could be right."

"Of course, Fulton justifies everything—every action—as necessary in the interest of national security. He's claimed that before the 'streamlining,' the agency's hands were tied—couldn't get things done without being hung up for months, or even years, in bureaucratic red tape. Now, however, they're operating on the very edges of the law. In the event of a terrorist threat, or on mere suspicion, the OSO overrides the Constitution. Anything to root out the enemy within, and individual rights be damned." Treadwell added, "I'm even hearing of new, 'improved' plans for Guantánamo Bay."

"I thought that place was being shut down," Ellen said.

"On the contrary, expanded," the Iowan said. "There are brand-new facilities on the drawing board for the expected brand-new terror suspects. However, as we're told, it's all for the good of the country."

Ellen thought of the Soviet gulags, her mind recoiling as she imagined the terror of the police state and, in the dead of night, the dreaded knock on the door in Cincinnati, Austin, or Des Moines.

"And that's the danger of a true believer with enough power," Treadwell said. "With Carl Satcher head of Homeland Security, Fulton will have a free hand. If he's elected President, he'll undoubtedly put the country on a wartime footing. Forget educating our kids, global warming, health care, and new technologies. Hell, forget the American Dream. He'll demand—and get—a steep increase in defense spending and homeland defense. The selling point to Congress will be full employment, likely to be at its highest since World War II—which is where we return to Kenny Stearns. Stearns's home state would benefit hugely by all this. He'll certainly be imagining those decrepit old factories newly refurbished, with the production lines rolling again, triple shift—even though they're producing missiles, tanks, and machine guns instead of automobiles. He'll be longing for it. *Greedy* for it. And I can't say that, in his shoes, I wouldn't feel tempted myself," Treadwell admitted.

"It's hard to believe the country would tolerate it," Ellen said.

"It's amazing what people will tolerate when they're scared—and when they're guaranteed good jobs and security. Though, of course, the OSO won't allow people to feel *too* safe," Treadwell reflected. "They'll always be reminding them of those out there who, given half a chance, will take everything away from them—which is why we need someone other than Kenny Stearns taking the lead at Satcher's hearing. Someone who will ask the right questions and call on the right witnesses. Someone like you. Your particular firepower is badly needed. Not only have you seldom missed an opportunity to make a mark professionally, but your personal life has always been transparent—until now, that is." Treadwell's pleasant face settled momentarily into implacable lines. "Although you have my utmost support, you need to come up with an ironclad defense against these accusations of hypocrisy and self-enrichment. And you need to do it pretty damn quick."

"I know," Ellen said. "And I will."

The meeting was over.

They rose together. The Iowan held out his hand and she shook it. He walked her to the door, where he turned to gaze longingly at his wall of photographs.

"You know," Treadwell sighed, "there are times when I'd so much rather be handing out prizes at county fairs!"

★ ★ ★

It was early afternoon when Ellen rode the train back to the Hart Building. From the speculative, shifting glances she received, she knew she was recognized, though nobody spoke to her. She preferred to think this was because they knew she was attempting to move around incognito and respected her privacy, though mud had a habit of sticking, Ellen knew——not only to those at which it was flung, but to all who came in contact with it.

As for Tom Treadwell, she was under no illusions. His duty was primarily to the Democratic caucus of the Senate, and if she was perceived as an embarrassment, or indeed a danger, he would have no choice but to withdraw his support. For now, however, he was squarely on her side.

He believed she could pull this off.

But suppose she couldn't? Suppose, in the end, she was forced to step down and relinquish the chair to Kenny Stearns?

She felt her shoulders sag under the invisible weight of the moment. This wasn't much of a new year.

★ ★ ★

Back in the office, she found a message from Ben on her voice mail.

"About dinner tomorrow night," he said, his tone carefully neutral. "Anita Hirsch called to cancel. She said maybe we could reschedule at a more appropriate moment, that she'd be in touch."

Whatever that really meant. *Oh, poor Ben.* Ellen suspected she knew only too well.

But she couldn't afford to worry about Ben's future as well. Not now.

She had work to do.

And, selfishly, she was almost grateful because she and Ben could have the evening to themselves.

She had the feeling it would be the last time for quite a while.

CHAPTER SEVEN

At his California ranch, Carl Satcher, wearing a battered Stetson with sweat-stained brim, canvas jacket, and jeans tucked into the tops of his hand-tooled size-thirteen Frye boots, swung his leg across the back of his big bay gelding Maximilian, then trotted out of the stable yard and down the long, tree-lined driveway.

Behind the white split-rail fences to either side lay the individual paddocks in which his stallions held separate court: Rush Hour, the black; Prospero's Book, the gray; and his favorite, the chestnut, Archangel, onetime winner of the Kentucky Derby and the Preakness, second by a nose at the Belmont Stakes, a magnificent animal, his thick winter coat gleaming bronze. Always curious, Archangel trotted up as Satcher approached, laid his velvet nose on the fence, and emitted a gentle snort and a chuff of warm, moist breath.

Maximilian pricked his ears and snorted back.

The horses rubbed noses across the rail, and Satcher leaned forward to pat his champion's glossy neck. "Later, fella," he said softly. "Catch you later!"

Reaching the bottom of the driveway, Satcher and Maximilian swung left toward the private airstrip where the white Gulfstream, with its navy-and-vermilion insignia *CAS* on the tail, lay quietly idle. Maximilian was used to coming this way and continued his ground-covering jog trot without a break in rhythm, Satcher riding loose-reined and swaying effortlessly in the saddle, allowing the horse to choose the route around the perimeter of the runway, onto the dirt track through the trees, past the paddocks where the few early-birthing mares nursed their foals, finally pulling up at the entrance to the beautifully maintained private racetrack.

His timing was good.

Cynthia, who had been watching the morning workout of their new two-year-old, was cantering gently toward him across the emerald grass. His wife wore impeccably pressed jeans, a faded blue flannel shirt under a denim vest, and thousand-dollar boots. She looked gorgeous. Satcher was immensely proud of her. She was twenty-five years younger than he was, and while she was stone beautiful with her sculpted cheekbones and thick fall of honey-blond hair, she was definitely no vapid trophy wife. To the contrary, they had become a formidable team through fifteen resilient years of marriage. Cynthia was ambitious and smart. She was a fine rider and could pilot a plane, held a master's degree in journalism from Stanford University, and before marrying Satcher and moving to Washington, D.C., as a Senator's wife, had run her own successful public relations agency in Los Angeles.

"He's a mean bugger," Cynthia said now of their new acquisition, who was small but fast, with a streak of temper which they hoped would be molded into a desire to win no matter what. "Just full of it. He bit Marcos in the arm. Would have torn a piece out of him if Marcos wasn't so quick."

"Maybe he thinks he has something to prove," Satcher said.

"Because he's small? Like Napoleon and Alexander the Great?"

"He'll do us proud—wait and see."

Cynthia reigned in alongside him and they trotted together in comfortable silence, knee to knee, up the steep trail. Soon these hills would be brilliant with spring flowers—purple lupine and the blazing orange of the California poppy. When the rains ended, they would become an undulating sea of golden grass punctuated by the dark green clumps of live oak thickets.

Beautiful! How Satcher loved this land!

If he turned in the saddle, he knew that every inch of what he saw belonged to him—to them—all the way down to the ribbon of Highway 101 where it skirted the coast. And that was but a small part of it.

Satcher also owned a chunk of Los Angeles County, with shopping centers, malls, and apartment buildings, as well as three prime acres in Bel Air upon which stood his eight-bedroom mansion with staff quarters and guest cottage, ten-car garage, tennis court, rolling lawn, and Italianate marble pool. Whenever possible, however, he preferred to spend time here on his ranch in Ventura County. It was the nerve center of his wide-flung interests, which included mining and oil-drilling interests in Utah, Texas, and Colorado, forestry operations in Northern California and Oregon, numerous housing and highway developments, and tracts of raw land in Montana and Wyoming, rich in shale oil and still virtually untapped.

Soon now, if things progressed as they should, the Satcher empire would extend north into Alaska, with its treasure trove of hidden riches—and so conveniently far away! No matter how loudly the environmental nuts like Ellen Fischer screamed, relatively few people actually went to Alaska, and when they did, they mostly stayed warm and cozy on their cruise ships, observing the glaciers, the caribou, and the grizzlies from a safe distance.

Only a relative handful made it into the hinterland, into those millions of square miles with their rich deposits of fossil fuels and minerals, and their potential for incalculable wealth.

But it wasn't only about the money.

When you got down to basics, it was the power that mattered.

Carl Satcher had spent the best years of his life in the U.S. Senate, until being unseated by that redheaded *nothingburger* (he could think of far worse names to call her, and had done so, but his mood right now was mellow), although a Senate seat seemed less important when, provided all went according to plan, he'd be confirmed as Secretary of Homeland Security within the month.

Personally, Satcher didn't care much for Craig Fulton and even regarded him with mild contempt. Satcher, from an old California pioneer family, had been raised with money, unlike Fulton, who was of lower-middle-class origins, with the narrow attitudes and pruderies of his station. Satcher wondered why a woman like Grace, from a different stratum of society altogether, would have married someone like that—though Fulton was undeniably handsome, relentlessly energetic, and so patently sincere, the kind of man you'd trust to sell you Florida property and know you wouldn't end up owning a piece of swampland that spent half the year under water.

And he was politically ambitious, too—Grace would have recognized his potential, and her possible ticket to the White House.

Satcher reined Maximilian in at a turn of the path, moving with Cynthia at his side to a grassy ledge from where he could look out over his vast holdings: house, stables, paddocks, and landing strip spread out below him like a landscape painting.

How small it all looked, how insignificant from up here, the magnificent horses and the grounded plane as tiny as toys, and in the middle of it all a diminutive figure, almost certainly resident veterinarian Gary Stonehouse, six-foot-five if he was an inch, crossing the stable yard to the barns.

Satcher smiled to himself and began to whistle through his teeth. "The Ride of the Valkyries." *DAH dum, dah diddy DUM dum, dah diddy DUM DUM, dah diddy DAH* . . . He had screened *Apocalypse Now* over and over again, loving those helicopters booming, fearsomely amped, across the rice paddies and forested ridges of Vietnam.

He considered it both an insult and an outrage that that little prick Slaughter used Richard Wagner's masterpiece to introduce his sleazy radio show.

No question, though, the show helped to stir up the fanatics and fools—the typical Slaughter fan was not the sharpest knife in the drawer—and the racket they made could be turned to useful ends.

Looking through Maximilian's twitching ears at the far blue reaches of the Pacific Ocean, Satcher said, "You did a nice job with that press release."

"It wasn't hard," Cynthia said. "Tacky and personal, the kind of stuff people can relate to. And you can be sure, when someone like Slaughter gets his dirty little paws on it, it comes across even tackier."

"So long as you got the main message across: that Fischer's corrupt and unreliable and not someone who should have *any* say at *all* in cabinet appointments." With the smallest tinge of anxiety, Satcher asked her, "You didn't leave any kind of fingerprint on it?"

"Don't worry. Nobody will make any connections with us."

"They'll certainly try."

"Then they'll be out of luck. Our guy's good. And he's loyal."

"When's the next bombshell scheduled to hit?"

"Tomorrow first thing. The copy's set to go and the picture looks really great."

"A touch of genius, that picture!"

"It's amazing what's available these days. It was simple. Thank God for Google Alert."

"So you just type in the person's name? And if there's a published photo—"

"—anywhere in the world, it comes right up. This picture actually appeared in some paper in Singapore."

"No kidding. Why Singapore?"

"Who knows."

"And who cares!" Satcher said, then added with satisfaction, "Fischer won't just appear corrupt, now she'll look like a fool as well. A dangerous fool."

Cynthia didn't deny it.

After a moment Satcher asked, "Are you looking forward to getting back there?"

"To D.C.? Of course." Cynthia leaned forward to stroke her mount's sturdy, chestnut flank. He snorted gently and leaned his neck to nibble grass, and she stared across the curve of his withers over the wide land she and her husband owned together. "Can't stand the weather, except in spring and fall, but I miss the action. We'll need a weekend place, though. I thought I'd look at properties out in Virginia, where we can keep horses. Around Warrenton or Middleburgh. Jackie Kennedy had a place there."

Satcher thought of Jackie Kennedy, trim and beautiful in her white breeches and bowler hat, out fox hunting. "Nice," he said. And with exasperation: "I've *never* understood how she could have been a Democrat!"

"We'll have to get an apartment in town, too," Cynthia said. "I'm tired of hotels."

Satcher contemplated the mansion on the grounds of the U.S. Naval Observatory, official home of the Vice President of the United States. "By the end of next year, we could be moving into the Vice President's residence. How would you like that?"

"You're certain Craig will make you his running mate?" Cynthia wondered.

"As certain as one can be of anything," Satcher said, letting the reins spool out between his fingers as Maximilian lowered his neck and also began to graze. "He needs me, and he knows it."

"Of course he does," Cynthia agreed. After a pause: "And then?"

"You mean, where do we set up housekeeping after the residence?" Satcher turned in his saddle to study her, so at ease in the saddle, so elegant, so accomplished on all fronts. "Maybe we'll move downtown. Somewhere more central. I can think of one particular address that would suit us," he said.

"That would do just fine," Cynthia said, and they smiled at each other in perfect understanding.

CHAPTER EIGHT

At 2:45 P.M., Ellen, wearing her defiantly bright jacket, strode through the Capitol corridors and up the wide marble staircase, her feet slipping with familiarity into the dish-shaped depressions worn by countless other feet over the centuries, on her way to the Senate Press Gallery located one flight above the Senate floor. This was the traditional venue for Senators to broadcast news good and bad; to report on bills passed or failed; battles won or lost; and to share personal crises, such as catastrophic health issues, with the nation.

Flanking Ellen, in a protective wedge, were David Makins in a smart new blazer, light blue Oxford shirt, and striped tie, and Derelle wearing a black leather jacket over an amber turtleneck the same shade as her narrowed, watchful eyes.

Ellen knew that by now her imminent arrival would have been announced, and she consciously made her mind go cool and distant.

People loomed up in her path and fell away, some known to her, most not; many were strangers on a tour of the Capitol for whom recognition of this newly notorious Senator would be the highlight of their trip. Voices faded in and out:

"That's her—that's Senator Fischer!"

"She looks taller on TV."

"She'd better resign or else."

"Hey, it's quitting time, Ellen!"

And, from a lone supporter, "Go, Ellen! Hang in there!"

Ellen had rehearsed what she would say, first silently in her office, then aloud in the privacy of her little bathroom. No notes. Straight from the heart.

They moved into the packed gallery now, into a blizzard of flashing light, then Ellen approached the podium, mounting the stool David had already set in place, since otherwise the tangle of microphones would be too high and too far back for her. When the dazzle of popping bulbs faded, she found herself facing at least thirty speculative pairs of eyes, many of them cynical, including those of Abner Calloway of the D.C. Times, her declared enemy, a thickset, almost thuggish presence seated front and center.

Ellen scanned backward from Calloway, row by row, trying to make eye contact with each and every individual, glad of the reassuring presence of David and Derelle, knowing their eyes were fixed upon her and that they were silently willing her strength.

She drew a resolute breath and gripped the sides of the podium with both hands.

"Thank you for coming, and I wish you all a happy new year. Although this is not exactly a good day for my family and me, I know we can only go up from here," she said, aware of a shifting impatience, and from the back of the room a stifled snort of skepticism.

"Now, about this blind trust issue. I'll be completely up front with you because I have nothing to hide. From the beginning, my husband's trust has been handled by the law firm where he worked before being elected to the House twelve years ago. At the time his investments went into the blind trust, his portfolio included no oil or energy stocks. Subsequently, according to the rules of the House, he was no longer allowed to know its makeup—that's why it's called a blind trust. And, of course," Ellen went on, "neither he nor I could exert any control over what was bought or sold. When we were married, my own assets—such as they were, and they weren't much, believe me—remained in a separate blind trust.

"Yesterday's disclosure, and the allegation that we have knowingly and cynically profited from oil and energy stocks, is both a stunning shock and of the utmost concern to us. Neither my husband nor I has ever been involved in any type of financial scandal, and I want to remind you that in this particular instance we have done nothing illegal, unethical, or even remotely improper."

Ellen drew a long, deep breath.

"Clearly, someone has attempted malicious damage." Her face devoid of expression, her voice deliberate, she continued, "We can only suppose that their motive is to discredit and damage me politically at such a crucial time. We have every expectation of finding those responsible. They have not only invaded our privacy, they have almost certainly broken the law."

She allowed her eyes to pass once again across the rows of faces. "In the meantime, I ask my colleagues, and the people of California who sent me to the Senate, to stick with me and not get distracted. We *will* get through this. Now, I'll be happy to answer any questions. . . ."

She called upon Abner Calloway first, to get it over with.

His question was much as expected: "Senator, do you seriously expect us to believe that you *never* discussed the contents of that trust with your husband?"

"I most certainly do. As I have explained, we did not know its composition. To know its contents would be illegal, and needless to say, neither my husband nor I would *ever* do that."

Ellen pointed at another reporter.

"Norene Parker, *San Francisco Chronicle*. Senator, how do you think the voters feel, since you always told them you were fearless against special interests and now it looks like those very interests were making you rich?"

California—her own state. That hurt.

"I always have been, and I always will be, fearless!" Ellen threw a quick glance at David and Derelle, who both silently urged her to stay cool, stand firm, and give as good as she got. "Are you suggesting that I have been helping the oil and energy industry? Is *that* what you're implying, Norene?" Without waiting for a response, she went on, "In this case, certainly my record speaks for itself. It will show that I never, at any time, did anything to help those special interests. And once again, let me say that I did *not* know what was in the trust."

A nod toward the press.

"Ava Nowicki, *Philadelphia Inquirer.* Senator, as a result of this disclosure, do you expect to be asked to step down as Chair in the upcoming hearings for Secretary of Homeland Security?"

Ellen had expected that one, too. "There is no reason for me to be asked to step down, since I have done nothing wrong," she answered.

"Marty Levine, *New York Times.* Senator, in view of your past hostile relationship with Mr. Satcher, do you not feel you should recuse yourself from these hearings?"

"I have no conflict of interest. If being of a different political party, or having run for office against somebody in the past, disqualifies you from doing your job fairly, we'd have to outsource most of the jobs in this town!" For the first time, she saw a few smiles, even heard a chuckle or two, and from that point onward it was relatively clear sailing.

Ellen answered each and every question calmly, candidly, neither fulminating against the injustice of the accusation nor attempting to disarm with smiles, as if this was just one more troublesome issue to take in stride on an admittedly difficult but not so unusual day.

And now, after forty minutes, David was bringing the show to a close and calling for just one more question.

"Anna Marcucci, Associated Press. Senator, you suggested that certain individuals would like to see you discredited at this particular time. Are you suggesting that Mr. Satcher, or the Vice President himself, could be involved in any way with this disclosure, and if so, do you have any proof?"

Ellen grasped the podium so hard, her knuckles turned white. Managing not to shoot an anxious glance at David, she raised her voice against the immediate clamor.

"I implied nothing of the kind. In today's climate of controversy, clearly some people would like me removed while others would prefer that I stay. I'm sure that comes as no surprise to anyone!

"And now, if you need any further information, ask David Makins—you all know David."

She glanced around the room with finality. Then, with a brisk nod and a "Thank you," she stepped down from the podium and was gone.

CHAPTER NINE

Ben decided to walk to Ellen's office in the Hart Building, and could cover the distance in half an hour if he moved briskly. He was glad to leave the apartment, where he'd spent most of the day on the phone with Judge Ray in Arizona. It was still only four P.M. there.

The investigator had met with the judge this morning and gone straight to work.

Ben was of two minds about his involvement. This Brown, or Browning, apart from hacking successfully into government files, had also been charged in the past with extorting large sums of money from various corporations whose systems had been contaminated by viruses he'd installed in them. However, Zachary Ray assured him that this had all happened a long time ago, that the man had turned over a new leaf and was now to be trusted.

He had certainly, so far, been productive.

He'd already run a thorough check on the individuals at the brokerage house who had approved access to Ben's portfolio. There were only five. Two were account managers, both over fifty, who had worked there for over twenty years and were approaching retirement; both were highly competent and, apparently, completely loyal. The other three were CPAs who also seemed low risk.

Brown, having requested a list of individuals who might, for whatever reason, wish Ellen harm—and what a list it was, including as it did the second most powerful man in the country—was now in the process of widening the investigation to include all employees of the law firm and the brokerage house, regardless of function. He would now be looking for what he described as lines of merge.

"For crossovers," the judge had explained to Ben, "the same names appearing in unexpected places and contexts. You understand?"

Ben had not returned the call from Anita Hirsch, and was not yet prepared to consider its possible significance. One thing at a time. The Hirsches had been the ones to cancel; let them get back to him when they were ready. And if the partnership offer was rescinded, then so be it, and he would write them off as fair-weather friends.

Anyway, he had now, perforce, made other plans for tomorrow night.

His spirits began to rise and his muscles to feel better from the exercise as he strode swiftly from block to block.

In any case, he always enjoyed walking down Pennsylvania Avenue, the Avenue of Presidents, the ultimate Main Street USA. He appreciated the variety of architecture, from the Romanesque Old Post Office pavilion, to the brutalist concrete bunker of the J. Edgar Hoover Building, to the graceful neoclassic facade of the Canadian embassy.

He liked the sense of connection with past events, stirring, tragic, or cataclysmic. He'd imagine the ghosts of marching suffragettes and the Depression-era unemployed jostling together with the Civil Rights marchers and the Vietnam War protesters, all mingled with the inauguration parades, the motorcades for national heroes and foreign leaders, and the funeral corteges for past Presidents who'd died in office. Ellen had said the same thing: "I like to feel I'm a part of it, too, that it's all going on and on, and that after I'm gone, my spirit will be marching along with theirs. . . ."

Ben wished he could have been at the press conference this afternoon to lend his support, but Ellen's staff had been adamantly opposed to that. His presence might suggest a dependency upon her husband, he'd been told; she must handle this one alone. He'd watched with helpless anger as his wife's hands gripped the edges of the podium, and fiercely but silently applauded her patience as she'd declared, time after time, that she and Ben had never known about the stocks, and that, "I always have been, and I always will be, fearless!"

It was her voice, and its sincerity, that he had found so arresting when they'd first met, over four years ago.

She'd worn green that time, too, a spring-like green jacket over a demure knee-length gray skirt and matching hose, and he'd thought her eyes were green, too, though he'd learn they were actually hazel, with clusters of honey gold and brown flecks around the iris.

He remembered the occasion so well—a conference committee between the Senate and the House to resolve the differences in a bill Ellen was sponsoring, the Child Protection and Enforcement Act, which had passed both chambers. The bill made any crime against a child a federal crime, and provided funding by the federal government, if requested by the states, for shelters, training, and intervention—and when necessary, the removal of a child from a lethally abusive home. Ellen had included a provision that some thought unconstitutional—the confiscation of all firearms from the offending households—but the provision had been upheld in legal challenges after the law was passed.

As a Republican member of Congress, Ben had gone into that meeting prepared to agree with the thrust of the bill—how could one disagree with the need for protection of children?—but not with that last measure.

He had changed his mind.

Or, rather, *she* had changed his mind.

He could remember every word of that closed-session speech, Ellen's voice growing deeper and stronger just as, at the same time, she'd appeared to grow taller.

"I *saw* firsthand the conditions these kids were living in, and what they suffered on a day-to-day basis," she'd said, "and it was impossible to imagine how anyone living in such hopelessness could even survive, let alone keep any sense of self and dignity. Add a gun into the mix, and it becomes even more lethal."

Her gaze seemed to be fixed upon Ben personally as she concluded, "I beg you, I *urge* you, to support me in *every* provision of this bill, especially the last one. Our children are our most precious resource. That's what we all say, right? But in the privacy of this room, we better not just say these words, we better mean them! Our children have a right to be allowed to grow up. They must have their chance. How can they be *our* future when *they* have none?"

Afterward, Ben found his way to Ellen's side. "You're very effective," he said. "Would you cross the aisle far enough to let me buy you a drink to celebrate your victory? I was, after all, the swing vote!"

The corners of Ellen's mouth lifted, almost impishly. "A drink with a Republican colleague? That would be a first for me!"

"On neutral ground, of course."

"I guess I could make an exception. . . ."

"Somewhere dark and very discreet where nobody will see."

"Are you mad?" She looked amused. "Someone *always* sees. They'd think we have something to hide—and we don't, do we?"

"Not yet," he said, "but we could work on it!" Ben realized he sounded too glib, and regretted the words the moment they left his lips.

"It would take a lot of work. Maybe some other time." Ellen had turned away.

Had she taken offense? Was she disappointed in him?

Ben had felt like he was sixteen again, all height and overlarge hands and feet and never able to come up with the right words until too late. "The truth is, Ellen," he said, determinedly following her, since he couldn't allow this chance to slip away, "I'd like to continue our conversation. Maybe about a follow-on bill?"

So she'd relented. They went to a bright, busy bar on I Street, where he knew half the people in the room and she probably knew the other half, and where of course they'd be noticed and their relationship, such as it was, speculated upon but dismissed as the innocent non-event it must surely be in such a place. They'd indeed discussed a possible follow-on bill while they each enjoyed a glass of California Chardonnay and nibbled on nuts until, hating to break it up and go home alone, he'd ended by inviting her to dinner.

She'd said no, she had plans. He couldn't decide whether she sounded regretful or not. Then she said, "But I'd like a raincheck!"

He'd walked home on clouds and called her the next day. "I know the dating rules say one's supposed to wait longer and play it cool—but I want to see you, and it's not like we're teenagers!"

But she was leaving for California that same afternoon, and when he called her the following week, she was in a meeting. They spent the next three days playing phone tag and leaving messages on each other's voice mail, and then Ben had to return to Phoenix.

When they eventually managed to get together, Ellen looking beautiful in a plain, scoop-necked black dress and bottle-green suede coat, Ben took her to the Four Seasons for dinner and, long before the crème brûlée and the decaf espresso, had fallen in love.

He asked her to marry him two weeks later, during inter-mission at a Rachmaninoff concert at the Kennedy Center.

Ellen looked genuinely stunned. She'd been holding his arm, and dropped it.

"Does this really come as such a surprise?" he'd asked.

"I hadn't thought about it. It's too soon for me to think about marrying again."

With quiet insistence, he said, "It's not too soon. Josh has been gone over four years."

"It doesn't seem that long."

"Because you never stop working. You cram your day so full, you don't have time to think. Or feel. I know how it is. I did the same thing."

Ben had been alone twelve years, twelve long years since Hilly, her beautiful body reduced to parchment skin stretched over bone, her lustrous black hair white and sparse since the chemo, had looked at him without a trace of recognition and murmured in a rusty voice something about how she was late and needed to get back to the dorm. He'd realized then that she had wandered in her mind back to college days long before he'd even met her. Soon afterward she lapsed into a coma and never returned.

"I didn't think I'd get married again, either," Ben told Ellen. "But there comes a time when you have to move on, and if you're really lucky, you find the right person to move on with." He held the point of her chin gently in his hand and turned her face to his. "I'm not getting any younger, you know, and neither are you."

She'd laughed. "Point taken! What a cowardly blow!"

"But true. For God's sake, Ellen, we've known each other a whole month already! We're wasting time!"

★ ★ ★

He asked her again the following week, over lunch at the private table way at the back of the ornate Senate dining room. He still remembered what they had to eat—a cup of navy bean soup, fresh crab salad, and one giant corn muffin split righteously between them—just as he remembered every detail of their too-few times together. He refused to call them "dates"—the word was inappropriate and childish and this relationship was anything but.

"Please try and understand," Ellen responded to this second proposal, raising troubled eyes to his, "that I'm scared of living with someone else, loving somebody else, and trying to meet their expectations. Suppose it doesn't work? Suppose, after Josh, there isn't enough of me left over for anyone else?"

At least, he thought, this time it wasn't an outright refusal. "You can have all the space you need. After a while, perhaps you'll find you won't need it."

"I've grown too used to being alone—it's become a habit."

"Habits are there to be broken."

"We disagree on so many things."

"Not the important ones."

"We argue all the time."

"Then I predict our dinners together will never be boring!"

They met each other's eyes, both laughing, then Ellen's laughter faded. She bent her head, spent a very long time meticulously spreading a thin coating of butter on her muffin, and suddenly he lost his patience.

"Listen, ever since I saw you across that room, fighting for your children's bill with every nerve in your body, I've loved you and wanted you and I can't stand the thought of losing you. But this is it, lady! This is the end of the line. I'm not just some colleague asking you to co-sponsor a bill. I'm asking you to marry me!"

And at last, finally, she said yes, and he vowed she'd never regret it.

★ ★ ★

It was almost seven o'clock as Ben cut past the Canadian embassy to Constitution Avenue. Another five minutes and he would be at the Hart Building, where he'd rescue Ellen from the rigors of her day. But before his husky, ex-security-guard driver could appear with the Lincoln and sweep them home to warmth, comfort, and privacy, Ben would have to face the ever-polite but shuttered eyes of Derelle, who had the ability to stare directly into his face while revealing nothing of what she was really thinking.

At the beginning, he had attempted to win Derelle's friendship, but although she was unfailingly polite, she maintained an invisible barrier between them and there seemed no way to breach it.

Though he'd still like to have a friendly relationship with Ellen's Chief of Staff, he'd given up and settled for her cool formality.

Did Derelle resent him for taking Josh's place? Was she jealous?

Ben was well aware of the long history between the two women, which went all the way back to Ellen's intervention and rescue when Derelle was an abused, violent child. He knew that over the years Ellen had nurtured Derelle, mentored and all but mothered her.

Now, in a reversal of roles, might it be Derelle who perceived herself as the guardian?

Although she had to be aware that Ben was blameless over this blind trust fiasco, might Derelle hold him responsible for destroying Ellen's peace of mind and, potentially, her career?

Well, he'd worry about her later, along with the Hirsches, when he had the time.

For now, he must tell Ellen that he'd made a reservation for the first flight out for Phoenix the following morning and would not be here to celebrate his birthday with her after all.

He wasn't looking forward to telling her.

He knew that, even without the Hirsches, she'd planned to make this dinner a special occasion.

However, under the circumstances, how could they possibly enjoy it?

There'd be another time, a better time, Ben thought.

For now, he could do far more to help Ellen elsewhere.

CHAPTER TEN

January 3

THURSDAY

David Makins, in mismatched pajamas—the top a subdued and faded flannel plaid in blues and grays with several buttons missing, the lower half navy silk patterned with prancing red-white-and-blue donkeys—hauled himself out of his rumpled bed, got himself his first coffee of the day, and headed for his computer.

He missed his wife and twin teenage daughters, but was glad they were still in Maine. He didn't need distractions, even the happy demands of family. And there was no time for such niceties as coordinating his pajamas.

He absently scratched his furry stomach with his left hand while scrolling the day's online news with his right.

Today's *Bridger Report* was muted.

Other feedback on Ellen's press conference was also restrained, much as he'd hoped.

He'd reasoned that, compared with the political scandals that regularly made the front pages, Ellen's situation was basically a non-event despite the rantings of shock jocks such as Sam Slaughter, and it seemed he was being proved right.

With a few exceptions such as, predictably, the *D.C. Times* editorials, reaction in the mainstream media to her press conference was favorable and the fires were dying down. There had only been cursory mention on last night's news shows, and the story had not been picked up by Letterman, Leno, Jon Stewart, or Colbert.

As to the regular shovelfuls of dirt so liberally applied by Sam Slaughter—*"Our Ellen's going down, down, DOWN! And if you want my opinion, it can't be soon enough, for me or for the country!"*—David knew that without fuel to keep the story alive, it would soon sink into the dead zone of old news, where it belonged.

He next scrolled through the swirling vortex of the blogosphere, checking up on the usual anti-Ellen blogs, glad to discover that not only had Derelle launched her e-mail campaign, but it appeared to be thriving.

Ellen had a huge following of young people, especially in California, whose lives she had touched directly or indirectly. Many were minorities, from impoverished and violent backgrounds, like Derelle herself. The oldest of them, who had self-styled themselves Ellen's Kids during her first run for the Senate, were in their mid-twenties now and could be noisily supportive, especially on the Internet.

Derelle had a list of thousands of names, which she could access with one click of the mouse. She'd e-mailed them all yesterday, giving the URLs for the most offensive blogs and links to the chatrooms. Their assignment, to be carried out with no undignified cyber slanging matches and, whatever the temptation, without the use of obscenities, was to counteract, politely but firmly, the negative views expressed in the blogs.

"Try to make them think," Derelle had ordered. "It's hard, I know, but do your best." David chuckled aloud now at the battle-lines being drawn on the screen:

What's wrong with you anyway? demanded Blufang, a seventeen-year-old ex–graffiti artist who, thanks to Ellen's intervention, now planned to go to art school, of Morningglory, whose misspelled prose had spewed its way through ten lines of vitriol. *So what if Senator Fischer married a rich guy? She never had peanuts before, she gave it all away. Would someone do that if she just wanted money? If you can think for yourself and don't believe all that crap just because its on TV then check it out. The info's all there. I dare you! And if Senator Fischer says she didnt know what the money was invested in thats good enough for me!*

Guerrero: *You got it all wrong. Senator Fischers a nice lady. She help my Mom when she was sick and the insurance run out and lost her job in the plant. She says it like it is and doesnt lie.*

Cinnamon13: *Dont you know a conspiracy when you see one? Someones out to get her with all of these mean rumers. Seems to me soon as a person tries to do some good in this country someone else is trying to get at them and close them down.*

Wizard: *People living in glass houses shouldn't be throwing stones. What do they have to gain? Lots, Im sure. Think about it!*

David hoped it would help; certainly it could do no harm.

He got up and went to the kitchen for more coffee and to grab a piece of yesterday's stale Danish, then to the bedroom to dress in comfortable flannel trousers, button-down shirt, and a tweed jacket. After putting a tie in his pocket in case of emergency, he hauled on his fleece-lined raincoat, jammed a knitted ski cap low down on his brow, and stepped out into the cold dawn.

He knew it would be another long day.

CHAPTER ELEVEN

Derelle Simba lay in bed, flat on her back with arms linked behind her head, staring at the opposite wall where she'd hung the blown-up photograph of the Taj Mahal, its jeweled dome and minarets milky pale in the dawn light.

Derelle herself was sitting on a bench in the foreground, the same bench where Princess Diana had once sat so poignantly alone in the most romantic location in the world, the memorial built four hundred years ago by a Mughal ruler for his beloved, dead queen. But while the lonely Princess of Wales had gazed forlornly at the camera with an almost audible sigh, she, Derelle, was smiling broadly.

Nor was she alone.

Salima was behind the camera, her elongated shadow aimed like a dart toward Derelle's bench and falling across her toes.

Derelle had known Salima for just two days.

As Senator Fischer's Chief of Staff, Derelle had accompanied her to New Delhi for a conference on global warming. Derelle had never before been on a trip such as this, and felt out of her depth with all the sophistication and ceremony. She also felt too tall and too drab in her sensible Western business clothes, her eyelids ached with tiredness, and at lunch that first day at the Oberoi Hotel she was dismayed to find herself seated beside petite, exotic Salima. What could they possibly talk about? Did the woman even speak English?

But there was no problem. Salima's English was not only excellent, but she was good company besides. She asked Derelle all the right questions and none of the wrong ones and, despite herself, Derelle found herself warming and expanding under the flattering attention. By the end of lunch, she had decided Salima was the best, if not the only, friend she had ever had.

If only she had a picture of her, but on neither of the occasions they were alone together did Derelle have her camera. How could she have been such a fool? Now, until Salima sent her a photo, Derelle must be content merely with her friend's shadow, endowing it with substance and color and motion, imagining the lively, dark face, the slender hands and feet, the golden, knee-length embroidered tunic over the slim-legged trousers.

Salima's traditional outfit was called a salwar kameez.

In the picture, Derelle was wearing one, too.

Hers was ivory colored, with russet and green embroidery down the front of the tunic and on the cuffs, and she'd been startled to see how well she looked in it.

★ ★ ★

That first afternoon, Salima had insisted on taking Derelle to a crafts fair during the brief window between lunch and the reception at the Chinese embassy, so while Ellen retired to her room to study her notes—she was giving a talk that evening on global warming and energy efficiency—Derelle found herself swept into a taxi and carried halfway across town. Or so it seemed. Maybe they hadn't traveled so far—how could she tell, since the streets all looked the same, congested with cars and fuming buses, overloaded bicycles, motor scooters, pedestrians, and casually wandering animals? All Derelle knew was that it had taken forty-five minutes to reach their destination and thus would take at least that long to return, probably longer since it would be rush hour by that time. She worried about the time, about Ellen waiting.

"We'll be late for the reception," she said to Salima.

"No one will care," Salima said. "The traffic is always terrible. Everybody knows that."

"I wasn't planning on going shopping, anyway."

"You're in India; shopping is a moral obligation."

"But I'm here on business!"

"Which means you're not allowed to shop? Nonsense. If selling is business, then looking, and maybe buying, must be business, too!" Salima laughed. "It always astonishes me how you Westerners live your lives, with your work, your play, your politics, and the worship of your God all in separate little boxes with no overlapping allowed between them. It makes no sense at all! You must at least look," she urged.

Derelle gave in. "Just ten minutes, then."

"Good—you won't regret it!" Salima said. "This is a very special event. We'll see the best fabric and crafts from all over northern India!"

She bought two tickets for fifteen rupees apiece and ushered Derelle through the gates.

Once inside, Derelle found herself in an enormous bazaar, a city in itself with one long main street and scores of branching alleys lined with stalls displaying all varieties of beautiful things— pashminas from Kashmir so fine they could be pulled through a wedding ring; rolls of sari silk; rainbows of scarves billowing in the breeze in an iridescent spectrum from scarlet through lemon and peacock blue to deepest purple. The sight of such colors all together stunned her senses.

Derelle forgot all about the time, as Salima had probably expected she would, and began to buy gifts. For Ellen, a long silk scarf, one side forest green shot with gold, the other side a shimmering gold shot with green. For David Makins, a traditional collarless shirt of finest lawn cotton. For Celia Chen's small son, a ferocious-looking puppet in a red satin robe and a tiny turban.

"Something for you now," Salima said.

"I don't need anything."

"I'm not talking need, I'm talking *want*." Laying a slim brown hand on Derelle's arm, she said, "Let's look at these!"

And there, swaying on hangers, were the tunic jackets of embroidered silk and the matching trousers. Salima chose a tunic and held it up against Derelle's body. "It looks so good against your wonderful skin!"

Derelle wasn't used to anyone praising her skin and she'd never before considered herself good looking, but she agreed to try it on. She entered the little compartment behind a prim curtain of striped cotton, changed with reluctance, and emerged almost shyly.

"You look lovely!" Salima cried, clapping her hands with pleasure. "Doesn't she look beautiful?" she demanded of the stall owner, a stout woman bundled in shawls, and of the pretty girl at her side with the gold nose ring and earrings and the scarlet bride-bangles tinkling up her arms.

"Oh my goodness, yes!" the woman agreed.

A bout of spirited bargaining ensued and an amount was settled upon in the thousands of rupees—a formidable-sounding figure, but not so frightening when translated to dollars. The girl, sensing opportunity, rushed to get more kameezes and tunics to hold up against Derelle's powerful, long-limbed, very un-Indian body, and all agreed that she would look great in those, too.

"Only one," Derelle insisted. "This one." As she reached for her purse, a small battle erupted with Salima over who was going to pay for it, a battle that Derelle lost.

"It's a gift," Salima insisted. "Please, you must allow me! A small souvenir of India! Of this day. After all," she pointed out, "you might never come here again."

★ ★ ★

So there she was, Derelle Simba at the Taj Mahal, grinning into the camera at Salima's silhouette with the dawn behind her, wearing her new Indian clothes, her head draped with the scarf she had bought for Ellen, which Ellen insisted she borrow back again because the air would be cool. "The colors are perfect. It looks even better on you than on me," Ellen had said. "And aren't you supposed to cover your head when you go to a temple?"

Derelle had wanted to give Salima a gift in return. Something personal. Perhaps a book? But the books Derelle saw in the hotel gift shops were all coffee-table souvenir tomes about India, which Salima didn't need because India was her world; it was all around her when she opened her eyes each morning, and was the last thing she saw at night.

A CD? But she knew little of Salima's musical tastes.

Jewelry would be inappropriate.

In the end, on impulse entering a small bookstore on a narrow side street, Derelle found a book of the poetry of Omar Khayyam, in Farsi with English translation, with wonderful illumined pictures in misty blues and gold.

She wrote inside, *For Salima, my guide and friend, with love and gratitude, Derelle.*

Altogether too flowery—but somehow right, at this time, in this place.

She'd given the book to Salima back in New Delhi, before she and Ellen left for the airport. Salima had taken Derelle's large, strong hand in both of her small ones and said she'd treasure it.

They'd exchanged e-mail addresses. Derelle had written at once upon returning home, and *please,* she'd begged, don't forget to send me a photo. So far she hadn't heard back, and with a feeling of hollow loneliness, she suspected she never would.

★ ★ ★

Now it was past time to get up.

The day was creeping in, a finger of wan, gray light sliding up Derelle's bedroom wall.

She must hurry or she would be late.

Still, she allowed herself just a few more minutes of lying in bed, gazing at that image of one of the wonders of the world, at the smiling woman sitting before it on a stone bench and Salima's shadow touching her foot and ankle like a blessing.

Just six weeks ago, but it might as well have been a lifetime.

That was why Derelle had gone to New York City over the holidays and, in a bookstore near the United Nations building, bought a book featuring Gujarat province, which included a photograph of the sixteenth-century Mosque of Sidi Saiyad in Ahmedabad, Salima's hometown.

Perhaps Salima had worshipped there, had admired its beautiful windows of carved stone filigree; perhaps her bare feet had crossed its cool tiled floor.

It brought it all back for Derelle. Or at least part of the way.

CHAPTER TWELVE

In the Vice President's residence, a little before noon, Grace Fulton sat across the table from her bewildering daughter in the breakfast nook, attempting to communicate with her.

Grace was wearing oatmeal-colored slacks and a heavy white cotton shirt, a navy cashmere cardigan slung across her slender shoulders. Her blond hair was smooth and blunt-cut, her makeup minimal save for pale lipstick and a touch of mascara on her light lashes, her only jewelry the thick gold wedding band on her left hand.

Brianna faced her mother, pallid and heavy eyed, lank black hair drooping over her thin shoulders, knees drawn up to her chest beneath a man's orange T-shirt which proclaimed: YEA THOUGH I WALK IN THE VALLEY OF THE SHADOW OF DEATH I SHALL FEAR NO EVIL—BECAUSE I'M THE MEANEST SON OF A BITCH IN THE VALLEY.

She cradled a mug of industrial-strength coffee in her long, spidery fingers. In front of her sat a shredded croissant on a plate— breakfast, and here it was noon already.

"I'm not hungry, Mom. I ate earlier," Brianna had said, which could have meant anything. The child didn't keep the same hours as most people for eating or sleeping. At three A.M., upon waking to sounds from downstairs, Grace might find Brianna at the refrigerator loading a plate with leftover chicken pot pie, or a banana and a slab of cake, or in late afternoon she might find her munching directly from a box of cereal.

In the past two years, since Brianna had left for Berkeley and become a rebel without a cause, Grace felt she'd entirely lost touch with her daughter.

Brianna used to be cheerful, sweet, and loving. Now she was remote and surly, and her face was far too pale for a girl going to school in California, where the sun was always supposed to shine. Although she'd gone to bed relatively early the night before, she appeared listless and tired. Grace hoped the child wasn't ill with a virus, something like mono; or worse, had an eating disorder; or worst of all, was into drugs. Grace liked to think she was an up-to-date kind of mother who would know at once if her daughter was using drugs, though she'd talked with too many mothers who had thought the same thing but then found, much to their surprise, that it was not so.

Or maybe it was just that Brianna had stayed up late e-mailing and text-messaging her friends like they all did. Grace told herself she must trust her daughter. And although the girl seemed far too thin, she showed no evidence of anorexia.

Unless, of course, she was bulimic?

Oh dear, thought Grace, and decided that if—no, *when*—she was First Lady, she would make protection of the young, including education about drugs, eating disorders, and sexually transmitted diseases, her number one project.

She watched Brianna select a Granny Smith apple from the fruit bowl in the middle of the table, take a large, crunching bite, then put it back again. At least her teeth were good; she had her father's strong, white teeth.

"Do you *really* want to go back to school early?" Grace asked.

A shrug. "What's there to do around here?"

Just everything, Grace thought in frustration. How could the child possibly be bored in the middle of the nation's capital? She ventured, "You really hate it so much at home?"

"Oh, *Mom!*" Brianna picked up the apple and took another bite. Her neck was so thin and white, Grace could actually see the shape of the apple as it slid down her daughter's throat.

"No," Grace said at once. "Don't put that back in the bowl."

"I'm not going to finish it."

"Nobody else will want it now."

Brianna heaved an eloquent sigh.

"Most young people would jump at the chance to have a life like yours," Grace persisted.

"Yeah, right. Like having photographers in your face all the time so you can't hang out with your real friends. Being set up with dorky guys who're only sucking up to you because you're the Vice President's daughter. And if you do get to have some fun somehow, somewhere, then the Secret Service is always breathing down your neck and screwing it up."

"I'm sorry," Grace said firmly, "but that goes with the job, and it won't get any easier when your father's President." For a while now, Grace had tried to think of Brianna as a White House daughter. She'd even allowed herself the dream of a politically dynastic match and a wedding either on the White House lawn or in the East Room, depending on the time of year. She had never mentioned any of this to Brianna, of course, and she waited now for the alarmed or excited response which ought to be forthcoming:

President?

Instead: "It's not *my* job," Brianna said.

"This isn't all about you," Grace declared, her patience finally fraying. "It's about your father."

"It'd be better if Dad was a Democrat. Or at least an independent."

Grace drew a deep breath and told herself that it wasn't really Brianna speaking, it was Berkeley, and peer pressure, and all the rest of it, and that it was so difficult to be young these days. She said firmly, "Your father didn't choose his politics just to annoy you, you know. He truly believes in this country—and by anybody's measure he's doing a fine job."

Brianna examined the apple again and sliced off a brown patch with her thumbnail. "He won't get to be President, anyway. Not the way people are talking about him." She gave her mother a speculative look. "I don't have to tell you what they're saying, do I?"

Where does she think I've locked myself away, Grace thought, and for how long? "No, you don't," she said sharply, "and please don't remind me. It's all untrue and it's not fair." She recalled the last few months of misguided accusations, all the unpleasant articles written from positions of ignorance, and, worst of all, the California trip.

Last fall, Craig had been invited to speak at a lunch at the Commonwealth Club in San Francisco and, that same evening, at Stanford University, and the demonstrations had been disruptive and obnoxious.

They hated him out there, and it had all been on TV—the ranting, sign-waving crowd (including, perhaps, Brianna's friends, even Brianna herself, though Grace wouldn't allow herself to think of that) seizing the opportunity to protest not only their perceived abuses of power, but all the other hot-button issues of the moment, as if it was all Craig's fault:

DOWN WITH FASCISM!

NO BLOOD FOR OIL!

GUNS KILL!

HANDS OFF MY UTERUS!

"Those poor, deluded children, they don't have a clue," Craig had sighed. "They have no idea how lucky and privileged they are. In Russia, or China, or in a host of other countries, they'd have been beaten and thrown in jail—if they weren't shot. To use their own words," he added, *"they just don't get it!"*

Craig had been and still was amazingly philosophical and forbearing, and Grace was proud of him, as Brianna should be also. Craig had his beliefs and was neither afraid nor ashamed to voice them openly.

"You must realize," Grace had told Brianna at the time, "that the San Francisco Bay Area is only a very small part of the picture.

It's *not* representative of the rest of the country!" Though it was certainly a strident part, especially with California Senator Ellen Fischer to stir things up.

A dangerous woman, Fischer, who'd come by her position by accident. A tragic one, it was true, but an accident just the same. It wasn't right that she should sit in a position of power and question either what Craig was doing for the country or whether Carl Satcher should join the Cabinet.

As if she'd read her mind, Brianna declared, "It's not fair, what they're saying about Senator Fischer, how she's a hypocrite."

"Secrets have a way of coming out, and if she's got something to hide, we'll know," Grace said. "She might just be the hypocrite they say she is—attacking Big Oil and laughing all the way to the bank."

"Mom, I *hate* when you get all righteous and say things like that!" Defiantly, Brianna placed the half-eaten apple back in the bowl, swung her bare feet to the floor, and had the last word. "I'll be glad to get back to Berkeley," she declared, "where people tell the truth and things make sense!"

CHAPTER THIRTEEN

Carl Satcher had canceled his customary morning ride and was at work in his ranch-house office before six A.M. Things would be moving fast from now on. He and Cynthia had to leave for D.C. before noon in order to arrive on the East Coast at a reasonable hour, and he still had an empire to run.

After finishing his regular business by nine o'clock, he rocked back in his chair and crossed his booted feet on the edge of the slab of black granite he used as a desk. Its surface was finally bare again, the way he liked it, save for a telephone, a television remote, and two news photographs—the first was of two women, a grainy, grayish computer printout; the other had been clipped from the cover of the January 1 edition of the *D.C. Times.* Satcher linked his arms behind his head, stared across the room at the triple row of horse-racing journals, bound in crimson-and-gold-tooled leather, and allowed himself a faint, satisfied smile.

He leaned forward, pressed a switch beneath the desktop, then watched the books divide down the middle and slide smoothly to either side, and the flat-screen TV they concealed move silently forward. A click of the remote triggered footage that had been taped the day before, and carried him into the Senate Press

Gallery, where Ellen Fischer stood at the podium, face pale and determined and eyes sparking with outrage. She was saying, "Clearly, someone has attempted malicious damage. We can only suppose that their motive is to discredit and damage me politically at such a crucial time."

"Well, good for you," Satcher said aloud. "You get it!"

"She's putting up a good fight," his wife said, entering the office. Cynthia was wearing a full-skirted robe of pink cashmere, carrying a mug of black coffee in one hand and a bowl of mixed berries in the other. She leaned her hip against the edge of her husband's desk, set the mug down, and began to eat the berries, one by one. "Most of the press corps are back in her pocket, as usual, and the blind trust story is dying as we speak."

Satcher tapped his finger on the picture of the two women. "This will do the trick. The blind trust dustup is just the first wound. Makes her weaker."

"The *D.C. Times* leads with the next wound tomorrow morning," Cynthia said. "All the media should have it before noon."

"Did that little prick Slaughter get everything he needed?"

"He's ready to roll."

"And of course there's been no direct contact?"

"No call, no e-mail, everything handled through our friend, as usual." Ever the consummate professional, even in the safety of their rural stronghold, Cynthia didn't mention the man's name. At times Satcher thought she should have followed a different career path, like running the CIA.

They watched the remainder of the press conference together in silence, then he clicked away the picture and watched the TV fold itself back into the wall and the layers of bookshelves reconnect as though they'd never been apart. "We leave in two hours," he said.

Cynthia finished her berries, left her mug and bowl on the desk, and ambled gracefully toward the door. "Then I'd better go finish packing."

Satcher disliked her habit of putting things down and leaving them, especially on the pristine surface of his desk. On the other hand, her serene expectation that someone would always pick up after her was a clear demonstration of her privileged pedigree—a circumstance he both appreciated and admired.

Occasional thoughtlessness, he had long ago decided, was a small price to pay when you'd picked a winner.

He smiled. Then he looked long and hard at the image of Ellen Fischer in the *D.C. Times,* caught at precisely the wrong—or the perfect—moment, and his smile changed to something calculating and cold.

Satcher had never returned to his old office in the Hart Building during Fischer's tenure and had no intention of doing so, but he knew she had hung a photograph of him on her wall, in equally unflattering mode. He made it his business, always, to know what was going on. He ripped the picture of Ellen Fischer across the middle, crossways again into four, then eight, and tossed the fragments into the black metallic-mesh wastebasket under the desk.

The gesture was foolish, of course, childish and quite beneath him. The political demise of Ellen Fischer wasn't even the primary objective of their campaign, but it would be a highly desirable side effect and Satcher smiled, showing teeth.

He could almost find it in his heart to feel sorry for her.

She hadn't a chance.

The phone rang. He stared at it in momentary annoyance, still enjoying the thought of Fischer's imminent downfall, then picked it up and barked, "Yes?"

The Vice President. It was clear evidence of Satcher's stature that the powerful Vice President should call him rather than the other way around. "Driscoll's flying in tonight," Fulton said. "Breakfast tomorrow at eight like we planned."

"Fine," Satcher said with a reflexive twinge. Breakfast at the Vice President's residence, as he well knew, would be granola, fruit, and yogurt and an assortment of vile herbal teas, and he vowed to have a man-sized breakfast at the hotel before leaving, despite Cynthia's warnings about cholesterol. He imagined that Brian Driscoll, a robust man, previously a senior lawyer for Ford Motors and currently top fund-raiser, adviser, and principal go-to guy for Ken Stearns, senior Senator from the state of Michigan, would do the same. "Any update on the Brits?" Satcher asked.

"No changes. Everything right on schedule," Fulton said. Then, his voice bearing a distinct undertone of anxiety, he said, "I'm *assuming* our next step is in progress? Photography-wise?"

Satcher gazed with satisfaction first at the ripped newsprint in his wastebasket, then at the second picture on his desktop. "Rest assured," he said, "we'll hit them where it really hurts, from a direction they'd never expect in their wildest dreams—and the best part is they've only themselves to blame!"

He hung up on the Vice President without farewell, his invariable habit with friends, acquaintances, his two ex-wives, his children, the executives of his far-reaching empire, and the President of the United States himself. Satcher considered it a weakness to say good-bye; neither did he bother with the niceties of identification and greeting. *Hi, this is Carl, how are you, good to hear that, thanks, I'm fine, too*—what bullshit! He expected people to know with whom they were speaking without being told, and as for all that social claptrap, it only took up valuable time. Who cared if he was considered peremptory and rude? His attitude kept people on their toes, off balance, and ideally questioning their own worth—and wasn't that the whole point?

Satcher stabbed a well-manicured finger at the intercom, instructed the immediately attending member of his staff to remove Cynthia's breakfast dishes, then handed him the wastebasket with the mutilated photograph. "Fix this up—glue it on paper backing or something, then mount it and frame it."

"I could get you a fresh copy of the newspaper."

"I want it just the way it is now."

"Yes, sir."

"And don't try doing too good a job of matching it up, either," Satcher said. "It's quite okay for the rips to show."

CHAPTER FOURTEEN

The plane angled into its final approach, and the vast, ever-expanding grid of greater Phoenix tilted below Ben from horizon to horizon, the snake trails of new developments reaching ever further into the stony, mesquite-dotted desert, the urban landscape an overall pinkish beige punctuated by the vibrant rust of sculpted rock formations and the brilliant emerald of well-irrigated golf courses.

The voice of the captain promised a balmy sixty-eight degrees.

Ben was one of the first off the plane, head down, looking neither left nor right. He headed through the gate into the terminal, almost running down the blond woman who stood firmly in his path and who could only be a reporter.

"Mr. Lind!"

He kept moving.

She trotted alongside him and actually grabbed for his sleeve.

Ben swatted her hand away and picked up his pace. "No comment."

"But Mr. Lind! Hey! Wait! *It's me, Margie!*"

Ben wheeled around to find his old friend Margie Street at his elbow. A short dynamo in navy pants, jacket, and black bow tie, Margie had driven for Judge Zachary Ray for the past ten years since his deteriorating eyesight forced him reluctantly from behind the wheel.

"My God, Margie, I almost didn't recognize you."

"New hairdo!" Margie patted her tight blond permanent.

"You're right," Ben said. "You've shed ten years!"

"Flattery will get you everywhere!" She grinned and wrung his hand as if he'd been away for months rather than a mere few weeks, and all the way through the concourse trotted alongside him like a small tug chivying an ocean liner into port.

In the garage, beside the judge's immense, unrepentedly gas-guzzling, infinitely comfortable vintage Lincoln Continental, she flung his bag into the cavernous trunk while he climbed into the passenger seat.

"I suppose you'll be coming home even less now that you've retired," she said after getting in the car. "That's too bad. We miss you here, Mr. Lind, and that's the truth! You ask me, if you'd stuck to your guns last spring, you'd have trounced that Phelps Lavalle and been back in the House sure as shooting."

"Thanks for the vote of confidence, Margie," he said as she expertly pulled into heavy morning commuter traffic on the 202, heading for the cluster of high-rises that marked downtown Phoenix.

"You're welcome. But I'd've rather had a chance to help vote you back into Congress."

Ben didn't respond at once. He'd hoped to sleep on the plane, but he'd been too edgy, too restless. He rubbed at his eyes, rolled down the window, spent a full minute breathing deeply, drawing the dry, rushing air into his lungs, feeling a little of the strain slip away.

As usual, Ben found that Phoenix—with its huge skies, its surrounding ranges of jagged mountains whose slopes changed color dramatically according to the light, its atmosphere of small-town friendliness despite extraordinary recent growth and the punchy frontier optimism—restored a sense of perspective after the pressure cooker of Washington, D.C.

Still leaning against the window, his face warmed by the winter sunshine, Ben said, "You always know everything. Fill me in, who's doing what to whom and why." Then he gratefully allowed Margie's voice to flood soothingly around and through him as she primed him with gossip on local characters and happenings, sports and scandals.

Everything had changed. Everything was the same.

Margie filled him in on the new speed traps on the 101 loop, the controversial new sheriff, and how construction on the light rail was still strangling the downtown streets. As she swung the car into the Seventh Street exit, she moved on to sports, to the Cardinals in the NFL Playoffs, how she hoped he'd seen that great touchdown pass in last Sunday's game, and what about their chances for the Super Bowl? Ben couldn't help but think, with newly awakened nostalgia, how once outside the Beltway, such was the reality of everyday life.

★ ★ ★

Zachary Ray's offices were on the fortieth floor of a bronze-and-glass building on Third Street immediately off Central Avenue, facing northeast across the city with a view of the distant McDowell Range. Ben was sure that, with a powerful telescope, he'd be able to see his own house in Paradise Valley.

"Congressman! Welcome home! Happy Birthday!" Judge Ray enveloped Ben in a bear hug, then clasped his hand in the hard grip of a man who had worked construction throughout college and who, though he had long given up carpentering, still enjoyed the heft of a rake or shovel while working in his yard. The judge's frame was tall and spare. He wore a well-cut though ancient pearl-gray suit and a black bolo tie. His abundant white hair needed trimming. A pair of thick-lensed glasses rested halfway down his jutting nose, above which gleamed ironic, piercing gray eyes. "You look like hell," he said.

"It hasn't been the greatest two days," Ben said.

"I'll bet," the judge said. Then: "Got somebody I want you to meet." He turned Ben to face a man who was getting up from a winged chair.

"John J. Brown," said the man in the tan oxford shirt, beige chinos, and shiny, chestnut-colored loafers. "Pleasure."

Brown was African-American, of medium height and build, and could have been any age, Ben thought, between twenty-five and forty.

"Likewise," Ben said, shaking the proffered hand, so smooth and light boned, such a contrast to the judge's powerful grip. "Do people call you J.J.?"

"No," Brown said.

The judge waved a casual hand over an assortment of muffins and scones on his black-oak coffee table. "Ordered us in some breakfast. Hope the airline didn't feed you too well!"

A meal had in fact been served on the first-class flight, but at the time, food had been the last thing on Ben's mind.

"Sure," he said now, "I could eat." He was hungry for the first time in days, perhaps because he found himself in the company of someone not only older than himself but surely wiser, who uncompromisingly cared about his welfare.

Zachary Ray settled himself into his battered leather sofa and patted the seat beside him—"Join me"—while John Brown passed around paper plates, napkins, and steaming mugs of coffee before returning to his chair.

"How's Ellen holding up?" the judge asked.

"It's hard on her," Ben said, "but she's tough. She's had to cope with worse than this in the past."

"That poor girl. I know she's a Senator, but I'm old-fashioned when it comes to small, pretty women, and I won't apologize." He sighed. "I can't tell you how much I regret this whole thing, and how I'm bound and determined to set things right—at least my part—and trace it back to its roots, which of course"—with a nod to Brown—"is why I got ahold of our expert here. He'll find just who the media is calling an 'authentic source,' and sooner rather than later."

"I'm not expecting any problems," Brown said with a small smile. His voice was easy on the ear, accentless, pitched in the middle range.

He sat in a relaxed posture, with the confidence of someone who knew he was very good at what he did and that his talents would always be in demand.

Ben experienced an inner flinch as he contemplated what those talents might entail. However, the judge had assured him that Brown had gone straight now and could be trusted, and Ben knew he could trust the judge. "Glad you were free," he said.

"For Judge Ray," Brown assured Ben, "I'm always free." He extracted a roll of mints from the breast pocket of his blazer and offered them around. With no takers, he unwrapped one and popped it in his mouth.

"Picking up where we left off yesterday," Brown said with a nod at Judge Ray, "I checked out previous employers, clients, political parties, clubs and affiliations, frequent repeat trips, unusual destinations, and other uncharacteristic behaviors of everyone on the list you gave me. And I think, finally, we have a candidate." Glancing from Ben to the judge, he asked, "Does the name Alan Sharpe ring any bells?"

"Not with me," Judge Ray said promptly. "Not one of ours. Has to be with the brokers. Damn, we screened those folks so tight, they were in knots."

"Sharpe's an independent contractor with your firm," Brown said, "but I'm not surprised you've never heard of him—there'd be no reason for you to meet him or deal with him. He's a freelance software designer and computer systems expert. He sets up Web sites, solves problems at need, and only comes into the office if there's trouble."

"So spell it out," Ben said. "What set off the alarm bells?"

Brown refused to be hurried as he ran through his findings. "C. Alan Sharpe," he related. "C, incidentally, for Clarence. I'm not surprised he prefers to be called Alan. Hometown: Oxnard, California. Graduated from CalTech. Parents both retired high-school teachers. No siblings. Regular churchgoer, mainstream Baptist affiliation. Registered Republican, subscriber to various right-wing publications including *The American Conservative* magazine and the *Cato Journal*—and he's a regular visitor to the ACDA

Web site. That's the American Conservative Defense Alliance," he explained. "Thought that might be of interest."

"Most definitely," the judge said.

"Is Sharpe married?" Ben asked.

"No record of any marriage."

"So—on to employment." Brown checked his notes. "Fifteen years ago, he worked for Cisco Systems in Silicon Valley as a software designer, but returned to Ventura County after eight months and went out on his own as a consultant. He seems to have done well. His major client was Tri-State Management, a big outfit that throws up housing developments in California, Arizona, and Nevada along with infrastructure and utilities, for whom he was creating computer models involving industrial development related to shifting demographics. Tri-State Management, in turn, is wholly owned by an entity called EastPac Development, which buys up large tracts of raw land in the West, from Alaska to the Mexican border. Corporate offices are in Santa Barbara. Sharpe probably liked that."

"Why?" Ben demanded.

"Because he seldom seems to stray far from his home territory of Central and Southern California," Brown said.

"And we're going exactly where with this?" Ben wondered.

"The big man behind Tri-State Management—Sharpe's major and possibly only employer—is Carl Satcher," Brown said. "He's at the top of your list of people who stand to gain. That's our first merge."

"I've never believed in coincidences," Ben said.

"Two years ago, Sharpe abruptly severed his connections with Tri-State and moved outside his comfort zone, to Phoenix," Brown went on. "He sought employment with this law firm—incidentally, there's no record of him approaching anyone else—where he has performed consistently well. In other avenues, he has worked as a volunteer for the Phelps Lavalle Congressional campaign, as well as being a significant campaign donor. That's another merge."

Ben and the judge exchanged glances.

"On the personal side, Sharpe drives a late-model Acura TL type S," Brown said. "He rents a three-bedroom house in Mesa for twelve hundred per month in a subdivision called Cerra Vista. I went there yesterday afternoon to check it out and browsed around a bit. Nice landscaping, a pool, three-car garage."

"I hope to God he didn't notice you hanging about," Ben said.

"He didn't," Brown said. "And even if he did, it wouldn't matter." He finished his muffin and wiped his fingers on his napkin. "Nobody actually notices anyone in those subdivisions. They don't usually know their neighbors. People drive directly into their garages, and the houses are designed so all the living happens in back. There's a high turnover in those neighborhoods, and with the housing situation so bad, there're a lot of Realtor signs and empty homes. Anyway," he concluded, "Sharpe wasn't there."

"How do you know that?" Ben asked sharply.

"I knocked," Brown said.

"We don't want you doing anything that's not completely legal," Ben said.

"I know the rules," Brown said. "The judge saw to that."

Judge Ray nodded but did not smile.

"What does Sharpe's lifestyle have to do with this?" Ben asked.

"I mention his lifestyle," Brown said, "because Sharpe could not live in such middle-class comfort if his only income stream was the part-time consulting fees from this office. In actual fact, he remains on Tri-State's payroll, though undocumented. He also travels a great deal. He has made in total"—Brown scanned his notes—"fifteen flights to Santa Barbara through LAX within the past year. In the past six months, he has made fifteen calls, ten of them in December of last year, to an unlisted number with an 805 area code which is a direct line to Mr. Satcher at his ranch in Ventura County. An additional three calls, very recent, were made to an unlisted number in Bel Air, California."

"Also to Satcher?" Ben asked.

"To Mrs. Satcher, at unusual times for normal business: Saturday evening at eight-thirty P.M. Mountain Standard Time; Sunday, ten-seventeen P.M. MST; and last Monday, at eight forty-five P.M. MST. The duration of these calls was fifteen, nineteen, and twenty-five minutes, respectively.

"There were also two calls this week to a Washington, D.C., radio station, WHAP A.M. 1050, duration eleven and fourteen minutes, respectively, and one call on New Year's Eve to an unlisted number in Chevy Chase, Maryland, at nine twenty-seven P.M. MST, or eleven twenty-seven on the East Coast. The unlisted subscriber is a Mrs. Elizabeth Rabich."

"And who exactly is Mrs. Rabich?" Ben asked.

Brown smiled before he answered. "The mother of Samuel Slaughter, the radio guy."

CHAPTER FIFTEEN

Douglas Brewer paced back and forth in his office in the J. Edgar Hoover Building, an austere room of gray steel and black leather, with a charcoal Berber carpet, and the only ornamentation being the photograph on his desk of his wife and two teenage sons.

"I need fifteen minutes," Brewer had told Chloe, his faithful gatekeeper, a sweet-faced woman from Dothan, Alabama, comfortably middle-aged with fluffy silver hair, who favored pastel cardigan sets and plaids, and who reminded all who saw her of a favorite aunt who'd spoiled them in childhood.

People were at first inclined to take Chloe, with her soft, Southern voice and gentle demeanor, for a pushover.

They never made the same mistake twice. Now she was again keeping the world at bay.

Fifteen minutes, Brewer thought, listening to the muted voices and ringing phones in the outer office, glaring at his closed door, which seemed almost to vibrate with the urgency of the breaking affairs on the other side.

He crossed to the window, gripped the sill, and gazed down Pennsylvania Avenue toward the dome of the Capitol, which glowed unnaturally white against the dark sky. There'd been little change in the weather for the past week, the quiet, brooding chill being a forerunner of the immense system of low pressure moving in slowly but inexorably from the northeast.

Brewer stared at the murk that lay over the city like a hemispherical bowl and imagined his mind as a bright hot-air balloon, drifting freely and silently through avenues and byways of thought and memory and sifting the information it found there. It was a practice he found valuable since, usually, ideas would occur and connections be made.

Something was wrong. Or, if not precisely wrong, then definitely awry, and as he had found himself doing for the past twenty-four hours, Brewer again pondered the significance of the Vice President's request. The Vice President had never before made such a general request for the names of terrorists. And just as his demand was unusual, so, too, had been Fulton's choice of the residence in which to make it.

The FBI Director believed in following rules and procedures, and Fulton, quite out of character, appeared to be bending them. A red flag went up in Brewer's mind, and he was a man who trusted his instincts, as any good law enforcement officer must.

Brewer had supplied that list of names without question, even though its compilation had taken time and energy he would have preferred to spend elsewhere. But what was the Vice President's reasoning behind it, and why the sudden urgency?

Of course, the new British Prime Minister would arrive tomorrow with his wife, but the visit was low-profile, planned as a meet-and-greet rather than an official state function, and it would involve a visit to Camp David for private, informal discussion of mutual global concerns. Until Carl Satcher's confirmation removed the responsibility from his shoulders, blame for any disaster befalling the visiting Britons would be Fulton's alone. Security was as vital an issue as ever, and it was understandable that Fulton should take every precaution for the visit, but that still didn't explain the request.

Perhaps the Vice President was reacting to more intense pressure than usual these days. In addition to his normal duties, including the running of OSO, he was acting head of Homeland Security. Fulton carried a heavy burden, no doubt enhanced by the expected fight over Satcher's nomination and the calls for his impeachment.

Just the same . . .

Brewer laid his forehead against the cold window glass. He'd had a good working relationship with the Vice President; moreover, OSO was an agile and effective addition to the fight against terrorism and it worked well in tandem with the Bureau. He remained skeptical about Carl Satcher, however.

Satcher seemed too driven by self-interest and too concerned with personal power, and Brewer sensed vindictive and loftier ambitions forming behind that gruff manner and the cold blue eyes that reflected everything but gave nothing away. When confirmed as head of Homeland Security, Satcher would have achieved his immediate ambition. But what did he really want, and how far would he go in order to get it?

Brewer sensed he was being deliberately left out of the loop, that something was going on he wasn't aware of—though he couldn't quite dismiss the thought that he was in possession of most of the facts, if he could only see the pattern.

Feeling distinctly uneasy now, the Director strained to see out into the dark afternoon as if he'd be able to make sense of what persistently lay in front of him if only he could penetrate the dense cloud cover.

There was no other choice but to wait, and watch, and be extra vigilant. His fifteen minutes of solitude, in any case, were up.

He buzzed through to Chloe. "You can let the world back in now," he said.

CHAPTER SIXTEEN

Ellen sat alone in the backseat of Ben's Town Car, grateful for the habitual, courteous silence of James, the driver. It was nine P.M. and she was finally headed home after a long, tiring day and an evening catching up with regular business. The nation's affairs rolled along as usual, and she had a mile-long list of calls to make and to return tomorrow.

Regarding her personal problems, she allowed herself to feel guarded relief, even optimism, for she seemed to be weathering the storm, and even Sam Slaughter, though still spewing his usual poison, was growing repetitive with no new material. "You can bet," David had said, "that a whole lot of folks are starting to switch stations by now."

Beside Ellen on the backseat lay Ben's birthday gift.

He was hard to shop for. He already had everything he could possibly need, and it had been with a feeling of triumph that Ellen had found the new biography of Beverly Sills, with whom he'd become friends through his involvement as a major donor both to the Metropolitan and the burgeoning Phoenix Opera.

He would love the book.

But now he would have to enjoy it some other time.

She supposed that was just as well. Ellen knew that Ben's interest in his birthday had vanished in light of the outrageous invasion into their personal financial affairs.

Even his sudden uncertainty about a future that had seemed so secure had paled in comparison.

"The future can wait," Ben had said. "I've known Joel since law school, and he's never lacked guts. Normally, he'd have been in touch with me himself, he wouldn't have left it to Anita. He'd have done it properly, over an expensive lunch."

★ ★ ★

James was expertly maneuvering the car through a system of one-way alleys between the major streets, approaching their apartment building from the rear in the event that reporters still clustered around the front door.

He pulled up outside the deserted delivery entrance, helped Ellen out of the car, held her arm across the treacherously icy curb, and walked her through the building to the elevator.

Without Ben, who filled a space just by his presence, the apartment seemed much larger than usual and coldly quiet.

Ellen could hear just the faintest sound of traffic beyond the double-glazed windows.

God, she was tired.

She laid the Beverly Sills book on Ben's nightstand, put a Bach Brandenburg concerto on the sound system, and retired to the bathroom, where she ran herself a deep tub with plenty of foaming bath salts.

She lay in the hot water, inhaling fragrant steam, and thought how different this evening was supposed to have been, with company, conversation, congratulations, and gifts.

She felt lonely and sad.

Part of her wanted to leave D.C. and never return. She thought of Ben's house in Arizona, its warm, terra-cotta-tiled floors and high ceilings, the yard with its pair of giant saguaro cacti riddled with holes where the cactus wrens built their nests, and the pool where Ben liked to swim sixty laps every morning when he was home. The sky would be blue there, and the air would be warm. Ellen wanted to sleep in Ben's huge bed with the canopy; to swim in that dark blue pool; to wear a colorful cotton caftan and silver jewelry and drink margaritas on the terrace at sunset.

But all that must wait for another time.

Ben had called her from Dulles before he boarded his flight to tell her to buy a disposable, prepaid cell phone. "You can get one for fifty dollars or so, with up to three hundred prepaid minutes. Send someone from the office to get one for you."

"Why?" she'd asked.

"It's safer. We'll talk tonight."

The thought that no phone was secure these days, that any and all conversations could be monitored, made Ellen feel creepy, as if touched by unseen and unwanted fingers. During the past year, she'd done her personal best to combat this "new normal" of eroded privacy by attempting to build a coalition in the Senate to challenge it, but had only managed to get twenty-five out of a hundred to go along.

She'd tried to call Ben on the new phone this evening, but had been sent directly to voice mail and he hadn't called back.

He finally returned her call around midnight, when she was in bed and trying, unsuccessfully, to sleep, but of course it was only nine P.M. in Arizona. Things looked good, Ben told her, his voice guardedly jubilant. There was this guy they'd tracked down, and when they actually located him, it looked like they'd be home free. "It's good news," he said, but Ellen was too tired really to follow his conversation.

Although she was exhausted, her sleep was restless and she woke again at three A.M. What had woken her? A sound? Her own thoughts? Ellen swung her feet to the floor and padded down the passage to the living room.

Across Market Square, the National Archives Building glowed back at her, its illumined marble pillars gleaming like bleached bone, the brightly colored banners advertising the current exhibit reduced to varying shades of gray.

Immediately below, a certain amount of traffic still moved down Pennsylvania Avenue, and she was reassured to see how many other people besides herself were still awake.

She switched on the lamp on the console table to her left and immediately the room sprang into being, the single low light source puddling the shadows deeply in corners and throwing furniture and objects into sharp and peculiar relief—the tall apothecary lamp beside the sofa, with its appended arm, looked remarkably like a gallows—and Ellen suppressed a shiver. She told herself she was being fanciful, that she was merely chilled and should have worn her robe and there was nothing sinister about this room, it was exactly as she had left it before going to bed.

Then, thinking once again of electronic bugs, she wondered whether the room felt alien because she might not, figuratively speaking, be alone in it.

Ellen pulled the drapes closed, made sure the fabric covered every possible gap and crevice, then deliberately made her way from wall to wall, running her finger lightly down the edges of the oak paneling, scanning the electrical fixtures and switches, the window and door frames. She paused in front of the fireplace and stared down at the brass peacock with spread filigreed tail which served as a fire screen. She grasped the bird by its neck and moved it to one side, dropped to one knee on the hearth rug and peered up the flue. She tried to recall when the chimney had last been swept, deciding it must have been at least a year ago, and thought how traces would have been left if the soot had been disturbed.

She wondered if it would be worth bringing a flashlight to search further.

Then she reminded herself that by current standards of surveillance technology she was decades out of date, that the days of implanting bugs into phone receivers or flower vases, attaching them to the undersides of tables and running wires around molding, under wallpaper, and up chimneys, was, as she herself had recently mentioned, *so cold war.*

Of course, it wasn't as if anyone would have entered their apartment on some clandestine errand, wearing a fake uniform and claiming to be a utility company engineer, building inspector, or exterminator. The security here wouldn't allow that, and anyway, these days, such people existed only in old movies.

It was absurd to tuck in the drapes so tightly; they might as well be opened wide to the world. If anybody wanted to know what Senator Ellen Fischer was doing up so late in her living room, and with whom she spoke on the phone, there would be remote devices undreamed of months or perhaps even weeks ago through which every movement could be monitored and each word overheard, from a van or truck parked blocks away, from a room across the city, or even from a listening post high in the stratosphere. A technological intruder could access this room from anywhere. These days, privacy was an increasingly unrealistic concept.

Ellen wandered from the living room into Ben's office, gaining comfort from the size and solidity of his desk, his big, comfortable, masculine armchairs, the shelves and shelves of books.

She touched the back of his office chair and swiveled it back and forth, and the movement must have disturbed his computer or the mouse, because the screen suddenly filled with light.

There was the iceberg again, and looking at it, Ellen knew, with a sharp pang of unease, that their opponents would not give up, that time was of the essence, that they'd move sooner rather than later.

But how, and with what?

It was four o'clock now and Ellen knew it would be futile to go back to bed, as she'd never be able to fall back to sleep.

She took a shower, thinking wryly that at least now she'd be facing the world doubly clean.

She spooned Colombian coffee into the filter and turned on the coffeemaker.

It was while checking out *A.M. America* on the kitchen TV that she discovered their enemies had moved even faster than she'd expected.

CHAPTER SEVENTEEN

January 4

FRIDAY

Derelle woke in darkness to the bugling of her cell phone, impossibly loud in the nighttime quiet.

For one joyful second, she allowed herself to believe it was Salima, confused about time zones, calling her from the depths of rural India.

But Salima was confused about nothing. Of course, it would not be Salima; nor, at five A.M., was it likely to be good news.

Derelle scrabbled for the phone, the dread possibilities flashing through her mind: An emergency. An accident.

That Ellen was in the hospital—though that was unlikely since she'd stayed home last night.

Derelle caught the phone on the third ring.

"Turn on your TV," David Makins ordered, his voice as tense as she'd ever heard it. "Channel Four. *Now!*"

Derelle fumbled for the light switch, then for the television remote—and found herself staring directly into her own face.

How could that be? But it was definitely her, her head draped in the scarf Ellen had lent her to cover her head at the Taj Mahal. She was embracing a similarly scarved, dark-faced Asian woman.

Salima.

". . . suspected Al Qaeda operative," the NBC anchorwoman was concluding. "We'll be closely monitoring this breaking story!"

Then the broadcast cut to a scene of snowy desolation and an airplane wreck in Colorado.

Derelle clicked off the TV and sat there with the remote clenched so hard in her hand she almost crushed it.

"Derelle! Derelle, damn it, are you there?" David's voice sounded faint and tinny from among her bedcovers. "What the hell's going on? Speak to me! Say something!"

"I don't know what to say," Derelle whispered. She shivered. "I don't understand."

"Then try, and think hard," David said, already sounding tired so early in the day. "The Senator wants to meet with you at Jimmy T's at six-thirty. This is a disaster, and we'll have to come up with a plan."

★ ★ ★

Jimmy T's was a cheerful, down-home-style breakfast place located in a pleasantly leafy neighborhood across the street from the Capitol Hill grocery, where the redbrick sidewalks heaved and twisted in serpentine shapes over and around the tree roots and posed a hazard for unwary joggers and cyclists. Today, however, before dawn in deep winter, most of the houses were still dark, and the streets were deserted.

Ellen parked around the corner from the café, pulled her coat collar up against the cold, and thrust her hands deep in her pockets as she hurried toward the glowing windows and welcome warmth.

Inside, she was greeted cheerily by the owner himself, against the hiss and gurgle of the coffeemaker. "Morning, Senator!"

"Hi, Jimmy."

"Early birds this morning!"

Another time Ellen would have allowed herself a moment of cheery give-and-take, but today she merely nodded in agreement.

"Coffee's about ready. And you'll want your usual blueberry muffins, right?"

"Sounds good."

Derelle, so far the only customer, was seated at a table in back, staring at the newspaper on the table in front of her. She raised shocked dark eyes as Ellen sat down and faced her across the scarred, red Formica table.

"Did you see this already?" Derelle asked, passing her the *D.C. Times,* with its front-page headline a black twenty-four-point scream:

FISCHER CHIEF OF STAFF COZY WITH SUSPECTED TERRORIST!

"I've seen it, and it looks really bad," Ellen said. "How did this happen?"

"They're saying she might be working with Al Qaeda," Derelle said. "That's crazy. Those people despise women."

"But they're not averse to using them," Ellen said. "They'll use anyone. But though she might well be innocent—"

"She *can't* be a terrorist," Derelle broke in hotly. "There's no way!"

"—the damage has been done, at least so far as I'm concerned," Ellen said. "In the eyes of this country I am now either knowingly harboring a terrorist sympathizer on my staff, or else I didn't know and I'm perceived as dangerously naive. I lose either way. The question is," she said, quoting one of Ben's legal sayings, *"Cui bono?* Who benefits?"

"Here we go!" Jimmy appeared with a pot of steaming coffee and filled their cups. Her head lowered, Derelle made a lengthy business of ripping open sugar and creamer packets and stirring.

"You're probably right about terrorist organizations not recruiting her," Ellen said. "I'm thinking much closer to home."

"You're saying Salima might have been recruited by Carl Satcher and the Vice President? In some kind of plot to get at you through me? That's just as crazy," Derelle said with conviction. "That's not what Salima's about. She'd *never* do anything that might help Satcher's nomination, or Craig Fulton to be elected President. She knows one of the first things his administration would do is cut back budgets for foreign aid—except for the military and weapons, of course. She'd be acting against everything she believes in."

Ellen wondered whether Derelle knew what Salima believed in. "There's no getting away from that photograph. Who took it, and how did the *D.C Times* get hold of it?"

"I don't know."

Derelle looked wretched. She added even more sugar to her coffee and watched her spoon as she stirred it endlessly round and round.

Ellen returned her attention to the picture. "It looks like you're inside some temple here."

"We're in the Taj."

"Of course you are. But not the first time, when we went with the group—it's the next morning, when you went back again. You're wearing your Indian outfit." Ellen was suspicious, as she had to be, wondering whether part of the deal—*but whose?*—was to persuade Derelle, innocently, to dress in such clothing, to add credibility. She also wondered whether somebody had made Salima an offer she couldn't refuse. Money was a great persuader, and who knew Salima's exact circumstances? She or her family might have been in desperate need—or could there be a more altruistic explanation? It would be helpful to know whether any of Salima's projects had received unusually large donations in the last few months. Ellen decided to put her researcher onto all those questions as soon as she got into the office.

The microwave pinged and moments later Jimmy appeared at the table with their muffins, hot and fruit filled, which he set down between them on the table beside the *D.C. Times*. If he had already noticed Derelle's picture, and recognized her, he made no comment. "Fresh from the oven!" he cried. "Enjoy your breakfast."

Ellen watched Derelle pull her muffin in half and crumble a piece in her fingers. "Were there any other people from our group on that second visit?" she asked her.

"No."

"There weren't, or you didn't notice?"

"I guess I didn't notice," Derelle said.

"Did anyone speak to you?"

"Only Salima. And the man outside, where we had to leave our shoes."

"She never, at any time, asked someone to take a picture of the two of you together?"

Derelle shook her head.

"And you never noticed anybody else taking a photo?"

"No, but it's possible. Perhaps someone with a cell phone . . . But why take a picture of two strangers?"

"Who knows? But the fact remains that *somebody* did, for whatever reason. Did you tell anybody else you'd be there?"

"Only you. We only decided to go the night before."

"Nobody else knew? No one at all?"

Derelle shrugged. "Just the cabdriver who took us there. And the doorman who called the cab."

"How about the hotel switchboard? Did you arrange for a wake-up call?"

"I used the alarm on my cell phone."

Ellen sighed. She felt as if she were walking through a maze where angles doubled back on themselves and nothing seemed to make sense.

What part did Salima, in fact, play in this mess?

Might she actually be a terrorist of some flavor?

Was it possible she'd been used by Fulton and Satcher to frame Derelle?

Could she have motives of her own?

Or might Ellen be creating her own sinister scenario where none existed?

After all, there was an old adage that went something like "Sometimes a tree is simply just a tree."

"Okay, let's leave the photo issue for now," Ellen said.

She cast her memory back through the early-morning meetings and press interviews in New Delhi, Derelle either at her side or within easy reach, and on to the lunch in that huge ballroom with its glittering chandeliers and its expanse of lush red-and-gold carpet.

She saw herself seated at the head of the horseshoe-shaped table between the ministers from Seoul and Singapore, Derelle halfway down the right-hand side, next to an elegant Indian woman with fluent hands. Had Salima somehow arranged that particular seating partnership? Had she bribed someone to put her beside Derelle?

"Tell me everything you know about this woman Salima, and try and remember every word—every *single* word—the two of you said whenever you were together."

"I'll try. But it was just talk, you know. . . ." Derelle extracted a piece of blueberry, ate it, then licked the purple juice on her fingers. "I'm sure there was nothing remotely significant."

"You might not have known what was significant."

"She mostly talked about her projects."

"She invited you to go shopping," Ellen said. "Then what?"

"She said I should see more of the city than hotels and official trips to monuments. She was right."

"And you had a good time," Ellen said, knowing that normally Derelle hated shopping, but recalling that this time she returned pleased and proud to have found Ellen the perfect gift.

That beautiful scarf. Ellen had worn it for several events.

In fact, she'd worn it just yesterday afternoon, at the press conference.

Most of the country would have seen it.

Would people remember? Would the connection be made with Derelle's scarf in the *D.C. Times?*

Of course it would, and that connection would be put to good use.

"Mostly what we talked about that afternoon was the people at the bazaar," Derelle was saying. "How they'd come from all over northern India. What clothes were worn in which regions, like the mirrored fabric from Rajahstan."

It sounded so harmless, but regional clothing, with its highly individual designs and colors, was often a valuable tool for secret and instant identification and communication. Ellen knew that such a method had been used by the indigenous protesters in Guatemala, and in certain parts of Africa. "I see," she said, carefully noncommittal. "And what else?"

"Nothing much." Derelle added after a pause, "Salima did say she didn't understand Western people, how we live our lives in boxes."

"Boxes?"

"She meant how Westerners like to keep everything separated—family, work, religion—not like Asian people, who see their lives as a whole, with everything working together and playing a part. But I know that was only talk. She was laughing at us, in a kindly sort of way."

A kindly sort of way.

Had that been the truth, or had Salima actually been voicing criticism of the West and encouraging Derelle to express certain negative opinions of her own?

Ellen supposed Salima's accusers—now Derelle's by association—could make a fairly good case. Her muffin sat in her stomach as solid as lead as she thought how easily Derelle might have fallen into a trap.

"Let's go back to Agra now," Ellen said. "That side trip was organized by the Minister of Culture just for us, the group from Singapore, and the Koreans. So how did Salima get to come along?"

"She came independently. She had business appointments there."

"She told you that?"

"I saw no reason not to believe her."

"What exactly *is* her job?"

"Banking. She makes micro-loans to women in rural areas and in the villages, especially in Gujarat province, where she's from and where not many tourists go. For example, for fifty dollars they can buy a good used sewing machine and supplies, go into business tailoring, and earn more money for their families. Maybe even employ other people, and eventually move into the middle class."

"How come she had appointments in Agra if she works mostly in Gujarat? It's a long way."

"I never thought to ask. And I didn't know where Gujarat was."

"You do now, don't you. It's on the Arabian Sea, bordering Pakistan."

"Do you think that's important?"

"It could be."

"You seem to think Salima's some kind of agent, too." Derelle regarded the cover of the *D.C. Times* with scorn. "Just like *they* do."

"You have to admit it's a possibility," Ellen said. "The work she does could be a convenient excuse not only to travel unquestioned around the country but to maintain contacts at every level. And, of course, a crafts fair, like the one you visited together, could be a convenient meeting place—everyone wearing and selling their special clothing, from Kashmir, Gujarat, Rajahstan, and wherever, and Salima harmlessly escorting her innocent tourist around the stalls."

Derelle's eyes narrowed. "You're saying she was using me for some purpose of her own. That I was *cover* for her."

That was exactly what Ellen feared, though she declined to take it further. Instead she asked, "Why did she suggest you two go back to the Taj?"

"Because the light is better first thing in the morning."

"And was it?"

"It was beautiful. Pearly, misty, and fresh—the air not so used up."

"That's when she took your picture, sitting on Princess Diana's bench?"

Derelle nodded, her face softening in recollection.

"Did you take any pictures of Salima?"

"No."

"Why not?"

"I was dumb." Derelle said with deep regret, "I'd left my camera in the room. She promised she'd e-mail me a photo."

"And has she?"

"Not yet."

Because Derelle had unknowingly served her purpose and there was no longer any point in staying in touch? Ellen wondered.

"And all this time, several hours walking about on your own, what were you talking about then?" Ellen asked.

"Various things. Her work again. And traveling. How I'd never been to India before, and how she'd never been to the U.S. and would like to go sometime."

"What did you say?"

"How that would be great and it would be my turn to show her around. And then she said she'd always dreamed of getting some kind of position with the World Bank. Or the U.N.—she wanted to see New York."

"She didn't specifically ask you for help finding a job in the U.S.?"

"No, she did not!"

Ellen suddenly wondered whether Derelle had been marked and set up before she even met Salima.

"Let's go back to when we first arrived in India," Ellen said. "Remember when we first arrived in Delhi, and we went to the hotel: Do you remember anybody approaching you for any reason, any unusual attentions or questions, anything *at all*? And I'm including those men in the embassy car." Though even as she asked, she knew this would be a dry well. How could Derelle know, arriving late at night in an unknown and exotic foreign country, what might or might not be unusual?

Ellen herself had been so tired that all she wanted was to get to the hotel. How glad she'd been for the reassuring presence of the man from the embassy, in his neat dark suit, white shirt, and tie, who had expedited their journey through immigration and customs, settled them in the limo, then sat up front quietly conversing with the driver in what she assumed was Hindi. She was almost positive Derelle hadn't exchanged a word with either man, but how would she really know? She'd been exhausted, slumped into the padded softness of the backseat and dozing intermittently throughout their long ride into the city.

As before, Ellen put herself back into the moment, visualizing them arriving at the hotel.

She recalled the mustached giant in scarlet turban, satin jacket, and pantaloons who had ushered them up the wide steps.

The vast lobby with its polished marble floors, trickling fountains, and bright shop windows—Cartier, Armani, Louis Vuitton.

Their suite with its tropical flower arrangements, tall windows overlooking lush lawns and fragrant trees, and the luxurious white bed. "Oh, thank God," Ellen had murmured, already visualizing blissful unconsciousness between smooth, freshly laundered sheets.

And Derelle had said—

—nothing. But Ellen now recalled the expression that had flashed, for one split second, across Derelle's face.

Revulsion? The opulence of the hotel, compared with the poverty of the streets?

At the time, Ellen had forgotten it. God, she'd been so tired. But she remembered now and wondered.

"Anything at all?" she repeated.

Derelle's face assumed the impermeable nonexpression Ellen remembered from the old days. "Nothing."

Ellen sighed. "All right, then."

Her neck ached. She realized she'd been sitting in one position, absolutely still, for half an hour. She stretched her cramped limbs and drained her coffee.

People were beginning to trickle steadily into Jimmy T's now as the regulars, most of whom worked on Capitol Hill, arrived for breakfast. They'd all have seen the news. Ellen intercepted a curious glance or two toward their table, though she knew nobody would say anything, nor would they approach the table unless invited, not here, where personal space was not only respected but inviolable.

Just the same, she and Derelle should leave soon.

Ellen folded the *D.C. Times* into a smaller rectangle and placed it in her briefcase under the table. "We'd better be going," she said. And in a rush of sympathy: "I'm so sorry, Derelle. Believe me, the last thing I wanted to do was put you through this third degree." She laid her hand on the table, palm up.

Derelle looked at it, then briefly touched Ellen's fingers. "I've told you all I can."

I hope that's true, Ellen thought. She rose to her feet and shrugged into her coat. "I want you to go home now," she said, "until all this gets sorted out. And I promise you it will be."

"Go home?" Derelle looked taken aback, even alarmed.

"It would be the best thing for you."

"But that's surely as good as admitting I'm—"

"You need to keep a low profile," Ellen said. "Come on. I'll give you a ride."

Stiffly, the new hurt showing in her eyes, Derelle said, "That's okay. I'll take a cab."

"Not today you won't!"

Derelle followed Ellen out of Jimmy T's, past tables filled with people who by now must have seen that picture in the paper or on a news show, and who, the moment she was gone, would plunge into talk and conjecture. She kept her head up, wearing her most defiant "don't mess with me" expression.

Once outside, she climbed into the passenger seat of Ellen's Prius and silently buckled herself in. Ellen backed out of her tight space, headed for North Carolina Avenue, and turned right toward the river, the Kennedy Center, and the Watergate, where, to avoid any reporters who might be clustered at the front entrance, she drove directly down and around the winding entrance into the garage.

Derelle's hand was on the door handle before the car had even stopped.

"Try and get some rest," Ellen said. "Make sure your cell phone's on, and keep it with you."

Thinking of Derelle's cell phone reminded Ellen of New Year's Day, Derelle's cell being off, and a thought suddenly struck her.

"Has Salima been to the U.S. since last November?" she asked.

Derelle froze, one foot on the ground. "If she has, she never told me."

"You said she wanted to see New York." After a pause: "She isn't in the country right now, is she?"

Derelle was out of the car at once, and wheeling to face Ellen, her face taut with misery, she said, "Who do you think I am? Do you think I'd lie to you? Or keep anything from you?"

You may not want to, Ellen thought, *but for whatever reason, you're doing it right now. I haven't known you all these years for nothing.*

"If there's anything else I should know," she said one last time, "please tell me. I don't want any more bad surprises."

"There's nothing!" Derelle took a deep breath and closed the car door with quiet deliberation. She wrapped her leather coat tight around her body, began to head for the elevators without another word, then abruptly turned and rapped on the window.

Ellen lowered the window.

"Senator," Derelle said with quiet formality, leaning in, gripping the door frame, "I can't tell you how sorry I am. In my wildest dreams, I couldn't have imagined something like this happening. How could they do this, and how could I fall for it? I've been around a long time, seen it all, you know?"

"It's okay." Ellen reached across the passenger seat and patted Derelle's cold, gloveless hand. "One way or the other, it's all going to work out." And knowing how foolish the words were before they left her mouth, she said, "Try not to worry."

CHAPTER EIGHTEEN

Carl Satcher drummed his fingers with controlled impatience against the buttery leather of his briefcase while his driver went through seemingly endless security rituals at the gates. But it was not until the yellow Labrador bomb dog had had a final sniff around the tires that the steel barricades lowered, like a drawbridge, so the big car could enter the driveway of the Vice Presidential mansion.

It was an attractive house, a turreted Queen Anne–style Victorian located on the edge of Rock Creek Park in Georgetown on the high ground of Massachusetts Avenue. However, despite its size and graciousness, and the twelve protective acres in which it was nestled, Satcher always felt confined and claustrophobic among the tall trees, since, to be honest, he found the entire Eastern seaboard encroaching and dark and the skies too narrow.

Give him the wide ranges, the rolling hills, the mountains and the ocean; for that matter, give him the vast tracts of his own housing developments throughout the Western states with their mile upon mile of turned earth and access roads where the bulldozers, cranes, and backhoes moved across the landscape like orange dinosaurs.

However, if his new position as Director of Homeland Security required him to live in these parts, he could adjust as readily as he had previously, when he was a U.S. Senator, and certainly he could arrange for a satellite office on the West Coast. And next year, when he was invited to share the Republican ticket with Craig Fulton, and when Fulton subsequently won the Presidency, then he, Carl Satcher, would be living here in the mansion himself. Nothing worthwhile ever came without a price, and this price was one he was quite prepared to pay.

"Good morning, sir!" said the rosy-cheeked ensign at the door. Satcher handed over his coat and allowed himself to be led to the dining room.

Craig Fulton, seated at the head of the table, rose as Satcher entered and extended a hand. "Carl! Glad you could make it."

"Good morning, Mr. Vice President."

"An okay flight?"

"Uneventful."

"Good, good . . . Bad weather out there. Pilots his own plane," Fulton explained to his other guest, a large man in impeccable navy worsted whose round blue eyes and smooth skin reminded Satcher of an overfed baby.

"Not these days," Satcher said. "Skies are too crowded. I leave the job to younger guys with faster reflexes."

"Nonsense!" Fulton said jovially. Then: "I'm not sure if you two gentlemen have met, but you'll certainly know of Brian Driscoll."

"Pleasure!" Satcher reached across the table to shake hands.

"Likewise," Driscoll said.

The two men exchanged congenial nods, and Satcher seated himself to the Vice President's left. He spread a snowy linen napkin across his lap, as herbal tea was poured from an antique silver pot, and chilled orange juice from a pitcher of faceted crystal.

"Brian was Chief Counsel for Ford Motors," Fulton said, "and now helps out Ken Stearns. You'll remember our friend from Michigan, who's also a member of a certain subcommittee." He made an expansive gesture across the table and invited, "Do help yourself!"

Satcher's quick glance took in the display of granolas, fruit, and organic yogurt, and he was glad, as he'd known he would be, that he'd availed himself of room service at the Willard Hotel. "Thanks," he said, "but I'll stick with toast."

"In that case, you must try the marmalade!" The Vice President pushed across a glass bowl of jellied brownish lumps. "Robertson's Chunky. I have it sent over from Scotland. Believe me, it's delicious." Fulton spooned a mound of granola onto his own plate, along with a scoop of mixed berries, topping it off with low-fat yogurt.

Across the table, Brian Driscoll did the same, adding honey.

"Do you gentlemen have everything you need?" Fulton glanced from left to right, then dismissed the two young ensigns, and declared it time to get down to business. "Now then, I've recorded the *Today* show for you, in case you've not yet seen it for yourselves. Here we go. . . ."

Of course, Satcher had made it his business to watch the broadcast, as indeed he had caught every news show since five A.M. He'd studied all the papers, too, but was not averse to hearing this latest news anchor, a crimped-looking blonde in a red jacket, explain once again, "Derelle Simba is, of course, Chief of Staff to embattled U.S. Senator Ellen Fischer, slated to chair the upcoming hearings of Homeland Security Secretary nominee Carl Satcher. Senator Fischer's office has no comment at this time and Ms. Simba could not be reached. . . ." And again the picture of the two women—Simba and the Indian woman—caught in an unguarded moment, smiling at each other with deep affection.

Brian Driscoll extracted a pair of narrow, gold-rimmed glasses from his breast pocket and perched them on his rosy knob of a nose. "Exactly how did they come by that picture?"

Satcher explained to Driscoll about Google Alert. "Ellen Fischer and her Chief of Staff were attending a global-warming conference in India. There're paparazzi there, too, you know— the picture appeared in the *Straits Times* in Singapore."

"And now it's everywhere," Fulton said. "All over the world."

"It doesn't hurt, either, that they're a couple of eye-catching girls," Driscoll said.

"Speak for yourself," Fulton said, and with an inner, ironic smile, Satcher recalled that the Vice President, for all his abilities and undoubted intellect, would have a narrow view of what constituted beauty.

"What do we have that actually connects the Indian woman with Al Qaeda?" Driscoll asked.

"Does it really matter?" Fulton responded. "Insinuation is as good or better than the facts, and like the genie, you can't stuff it back in the bottle. That image, and all it might mean, is out there now. Women in head scarves. One of them an American!"

Fulton helped himself to more herbal tea and a piece of whole-wheat toast, which he liberally coated with his special chunky marmalade. He went on, "Many would figure that Simba has the ideal credentials for terrorism. She certainly has the background. If she hadn't been a juvenile when Ellen Fischer got hold of her, she'd have done prison time for assault."

"Fischer will certainly find it tough to talk herself out of this one!" Satcher said.

"No love lost between the two of you, then," Driscoll observed.

"Senator Fischer, for obvious reasons, is no friend of mine," Satcher agreed, "though I surely sympathize with her over the poor timing of these disclosures, as indeed we all must. It's now likely she'll be forced by public opinion, to say nothing of her party leadership, to resign as chairman of the subcommittee. That responsibility will then, necessarily, devolve upon Senator Stearns as next senior Democrat—and he'll be the one to wield the gavel at my hearing."

Driscoll gazed patiently at him across the table, his wide blue eyes expressionless.

"Carl wants to lay out some ideas he has in this regard," Fulton said.

"Yes indeed." Satcher laid down his knife. "We're here this morning to consider the big picture. The country needs me as Secretary of Homeland Security just as next year it needs Craig Fulton as President. Working together, we can achieve a great deal."

Driscoll glanced from Satcher to the Vice President and waited patiently, hands clasped loosely across his stomach.

"I'd like you to convey to Senator Stearns," Satcher continued, "how President Craig Fulton's agenda, with its focus on antiterrorism, would greatly and positively affect his constituents in the future and how he—the Senator, I mean—could soon be in a position to bring great hope and progress to his state, with many thousands of jobs. Craig and I look forward to working hand in hand with Ken in protecting and rebuilding this great nation."

Satcher watched the man across the table, whose face betrayed no trace either of emotion or conjecture. Then he thought of Senator Kenny Stearns, spare and balding with tired eyes, an aging man with no future beyond the next two years, after which he would undoubtedly lose his seat to someone younger, brighter, and more telegenic—unless by some miracle the Senator was able to revitalize and retool those decaying industries on the shores of Lake Michigan. Abruptly, Satcher added, "Senator Stearns is a union man, right?"

"UAW. Still has his card."

"And if I'm not mistaken, his father was a foreman for General Motors?"

"Correct." Driscoll allowed, "You do your homework!"

Fulton broke in wistfully, "Those were the days. God, how I loved those cars!"

"And in those days," Satcher said, "this country owned the industry, but we've been overwhelmed for a long time now by the Japanese and the Koreans, and the Chinese are standing in line. Under certain circumstances, however, a whole new era could open up for our auto companies. There'd be government grants, *huge* grants—we're talking billions here."

He leaned forward, elbows on the table, steepled his powerful fingers, and stared across them into the future. In a soft, almost mesmeric voice, he said, "Imagine: Armored trucks to control every inch of the U.S. border, our ports, airports, and train stations. Vehicles to patrol our cities, equipped with surveillance cameras. Newly designed tanks—we'll call them Urban Protectors—to guard potential terror targets such as schools and sports stadiums. City buses—all across America—redesigned and rebuilt in the Senator's state to withstand armed attack. The list is endless—troop transports, helicopters. . . . And we're not about to trust our future and our national security to foreign manufacturers. No, sir!" Satcher thumped the tabletop. "Everything, and I mean *everything,* down to and including each last bolt, rivet, and truck tire, will be made in the U.S. of A. with American know-how and muscle, factories coming back on line, full speed ahead, working triple shift—and that's just the beginning."

Satcher leaned back in his chair, arms folded across his chest. "I hope you'll convey these thoughts to Senator Stearns," he said.

Driscoll nodded. "I'll certainly do that."

★ ★ ★

When Brian Driscoll had been ushered out, the Vice President said, "I think we can expect some cooperation in that quarter."

"Naturally." Satcher pushed his plate aside. "Stearns has nothing to lose and everything to gain. He's fifty-eight and looks ten years older. Next election year, he'd have been headed off to the glue factory like a worn-out old horse, but with defense contracts to throw around, he'll be a Goddamn hero. It's our job to make sure it all happens."

Fulton nodded.

Satcher poured himself some more herbal tea, remembered how much he disliked it, and set his cup down again. "Craig," he said thoughtfully, "can you get that TV picture back of the girls and freeze the frame?"

The Vice President clicked the remote, and a few moments later, Satcher gazed at the two faces. "See how they're *looking* at each other?"

"I'm not sure what you mean," Fulton said.

"This could be even better than we first thought," Satcher said. "Do you suppose she's a lesbian?"

"Who? Simba?"

"Or both. Doesn't matter."

"I wouldn't know."

"It could be useful," Satcher said.

"If you're talking security risk, it's not against the law in this country."

Though the Vice President would routinely insist that he was not homophobic, that he had many gay friends and was a strong supporter of the Log Cabin Republicans, Satcher wasn't fooled. "It would work for us nicely," he said. "Simba has a high-profile job. If she was gay, she'd most likely want to keep her private life exactly that, private—which is next to impossible in a fishbowl city like this one. The alternative is to *have* no private life at all, which, so far as we can find out, she doesn't. No boyfriend. No friends. No socializing." After a pause: "You see where I'm going with this?"

"Not yet," Fulton admitted.

"She may not realize how lonely she is," Satcher suggested, "and how she's missing out on life. Then she finds herself in an exotic country on the other side of the world, with the apparent freedom to let down her hair with nobody noticing. A fantasy, of course, because the whole damn world's a fishbowl these days. And suddenly she meets a beautiful woman and falls in love. And this Salima, by no means the innocent she might seem, seizes her opportunity and moves right in. Who knows what Simba might have confided to that woman in a moment of passion? It opens up a whole new realm of possibilities."

"I didn't think this Salima woman *was* in fact an operative."

"That's the beauty of the thing," Satcher said. "Like you said, it really doesn't matter. Particularly now that we have that picture."

Fulton nodded seriously. "Salima Aboud and Derelle Simba— Senator Fischer's Muslim pit bull."

Satcher chuckled. "For all anyone knows, Simba could have been a terrorist sympathizer for years. And you know what's best of all, the clinching detail? Look at what the woman's wearing."

"Simba?"

"Of course Simba."

Fulton gazed at the picture again. "An Indian outfit."

"And?"

"One of those hijab things."

"It's not actually, it's just a scarf. Look more closely."

"A green-and-yellow one."

"Ellen Fischer has one exactly like it. It could easily be the same scarf." He thought for a moment, then said, "Good God, man, she wore it to her press conference the day before yesterday!"

"You're right!" the Vice President exclaimed. "I thought it looked familiar."

"So there we have it," Satcher said. "The two—or three—of them are packaged neatly together, they even appear to share each other's clothes. Senator Fischer's caught like a fly in syrup, and no matter how hard she struggles, she'll only get herself sucked in deeper!"

CHAPTER NINETEEN

David Makins climbed the flight of narrow steps to Ellen's second-floor offices, the passage lined with workstations occupied by her specialists on foreign policy, defense, NASA, the environment, trade, transportation, and energy. At the end of the passage sat researcher Rachel Adoni, a greyhound of a woman with close-cropped pewter hair, wearing black drawstring pants, high-top sneakers, and a T-shirt decorated with planets and lunar landscapes, no doubt acquired at one of the science fiction conventions she frequented around the country. Adoni was physically awkward except in front of the computer screen, where her long, unkempt fingers became suddenly as graceful as a ballerina's.

She rolled her office chair back and forth between three screens, one displaying the elegant figure of Salima Aboud in a head scarf of buttercup yellow. On the other two screens scrolled names, statistics, news reports, and other information in English, Hindi, and Urdu.

"Aboud was born in Ahmedabad, Gujarat province, in 1969," Rachel reported against the counterpoint of techno-rock faintly emanating from the bud in her left ear. "Her parents are Hassan and Saida Aboud, both schoolteachers, both retired. She has three siblings. B.A. in English at the state university in New Delhi, with a master's degree two years later from the London School of Economics in London, England."

"And then?"

"Not much for a while. She's listed as attending a few conferences, gave a paper in Bombay on emerging economies, is an officer of something called the League of University Women, a national organization. There's no substantial data until the end of 2002." Rachel leaned dangerously far back in her chair and linked her fingers behind her head. "Since then, however, she's been busy. She's currently connected with the SEWA Bank in Ahmedabad, is a consultant for various NGOs, including BASIX in Hyderabad, Sadhan in New Delhi, and for something called MASS, also in New Delhi."

David wondered, "MASS?"

"The Movement and Action for Social Services. It's a fairly comprehensive agency covering land and water rights, livestock, infrastructure, and human development. It seems benign. She doesn't show up on any watch lists. And so far I've come across nothing that might suggest a connection with terrorist organizations—though, of course, I've just gotten started." Rachel rubbed her skinny right calf with the toe of her left sneaker, retrieved a Snickers bar from a cache in her desk drawer, unwrapped it, crumpled the paper, tossed it at the wastebasket and missed, took a bite, and hospitably offered it to David. Want some?"

"No thanks."

"Three Musketeers?"

"No candy before lunch." He patted his midsection, then urged, "Keep digging. Dig deep. If you find anything remotely questionable, anything at *all,* let me know at once."

"You got it."

★ ★ ★

Ellen sat at her desk, grim faced, scanning a pile of newspaper clippings. In the background, Sam Slaughter's fulgent baritone:

"So not only does our one and only Senator Ellen Fischer play fast and loose on the financial front, but she seems to employ terrorists, too, not only as office flunkies, either, but right-hand members of her staff—Chief of Staff, no less! Whoops—what an embarrassment this particular little lady has turned out to be! If you can call her a lady, and I'm sure you can figure what I'm saying here, folks!"

David winced. "Want me to switch that little turd off?" he asked.

"Of course I do," Ellen said, "but I also suppose we need to know what he's saying."

"Too bad he's only on radio. If people could see him in the flesh, he'd be off the air tomorrow."

Ellen gave a wan smile. "So get him a TV program."

"I'll work on that. Where's Derelle?"

"I took her home and told her to stay there. I want her protected from the media while this mess gets straightened out. Any plans for how we might do that?"

"Sure. I'm arranging an informal breakfast press avail for tomorrow morning for the California media," David said. "Not in the Senate Press Gallery. This is about a staff member this time, not about you. Coffee, bagels, and cream cheese, in this office at nine A.M. Okay? Give you enough time?"

Ellen sighed. "If only we knew what we were dealing with here."

"Regarding Salima?"

She nodded. "It could be everything—or nothing. If she really is a terrorist, or has terrorist sympathies, we could be in big trouble. Alternatively, the situation could be exactly as it appears on the surface: Two bright young women from different backgrounds meet and like each other, go shopping and sightseeing, and have some fun. So far there seems to be no proof that Salima is anything but an idealistic mid-level operative of various humanitarian agencies. Damn it, David, from everything Rachel tells me, they're perfectly innocent. Nobody can prove a thing."

"Then that's your position tomorrow," David said. "Just like with the blind trust situation, your best defense is complete transparency. Go with the facts as you know them."

Though he knew there was a big difference. Over the blind trust issue, Ellen had simply told the whole truth. This time she would go with the facts *as she knew them*—but there was so much she didn't, and couldn't, know.

"Poor Derelle," Ellen said. "It's not fair. I hated to send her home."

"Fair or not, she needs to keep her head down—at least until after the first wave of craziness. If she sticks around, she'll only make things worse." David added, "We have to admit she's not a born diplomat."

"Slaughter calls her 'the Senator's pit bull,'" Ellen said.

"Don't knock it—you can sure use one." David glanced through the window at the facade of the Supreme Court building across Constitution Avenue, its white marble stark against the dingy sky. He couldn't remember when they'd last seen the sun. He wished it would either clear up or snow.

He said softly, "But I wish this time the pit bull had stayed in her cage."

CHAPTER TWENTY

Home in her kitchen, Derelle set the coffeemaker to brew, changed into jeans and a spotless white T-shirt, and restlessly paced the confines of her living room.

When the coffee was ready and its fragrance had permeated her small apartment, she poured herself a cup, straight black with tons of sugar, exactly what she didn't need but what her body craved today. Then she carried it to her bedroom, sat on the bed, and stared at the picture of the Taj Mahal. She wondered what Salima was doing at this moment. She imagined her in one of those poor, dusty villages where the tourists never came with their infusions of dollars and euros, seated in a circle of women, explaining the principle of success and reward, offering more than an elusive dream of hope.

Or perhaps she was home in Ahmedabad. Derelle tried to work out what time it would be there, yesterday or tomorrow, she could never remember. If it was evening, might Salima be relaxing with a cup of tea as she leafed through Derelle's gift and enjoyed the softly mystical illustrations of the Rubaiyat of Omar Khayyam?

At least one good thing had come out of this mess: Derelle now had a photograph of Salima. She'd bought three copies of the

D.C. Times and carefully cut out the front-page picture from each one. Tomorrow, or very soon, she would have a decent print made on good paper, mount it, frame it, and keep it close. It was the only ray of light in her current dark predicament.

She had never before felt for anybody, man or woman, what she felt for Salima.

She hadn't known it was possible—such joy, combined with self-revelation. It was a gift, and even if Salima had been using her, even if Derelle never saw her again, nobody could take it away from her. Ever.

Restless again, Derelle returned to the living room. She leaned moodily on the windowsill, staring down into the lower courtyard, watching the occasional well-wrapped figures scuttle in and out of doorways, and the fountain, where the water trickled in a thin stream down and down through a succession of saucer-shaped dishes. She was vaguely surprised that the water hadn't frozen.

In Oakland right now it was sixty-two degrees.

Derelle wished she was back there.

Then she realized she might be back sooner rather than later.

What was going to happen to her?

She couldn't imagine a future without Ellen—Ellen, who had given her a future in the first place—but perhaps she'd have to try.

CHAPTER TWENTY-ONE

"*Make no mistake about it, folks, you and I and the whole country are in deep doo-doo—there's a more descriptive word, but remember this is a family station—when a Senator—yes, that Senator—places a street thug in a position of the highest trust, responsibility, and authority. Chief of Staff, no less, managing the Senator's life and career, mixing with the highest in the land, traveling to faraway places on the nation's business and on the nation's payroll.*

"*So what are we to think, folks? What does this tell us about that so-called paragon of virtue, Senator Ellen Fischer?*

"*Her Chief of Staff, this woman Derelle Simba, could be tight with some very scary people. We see her all lovey dovey—yes, check out those faces, all sweet smiles, at the Taj Mahal no less, the most romantic spot on the globe—with a politically connected and politically active Pakistani woman, a Muslim, too, name of Salima Aboud. Now, Ms. Aboud spends her time traveling around India and Pakistan—and for all we know, through other unfriendly neighboring countries where our brave young men are at risk! They say she's handing out loans for village women to start businesses, to fund medical care for the poor, which sounds all fine and dandy till you read the fine print and find that's merely a cover for funding abortion clinics, and I don't have to tell you whose tax dollars are paying for those! But*

our sources in Asia tell us this is all a cover for a whole lot more, like carry-
ing information for our enemies and even smuggling weapons. And now
Ms. Aboud has good connections in our government—on account of her new
best friend, Derelle Simba, Senator Ellen Fischer's trusted Chief of Staff!

"So, folks, is this particular Senator someone we want setting our
nation's policies and directly affecting our lives?

"Is this Senator the person you want picking our future leader of
Homeland Security? Does that make you feel safe? Does it make any kind
of sense to you?

"Think about it!"

★ ★ ★

Ellen could take no more and clicked Sam Slaughter off in
full flight.

Quite apart from the slanderous allegations against her, how
dare Slaughter attack Derelle, who wasn't even in elected office.

Ellen wished Slaughter's remarks were actionable but knew
they were not, and that he was safely using—and abusing—the
First Amendment.

He not only disgusted her, he infuriated her. Sam Slaughter
routinely distorted the facts, derailed important discussion, and
incited the public over false issues, the accompanying noise and fuss
resulting, more often than not, in the mainstream press picking
up right behind him.

Ellen had warned her staff of the impending avalanche of dirt,
and now that it was upon them, she could see it was not only the
young people in the office who were shaken by the volume and the
vitriol of the incoming calls.

In addition, rumors of divorce were now surfacing about Ellen
and Ben. "This is a download of the *Bridger Report*," David had told
her just that morning as he handed her a computer printout. "The
bloggers are having themselves a ball," he said in disgust. "Needless
to say, this *Slaughterhouse* garbage has sparked off a whole bunch of
gleeful gossip. I hate like hell to be the one to break it to you, but
someone has to be the messenger."

"I'm not shooting at you, David."

"Don't make promises you can't keep. But it'll be all over the country by now, complete with juicy faked-up pictures."

STRATEGIC WITHDRAWAL?

Ex-Congressman Benjamin Lind, on his way home to Phoenix, Arizona, had no comment when asked whether his marriage to Senator Ellen Fischer was under stress due to recent revelations of alleged blind trust misconduct. Today new charges linked his wife's office to a suspected terrorist. Mr. Lind has no plans to return to Washington, D.C., at this time . . .

And in the accompanying photo, there was Ben, about to enter the airline terminal, dark brows drawn together, mouth a grim line, hand raised as though to smash the reporter's microphone to the ground.

"Oh God," Ellen said, wondering whether Ben had seen it yet and guessing he must have. "They've certainly wasted no time."

"In these days of instant messaging," said David, "anybody remotely in the public eye can expect to have his or her picture taken and that picture transmitted to the press or a celebrity-watch service bureau 24/7."

"You don't need to tell me that." Ellen crushed the paper into a ball and tossed it in the trash, though she would have preferred to rip it to shreds, or set fire to it. A public figure had to expect this kind of harassment, but it never failed to hurt. "So Ben traveling to his hometown, without a return reservation because he doesn't know how long his business will take, automatically means we're getting a divorce?" With a mirthless laugh, she added, "Is he supposed to have left me, like the rat leaving the sinking ship, or have I thrown him out?"

"Take your pick. And this means one more idea has now been planted in fertile soil, one more indication that your life is unstable and you're the wrong person to be trusted to lead Satcher's hearing."

So faces were grim as Ellen climbed the stairs to her upper suite of offices and glanced down the passage to where Rachel Adoni, probably the only member of her staff who was both oblivious and immune to *the Slaughterhouse* and the venom of the hostile blogs and tabloids, shuttled between her computer screens, all elbows and dedication, as she threaded her way through the lives and careers of Salima Aboud and her family.

Ellen let herself out into the second-floor corridor and made her way to the elevator, which opened upon two young office staffers carrying Styrofoam containers of coffee, heads together in intense and hushed conversation. They got off at the next floor and Ellen rode up to the top of the building, to the conference space, a neutral area of gray carpet, walls, and ceiling, which was mercifully quiet. Once there, she leaned her elbows on the parapet overlooking the atrium and tried to quiet her thudding heart.

This eagle-eye view invariably worked for her and brought things into perspective.

From here, even the Calder sculpture, now below her, seemed unintimidating. Ellen gazed onto the upper sides of the cloud shapes, which as always reminded her of giant Frisbees, and noted that they were dusty, which pleased her, as it brought the whole thing into mundane perspective to think of cleaners suspended from the rafters with mops and pails, while the people scurried far below her, looking tiny, their bodies foreshortened to heads and busy feet. For this moment at least, Ellen felt as if she stood outside the world, remote and safe.

She thrust aside both the image of Sam Slaughter spewing hatred from his desk at WHAP and the upcoming command meeting with Majority Leader Tom Treadwell, and seized instead upon thoughts of those who loved and supported her. She recalled the phone messages from her mother and from Ruthie, both telling her not to worry, that everything would be all right in the end.

Ellen thought of Ben in Phoenix, pictured his disgust upon seeing that photograph of Derelle and Salima on the front page of the *D.C. Times.* She wondered whether he had already seen today's

Bridger. She wished he were back. She visualized the birthday dinner they might have had together, and the good-humored give-and-take through which they routinely aired their political differences.

"We're still the Grand Old Party," Ben had loftily maintained very recently, "the party of Lincoln"—as if to say, *Try and top that!* They'd been having breakfast. Where? California, she thought, in her apartment overlooking San Francisco Bay.

"These days GOP stands for Gasoline, Oil, and Petroleum," Ellen said. "Though I guess I have to give you Lincoln."

"And that didn't stop you guys from using the Lincoln Bedroom for some bucks," Ben had countered in a snap, and they'd both laughed.

Well, there wasn't much to laugh about now.

★ ★ ★

Ellen left her reassuring overview, took the elevator down to the basement, and again rode the train to the Capitol, where she avoided the more traveled pathways and thoroughfares and entered Tom Treadwell's office through an unmarked side door.

This time he was not so sanguine. He didn't smile, nor did he offer root beer.

The Iowan led her into what he called his troubleshooting room, a small chamber in which he addressed pressing, confidential business. He sat her down in one of two royal-blue armchairs that faced each other before the tiled fireplace, took the one opposite her, and hitched it forward till their knees were almost touching.

"First off, Ellen, let me say how sorry I am about what you're going through. This is one big swamp we're slogging through, and it's getting stickier and dirtier by the minute."

"Speaking of dirt," she said, "I'm assuming you heard, or were told about, today's *Slaughterhouse?*"

"That little shit! Excuse my French. No, thank God I didn't hear it, but I've been given a transcript—a masterpiece of filthy innuendo, which of course would have been delivered in that righteous voice of the preacher and accepted by millions as gospel truth." His face turned stony. "By now Slaughter will have done an unconscionable amount of harm. So, what are you doing about Derelle Simba?"

"I've told her to stay home for now."

"That's good, as far as it goes——"

"For her own safety, as much as anything."

"——but you need to go a lot further. I'm sorry, Ellen. I'm well aware of your long and special relationship with her, but we must be realistic here. You need to disassociate yourself from her at once."

"I'll have her take a leave of absence till this situation is cleared up."

"Not good enough." Treadwell sought her eyes. "I believe you have a press avail tomorrow morning?"

Ellen nodded.

"That would be the appropriate time to announce her resignation."

It was only what she'd expected him to say, but just the same, it came as a shock. "I can't do that," she said flatly.

"You not only can but you must. That woman is not just a loose cannon but a dangerous liability." After a pause, he said, "Are the rumors I'm hearing true?"

"I'd stake my life on Derelle—no way is she involved with terrorists."

"I was talking about her sexual orientation."

"Derelle's private life is her own business," Ellen said stiffly.

"In the world we live in there's no such thing as a private life. You of all people should know that. Ms. Simba is vulnerable. She's an accident waiting to happen."

"Mr. Leader, with all due respect——"

"In the parts of the world where she seems to be involved, Derelle Simba's alleged lifestyle is not only against the law but a grave danger to herself and others. Listen to me—listen as a friend!" The Iowan leaned forward, impulsively reaching for Ellen's hands. "I freely admit that it's not fair, and neither is it right, but you have no choice but to remove her, or in effect *you're* history."

Ellen was quite aware of the dilemma in which he found himself, but the anger welled inside her as she withdrew her hands.

Treadwell gave a small sigh but continued implacably, "Needless to say, I'm still under pressure to replace you as leader of Satcher's hearings. The calls are coming in fast and furious from both sides of the aisle now."

"No surprise there."

"Which will mean Kenny Stearns has the gavel—not a comforting thought, in view of the government contracts that will be dangled in front of him as bait. I'm sure that no time is being lost to reel him in. Although Kenny cannot ethically meet with Carl Satcher, on account of Kenny's position on the subcommittee, there's no such prohibition against Satcher meeting with an intermediary." The Iowan leaned his large head forward with an air of confidentiality. "I have it on good authority that Kenny's chief fund-raiser, Brian Driscoll, met with the Vice President and another individual for breakfast at the residence this very morning."

Ellen raised her eyebrows. "How do you know that?"

"Secrets are hard to keep in this town. Nothing is private anymore."

"Including this conversation?" Ellen wondered.

"You're as safe in this room as you can be anywhere. And for your information, we regularly sweep for bugs."

"Have you ever found one?"

"Not yet. Of course, we don't expect to in these more sophisticated days. But the very fact of taking such action, and making sure it's noted, is at least sending a message."

"I suppose I should find that comforting," Ellen said.

"Nothing is comforting these days, and we all spend far too much time fighting each other. It's tiring and wasteful. But in the meantime, you have to get rid of Derelle Simba."

Ellen retraced her route back to the Hart Building on the

train, then took the elevator to the second floor, her mind filled with reluctant thoughts and conflicting emotions.

She must hang on to her chairmanship at Satcher's confirmation hearing—but would the cost be too high? She didn't want to pay with Derelle.

I'm sorry, Derelle, please understand I have no choice. Personally I trust you absolutely and I hate to do this, after all we've been through together and your years of total loyalty, but people see you now as a security risk. As I'm sure you understand, I just can't keep you on my staff. Of course, I'll give you a great reference. I promise you'll have nothing to worry about—

Even forming the words into a speech was difficult and painful. How was she going to look Derelle in the eye and say all that?

I can't do it now, Ellen thought; I'll sleep on it. I'll meet with her first thing in the morning. Perhaps by then I'll be able to make it sound better.

But she knew there was no way to make that happen.

CHAPTER TWENTY-TWO

Alan Sharpe was a slight man with thinning, pale hair and a prim mouth. He wore tan slacks, a blue-and-white-striped golf shirt, a pair of steel-framed sunglasses, and an expression of deep annoyance as he was ushered into the judge's office.

"They told me there was an emergency, that your whole system had crashed and it couldn't wait," he said once inside. "I was in Oxnard for my parents' forty-fifth anniversary. I came directly from the airport," he complained. "I haven't even been home yet."

"Sit down," the judge said tersely.

Sharpe blinked in confusion but obeyed, then for the first time noticed Ben standing quietly beside the window, noticed his height, the breadth of his shoulders, his stony expression, and how he held his hands at his sides, bunched into fists.

Sharpe's face blanched to an unhealthy pallor.

"I see you recognize my friend Congressman Lind," the judge said.

"We haven't actually met," Ben said.

Sharpe looked from Ben to the judge and visibly gathered himself. "You had better tell me what this is all about," he challenged with unconvincing bravado.

"Of course we'll tell you," Ben said, moving toward Sharpe, who instinctively reared back in his seat. "And I'll cut right to the chase. We now know it was you who leaked details of my portfolio to the media."

Reflexively, Sharpe reached into his breast pocket, withdrew a ballpoint pen, and rolled it between his fingers like worry beads. "That's outrageous."

"We also know," the judge said, "that you planted malicious and untrue rumors in the media concerning Senator Fischer's Chief of Staff."

"You can't prove that," Sharpe asserted.

"We certainly can," the judge said. "Apparently, everyone leaves a trail, and we've found yours."

"I don't know how much Satcher was paying you," Ben said, "or whether you thought you were doing something noble. But you must be aware that what you were doing was against the law."

Sharpe glanced from the judge to Ben, sliding his pen between his index and third finger, then tapping it against his kneecap. The silence strung out. Finally, with a thin tone of desperation, he said, "I could sue you for invasion of privacy!"

"So you could," the judge agreed genially. "But you won't, for no other reason than that you'd be committing professional suicide. For God's sake, man, do you think you'd ever have another client if they had even a whiff of your abuse of confidentiality?"

"And been caught," Ben added drily.

Sharpe drew breath to deliver what might have been a fierce response, but clearly thought better of it.

Ben and Judge Ray glanced at each other over the top of Sharpe's head.

The judge moved from behind his desk and pulled up a chair adjacent to Sharpe's. "You know," he began in gentle, almost confiding tones, "I was on the bench for a long time, and I like to think of myself both as a good judge of character and a pretty understanding person. You don't strike me as someone who is out to break the law for personal gain—you could have used your talents to accumulate a lot more money and right now be living high on the hog. Nor do you strike me as being stupid or careless. I'm inclined to think, in this instance, that you acted under an honest belief that you were doing the right thing."

"Everything I've done," Sharpe said with a certain dignity, "has been with the ultimate good of the country in mind."

"We believe you," the judge said. "Carl Satcher would have been very convincing on that subject. I can hear him." And for the next ten minutes he slowly, methodically, and at times vehemently explored the rationale that Satcher would have laid before Sharpe to justify his actions: how America had fallen upon difficult and dangerous times; how the country must be guided back to a position of strength and greatness; that the occasional legal technicality should not be allowed to stand in the way. No doubt, Judge Ray suggested, Satcher had pointed out that there was no need for Sharpe to know the big plan, that he merely needed to perform his allotted tasks loyally and effectively, and everything would work out just fine.

"You've done some work in the past for various security agencies of our country," Ben put in, drawing on background details uncovered by John Brown, "and you know how security operations are conducted. You no doubt figured that Mr. Satcher was simply asking you to do the same type of work for him, with a similar result, even though you'd be operating without governmental authority."

Silence. Sharpe neither agreed nor disagreed and continued, head bent, to play with his pen.

"Satcher had been an important elected official," Ben continued, "and now he's on his way to being Secretary of Homeland Security. It's easy to understand, when dealing with a man in such a position, how the lines between the official and the personal can blur, or be made to blur, and the line between right and wrong can seem forgiving. But let me assure you," he said, his voice hard with sudden authority, "that there *is* a line. Let me further assure you that it is maintaining that line that truly makes our country safe, strong, and great, and that, despite everything, we *must* continue to respect the laws by which we live."

The judge picked up the ball. "What Congressman Lind and I are offering you now is the chance to come back across the line and do the right thing for your country—for *our* country."

Ben and the judge waited. The silence drew out to a full minute.

Sharpe fingered his pen one last time, then suddenly returned it to his pocket, which suggested to Ben that a decision had been made. The inclination of Sharpe's head suggested that it was a negative one.

Before he could speak, however, Judge Ray pointed out, "There's another factor you need to consider. Mr. Satcher has been proven, over and over again, to be not only ruthless but also quite unprincipled. His respect for the Constitution, and for our country, lies in direct relation to his own ambition. Think whose name appears on the phone, travel, and e-mail records. It's not his. Do you seriously imagine, when your contribution to this sad business is exposed—as inevitably it will be—that he will hesitate, for one second, to throw you under the bus? You need to protect yourself."

"You don't have as much understanding of the situation as you think you do," Sharpe replied, sounding resigned and almost sad.

"Are you saying there's more?" Ben replied. "Something else?"

Sharpe nodded reluctantly. "There's more."

"Then you'd better tell us the whole story," the judge said firmly.

★ ★ ★

Grace Fulton sat quietly in the cozy darkness of the heavy car, gazing between the shoulders of the driver and the armed Secret Service man in the passenger seat as she wondered how to answer the woman at her side.

"I know he's a foul little man," Cynthia Satcher had just said of Sam Slaughter, "but they do say that where there's smoke there's fire. And if there's even a germ of truth in what he says, don't you feel the information should be out there, so people can make up their own minds?"

Grace had known Cynthia for many years. She admired her beauty, her intellect, her drive, and her reserves of patience. It would have been hard for her when her husband lost his Senate seat. Carl Satcher was neither an easy man nor a comfortable one, and was lethal when crossed, but you'd never have known that from Cynthia's public demeanor. She had bowed out of Washington society, where she had been a leader, and returned to Los Angeles, to resume her life as patron of the arts and dynamic fund-raiser for her various good causes, and she'd done it with neither bitterness nor complaints, as far as Grace knew.

But, of course, there would have been bitterness—how could there not be? Grace began to realize for the first time just how much there must have been when, two hours earlier, the two women had been standing together on the White House lawn, Grace wearing a knee-length shearling coat and black slacks, Cynthia a full-length, dark ranch mink coat and matching hat, watching the Presidential party board the two helicopters.

The President and First Lady, with Johnathon Ewing, the handsome, young Conservative Prime Minister of England, climbed up the steps into *Marine One*. They paused in turn in the open doorway for a farewell salute and smile for the cameras, before ducking inside and buckling in for the seventy-mile, fifteen-minute flight to Camp David, while Craig Fulton boarded *Marine Two* accompanied by Frances Ewing and Carl Satcher.

With the exception of the Prime Minister's diminutive and engagingly cockney wife, they were all tall, imposing people, exuding an air of privilege and power. The Presidential helicopters were also redolent of power: olive-bodied and white-topped, emblazoned with the national flag and UNITED STATES OF AMERICA along the bodywork.

It was a great photo op.

"This will certainly do our husbands no harm," Cynthia Satcher had said at the time. "You can't have enough positive, reinforcing imagery, and the whole country will see Craig in his role as trusted second in command, flying off to spend quality time with the President and Prime Minister."

Grace had summoned her radiant public smile for the cameras. "Absolutely no harm at all!" she agreed.

"And Carl is obviously expected to be confirmed to Homeland Security, or why would *he* be going to Camp David?" Cynthia said.

The engines of *Marine One,* and then *Marine Two,* had then roared into life with a blast of sound and whoosh of air. The steps folded up into the cabin wells and the doors closed. Onlookers moved aside to give the aircraft a wide berth. The Marine Guard saluted. The President's smiling face could be seen at the window, his hand waving.

The helicopters rose sedately, then banked into a steep turn toward the northwest, at which point the photographers turned their attention to the two wives left behind on the ground, who, backed by the pillared elegance of the White House, waved to their men, with whom they would reunite in two hours or so after driving up in the Vice President's big black SUV.

Another good photo op.

Cynthia had said, "It's been a rough few months for us all. Thank God it'll all be over in the next couple of weeks—then you and I can make some serious plans." With a charming, conniving grin, she added, "We'll be spending a lot of time together, you know."

Grace, ever cautious, wondered, "You definitely think Carl will be confirmed?"

Cynthia's eyes had widened in genuine surprise. "Of course! Fischer's goose will be well and truly cooked by then, if it isn't already, and she's the one who's holding him back. When that woman's current term ends, I predict she'll find herself either bounced back to California to tend to her castaway children, or taking golf lessons in Phoenix. Provided, of course, that she still has a husband."

Some quality in Cynthia's voice prompted Grace to angle her a sharp look, and she noticed for the first time that Cynthia's beautiful blue eyes could look as cold as arctic water.

She suspected that, despite her apparently gracious retirement from political wifehood, Cynthia had never forgiven Ellen Fischer and probably even hated her for, in Cynthia's eyes, supplanting her husband from his rightful place in the nation's highest legislative body. Clearly, revenge was playing a part here.

And yet revenge definitely took a backseat to red-hot ambition.

Grace had found herself thinking of Lady Macbeth, who would do whatever it took, including multiple murder, to see her husband crowned king.

But that made no sense because it wasn't Cynthia's husband, was it, who planned to become President of the United States.

★ ★ ★

Now, in the Vice President's car, Cynthia prompted, *"Don't* you believe the people have a right to know what's going on?"

"Perhaps," Grace said unwillingly. "But that man Slaughter is a disgrace. Must there be all this unpleasantness and insinuation, such as accusing Ellen Fischer of being connected to terrorists— or as good as accusing her—which is stretching it to the limit, you have to agree. And now this rubbish about her and her husband having marital problems—that's downright sleazy!"

Cynthia said serenely, "It goes with the job. If you can't take the heat, then, you know, stay out of the kitchen." She began to shrug out of her beautiful coat. "I never thought I'd take this off, but I'm actually warm for the first time today! I have to admit I'm not looking forward to East Coast winters again."

"It could be a lot colder than this, and for much longer— think Vermont or Minnesota."

Cynthia laughed. "You're right, but I'm a California girl." She opened a compartment in the walnut paneling behind the front passenger's seat and withdrew a silver flask and two cups. "Goody—they said they were packing Irish coffee. I could use some. Couldn't you? It's past cocktail time!"

It occurred to Grace that Cynthia was making herself rather too much at home in her own husband's, the Vice President's, car and she wondered whether she should feel affronted, then decided that would be petty. Cynthia had been chilled and she wanted a hot drink—what was the big deal? She, Grace, should have thought of it herself and been a good hostess. And it must be at least seven o'clock.

However, she wasn't about to dwell on Cynthia's attitude, nor did she care to discuss the weather, so Grace returned firmly to the topic at hand. "Putting up with spiteful lies and gossip *shouldn't* automatically go with the job. It's hateful. And Sam Slaughter is truly the bottom of the barrel. The things he says are vile—and could be dangerous. Too many people listen to him, too many believe him and buy right into all that filth just because they want to." She recalled Brianna's face yesterday when they discussed Ellen Fischer: *How can they say those things on the air?* she'd demanded. *Aren't there any laws about that?*

Grace had been as shocked as Brianna. She said now, "Sam Slaughter came right out and called Derelle Simba a terrorist lesbo. How can he say that and get away with it?"

"The blessing and curse of the First Amendment," Cynthia said. "Simba is a public figure, and there is no limit on speech about a public figure. Anyway, being gay isn't exactly an issue these days, you know."

"But a lot of people still get awfully riled up—there're fanatics out there, and that kind of stuff stirs up the worst emotions in the worst people."

"Too true—but the advertisers love him! Sam Slaughter is pure gold!" Then, in a casual tone Grace sensed might be masking an altogether darker emotion, Cynthia said, "How much do you really *care* what happens to Ellen Fischer?"

"I just want her out of Craig's life—and Carl's, too," Grace said. "But not this way."

"Then you'll have to look at the big picture, won't you, which is to get my husband confirmed to Homeland Security, and yours elected President." Cynthia Satcher tapped Grace's knee with a beautifully manicured finger. "And you *know* you can't make an omelet without breaking eggs!"

★ ★ ★

They were seated so close that the Vice President was sure he could feel the warmth emanating from the thigh of Britain's First Lady.

"Pity we couldn't persuade your wife to come with us," Frances Ewing yelled above the racket of the engine, and turning to Carl Satcher in the seat behind, she added, "Yours, too. Hope it doesn't snow and they get stuck on the way up."

"Grace doesn't care for helicopters," Fulton roared back. "Hates the movement. Makes her feel sick."

"Poor thing," Frances said.

"And even if it does snow, the Marines will get them up there somehow."

Frances shifted in her seat to gaze at the dark landscape. "Must be pretty country!" she shouted.

"Beautiful!" Fulton agreed, whereupon the effortful conversation died, which was fine with him.

Usually, Craig Fulton loved going to Camp David, lush and leafy in summer, stark in the winter with dry, crackling air, the tops of the pine trees powdered with snow. He enjoyed the healthy activities always available: the workout room, the hiking trails, the stable of horses, the lap pool, and the tennis court where one might find oneself rallying across the net with a visiting king or head of state.

More important, it was a place where the serious work was done, a high-security refuge guarded by Marines where one could walk the extensive grounds without a bodyguard or fear of press intrusion, and speak one's mind, off the record, without fear of being misquoted.

Best of all was the guest book he would sign upon departure, where his own signature would share space with those of Vladimir Putin, Tony Blair, and King Abdullah of Jordan.

If he handled it right, he, Craig Fulton, grandson of a laborer, would soon be hosting such illustrious company himself.

"This visit's a natural opportunity for you to cozy up to the Prime Minister," Satcher had observed on the way to the White House this morning. "You being a Brit yourself."

"I'm an American," Fulton had insisted. "I was born in Wilkinsburg, Pennsylvania. And so was my father."

"Don't quibble—your roots are British. You can get together over tea or whatever and establish a relationship for later on."

For when I'm President, thought Fulton, and wondered why, this time, the thought didn't send off incendiary rockets of excitement through his body.

"It's all coming together," Satcher said, sounding so confident. He always had a knack for brushing away problems and irritating truths like lint off his coat sleeve—though sometimes lint had a habit of sticking, and Ellen Fischer was nothing if not tenacious.

Fulton wished he could share the Satchers' confidence, but instead he had this deep, dragging doubt in his gut when contemplating the next step.

He thought of himself as a nice guy, doing the right thing. He had never really approved of going negative in a campaign. He considered such tactics dirty pool, and preferred to feel he was above all that. And yet those kinds of campaigns usually seemed to work, and so, with some reluctance, he'd played along.

Lately, he'd persuaded himself that what he and Carl Satcher were doing was little different, that it was just another campaign, though with greater stakes, and although he personally abhorred both the clandestine releases sent to Sam Slaughter and that business with Derelle Simba and the Indian woman, he had tacitly signified his assent by his lack of resistance.

And now the end play, the final clincher, was coming up.

It had been inevitable from the moment he made the casual observation to Carl Satcher, over drinks late at night in Los Angeles two years ago, how another subway, stadium, or airport incident—successfully thwarted, of course—wouldn't be a bad thing. Not merely to restore Fulton's sagging popularity—absolutely not—but as an urgently needed wake-up call for the nation.

"A wake-up call," Satcher had said, regarding Fulton with unusually marked respect. "Not a bad idea!"

Fulton should have remembered that Satcher was not some-one with whom you spoke idly.

"I should have thought of that myself," Satcher had added.

With a mild attempt at humor, Fulton added, "Unfortunately, we can't rely on a terrorist to meet our time requirements."

"No. We'll need to arrange one for ourselves," Satcher agreed.

"Carl, you're mad!" And when Satcher didn't at once reply, Fulton said, "Or joking. You're joking, right?"

"Not an *actual* terror event," Satcher mused. "An alleged plan or plot is enough, something the OSO can crush before it happens."

"Forget it! You can't pull off something like that. It just can't be done. Anyway, I won't tolerate it."

"Don't pull that righteous crap with me," Satcher said. "Of course it can be done, and don't think like a girl, look at the big picture. Whether the conspiracy is real or not is quite irrelevant. Nobody would deny that a terrorist organization or cell could attack anyone, anywhere, at any time. Think in terms of prevention—prevention is the name of the game. Think of the message it'll send to all the guys out there who want to kill us. Think of what such a plot, uncovered just in time by you, would mean for this country.

"Though, of course," Satcher had mused, "we have to pick the moment. Timing is everything."

And the time had now arrived. Soon, thanks to Carl Satcher and the organizational abilities of his clever wife, Fulton's star would shine brightly once again—provided nothing went wrong.

Fulton felt a little queasy as he thought about the next forty-eight hours. Then he ordered himself to get a grip, to remember that heady time early in the administration when, a hero, he'd laid out his plans for the future protection of America—and the country had listened.

The country had needed him then, and it needed him now if it was ever to return to that time of unquestioned power and extravagant dreams, to those golden years when America was the land of opportunity and riches, when the streets were, indeed, paved with gold and everything—ambition, fortune, buildings, roads, automobiles—was supersized.

Cling to that thought, he ordered himself; have faith, even though it's hard. The editorials and blogs attacking his stance on privacy and constitutional rights were a mounting distraction. And the Homeland Security hearings on Satcher, no doubt intended by Ellen Fischer as an inquisition, could only result in real damage to the country. People just didn't understand what was at stake, what had to be done.

As the tips of the pine trees rushed below him in the darkness, Fulton willed himself back to an earlier, safer time, himself ten years old, seeing Uncle George and Aunt Ceecee off on their first European vacation. They were sailing from New York to Southampton, England, on the ocean liner *Queen Mary,* immense with its row upon row of portholes and three raked funnels towering over the Fulton family down on the dock, while the tall cranes swung overhead loading the goods, the luggage, and, finally, the automobiles. People often took their own cars on vacation with them then, and he'd watched a bright-pink Cadillac swoop up and over in a cradle of steel and rope, hundreds of feet in the air as the longshoremen directed its passage, and Fulton had actually ducked as its huge dark shadow swept over his head and he'd thought proudly, We're Americans!

We're the best!

★ ★ ★

The aircraft rocked in the cold downdraft from the mountain, and the lights of Camp David came into view below them.

Frances Ewing shouted, "I could fancy a nice, hot cuppa tea! Think that'll be on, then?"

"You can have whatever you like!" Fulton yelled back. "They'll show you to your cabin, then after you get settled, you'll come to the main house and have coffee, tea, drinks, or whatever with the President." And sometime this evening, or tomorrow, he and Satcher would meet for a brief conference of their own.

The aircraft circled the area and the Prime Minister's wife leaned across his lap with unabashed enthusiasm to gaze out and down at this island of civilization in the surrounding darkness. "Looks ever so lonely from up here!"

"But comfortable," Fulton said. "Cozy. You'll like it." He thought of how next year, if everything went as planned, he'd no longer be a forgotten man written off as a footnote of history, he'd be getting ready to be Commander in Chief.

Camp David would be his own private getaway spot then.

CHAPTER TWENTY-THREE

January 5

SATURDAY

For the second morning in a row, Ellen rose before dawn to meet with Derelle.

She felt cold, inside and out, but didn't attempt to warm herself with a cup of coffee, as if to punish herself for what she was about to do.

Ellen glanced down at the papers lying at her feet in the small lobby but didn't gather them up and take them inside. Instead, she just stepped over the *D.C. Times* with its gloating banner headline, FISCHER-LIND MARRIAGE TERMED OUT?, and rode the elevator down to the garage.

It was before seven o'clock on a Saturday and there was little traffic. The city was dank and cold, with the bellies of the clouds pressing down.

Ellen dreaded this meeting. She had lain awake all night, because this was Derelle, still and always the child she had saved. How can I do this? she wondered.

Yesterday had been bad altogether.

At least Ben would soon be home. He'd called her last night and said he hoped to be home by midmorning. "Stop worrying, everything will be fine," he had said. "A lot is happening. I'll tell you when I see you—we're not trusting the phones."

"Now that you're coming back, those scandalmongering idiots will have to stop saying you walked out on me," Ellen had said.

"Or that you threw me out," Ben said.

"Not that it makes much difference. They invent their own reality as they go along—anything to raise circulation and please the advertisers."

"What's happening about Derelle?" Ben asked.

"They say I have to let her go. They say she's a loose cannon with poor judgment and dangerous connections and I don't have a choice."

"What will you do?"

"I don't know. I *hate* to let her go for some trumped-up reason, especially when she's given so much, and been so loyal over the years."

"You'll do the right thing," Ben said. Though Ellen guessed he wouldn't mind if Derelle was out of her life. Her Chief of Staff neither liked nor approved of him, and he'd tried so hard with her, too.

★ ★ ★

Now, relieved that Ben would be back soon, Ellen turned off Constitution Avenue onto Henry Bacon Drive and pulled in behind the single car parked there, which was Derelle's dark blue Infiniti.

"The Vietnam Memorial?" Ellen had asked when they made plans on where to meet. What a terrible place to have to give bad news! she thought. "Are you sure?"

"I have to get outside. I'm going stir-crazy in here. And so early in the day, in that place, nobody's going to bother us."

Derelle was standing at the angle made by the two black granite walls, hands shoved deep in the pockets of her leather coat. She was alone save for a gray-haired man in a shabby raincoat further along the wall, a black woolen watch cap clutched in his hands, a mayonnaise jar at his feet containing two red roses, so bright they must be artificial. Had he come here all the way across the country? Did he stop by in routine pilgrimage? As Ellen watched, he leaned forward to touch the polished stone and trace one of the names engraved there. She saw his lips moving, thought he might be weeping, and turned her head away.

She told Derelle, "Let's walk."

They paced silently down the tiled walkway to where the shorter, eastern length of the wall lowered to a height of eight inches and came to an end, then slowly returned.

Ellen wished Derelle would say something. Anything at all. She tried to formulate her opening words, but her mind recoiled.

Imperceptibly, the sky was lightening; she could feel the chill moisture in the air and hear a muted dripping from the naked trees.

"I saw Tom Treadwell yesterday," Ellen said finally.

Derelle remained silent.

"You can probably guess what he wanted."

"I'd be some kind of a fool not to guess."

"I'm supposed to tell you——"

Derelle halted, and held up a hand. "You don't need to say it. What else can you do? You can't afford to have me around anymore. I was careless and took a risk; it's my fault. I suppose I thought I was so far away from home across the world in India, I could do what I wanted and it wouldn't matter. Not smart: I understand that." She added, "And you know something? I'll be glad to go."

It should have been a relief hearing that, but if anything, Derelle's understanding and forbearance made Ellen feel so much worse. She felt a dark, deep pit opening up at her feet as she thought of her life without Derelle in it with her candor, her strength, her guts, and her loyalty. She asked, "Will you really be glad?"

"I don't want to leave *you*—that will be worse than anything I can imagine—but I can't stick around with things the way they are now." Derelle met Ellen's eyes squarely. "There's too much hate. It's like a disease. Everything gets twisted and warped, and the very best people, people like you, don't have a chance." She drew a long, deep breath. "So I'm resigning—you don't have to fire me. Then I'm going back to Oakland. I've made up my mind.

They need people like me in that community, and I can make a real difference, working with families like you did for so long. Maybe I never should have left." In a flat voice, she added, "Of course, you'll be in California a lot, like always, and we'll stay in touch."

Ellen thought about arriving at work in the mornings and finding Derelle's desk empty—though, of course, it wouldn't be empty, there'd be another person sitting there, the wrong person. Ellen supposed she'd have to start interviewing at once unless she promoted from within, but she couldn't imagine anybody she'd want in Derelle's place.

She remembered their late suppers at Marty's on Capitol Hill when, over platters of pork ribs, garlic mashed potatoes, and cole-slaw, even the knottiest problems seemed to untangle and be discarded among the piles of chewed bones and crumpled napkins.

She recalled midnight sessions in her own office, Derelle's keen mind seizing the issue of the day, running with it, considering it from all angles, and stripping away the nonessentials, her valuable instincts honed from years of street living when a wrong call could have meant injury or worse. How often were you blessed with a staffer like Derelle, who could be counted on always to tell the truth—even when you might not want to hear it?

Above all, she remembered Derelle's kindness after Josh's death, and all the acts of friendship, large and small, over the years. People like Derelle were more valuable than diamonds.

The man—the veteran?—was leaving now, knitted cap pulled down over his eyes. He passed them, looking down, not seeing them. They stood aside to let him go, then moved together again.

"You really don't have a choice," Derelle said, eyes following as he faded into the mist like a ghost. "It's the only thing to do."

"You're welcome to hand in your resignation," Ellen said, "but I'm not going to accept it."

Derelle wheeled around, and for one of the few times in her life, Ellen saw her eyes dilate with astonishment. "You're not?"

"If you truly want to go back to Oakland, then of course go with my blessing," Ellen said. "I'd never try to stop you. But I need you to stay. Senator Treadwell tells me, and now you're also telling me, that I don't have a choice. But that means it's my opponents who are making my choices, not me—and that's unacceptable." She took a deep breath and felt the cold air rush bracingly into her lungs. "The next few weeks are going to be rough, and I'll need all the loyal friends I can get. That especially means you. Later this morning, as you know, I'm meeting with the California press. I'll be telling them that I don't believe you have now, or have *ever* had, any connection whatsoever with a terrorist organization. That I believe in you totally, that I value and support you and have no intention of losing you—unless you choose to resign, of your own free will, at which time, believe me, I'll try to talk you out of it."

"You're serious, aren't you?" Derelle said.

"Never more so in my life!"

"Mr. Lind won't like it."

"Ben will want me to do what's right. I know you don't think of him as a friend—though I wish you would try—but he respects you a lot."

"He does? Really?"

"He knows how well we work together, how lucky I am to have you, and how hard it would be for me to replace you. And so far as Senator Treadwell is concerned, for all I know, he's testing me, to make sure I have what it takes, to stand up for what's right. That happens, you know." Ellen looked up into Derelle's face and for once felt the taller of the two. She'd made up her mind and the decision felt good. Very good. "So take it from me, I'm not prepared to lose you!"

Derelle, at a loss for words, pressed her lips together till they almost disappeared; when she relaxed them, they trembled. "Are you sure? *Positive?*"

"For God's sake, yes, I'm sure," Ellen cried. "And now, please, Derelle, just say something like 'Okay, right on,' whatever. Then go home, get some rest, be prepared to start in again first thing Monday morning, and work harder than you ever have in your life."

She added sternly, "Are we on the same page here?"

CHAPTER TWENTY-FOUR

Derelle did not go directly home after leaving Ellen at the Vietnam Memorial. In her present mood, returning to the narrow confines of her apartment seemed quite impossible. Instead, she drove across the Roosevelt Bridge, turned onto the George Washington Parkway, and headed toward Langley, Virginia.

She pulled into the view area at the Potomac Overlook, climbed from the car, belted her leather coat tightly around her waist, and leaned over the wooden railing, gazing at the slate-gray river sliding swiftly and silently below her.

She followed the beaten dirt track around the railing and partway down the twisting trail leading to the riverbank. It was slick and icy, and her booted feet almost shot out from under her. All she needed right now was to slip and fall and end up with a broken leg or worse, so she struggled back up the trail and once more leaned on the railing, watching the river, thinking she had seldom felt so happy.

Ellen still trusted and believed in her.

She was going out on a limb for her, acting against the dictates of the party leadership.

It was possible, of course, as Ellen said, that Treadwell could be testing her grit and determination to stand by her friend and colleague, though personally Derelle couldn't quite buy it. She suspected that Ellen didn't really buy it, either, which made her decision the more meaningful.

Even the warmth of Derelle's feelings, however, couldn't indefinitely block out the cold.

She returned to her car, switched on the engine, and turned up the heat.

She sat there for another ten minutes, hers the only car at the Overlook, still not wanting to go home, but knowing how much easier it would be now to get through the day. There were errands to run, e-mails to send, such a lot to do in preparation for Monday, when, as Ellen promised, she would have to work harder than ever before and wouldn't see her own home except, as usual, to sleep.

A few fat snowflakes settled moistly on Derelle's windshield. Although still early, it was as dark as late afternoon and she switched her lights on before shoehorning her way into traffic on the westbound parkway. As she did so, with only the briefest flurry of warning, the sky let go with an almost solid cascade of snow and the cars slowed down, crawling toward the city through a deepening whiteout.

Derelle didn't care. She had plenty of gas. She followed the glowing red taillights ahead of her, found a gospel station on the radio and sang along, safe and warm and protected from the weather. She didn't normally care for gospel—she had never been religious—but today the music, so uplifting and full blooded, called to her and enhanced her mood.

It was at least an hour before Derelle pulled into the garage at the Watergate, still euphoric, still singing, counting her blessings, making vague plans to actually visit a church tomorrow and give thanks for a life that until recently had seemed so dark and joyless.

She eased skillfully into her space, a slot beside a pillar which called for tight maneuvering, and switched off the radio. She climbed out, slammed the door, and locked it with the remote, at which point the Infiniti gave its usual affirmative toot and flash of taillights. Derelle patted it absently on the fender, hefted her purse over her shoulder, and for one of the few times in her life didn't mentally grumble about her space being about as far from the elevator as it could possibly be.

She was humming, actually humming, as she'd remember later—*Amazing Grace, how sweet the sound*—high-stepping along and swinging her purse on its strap. *I once was lost but now I'm found*, so happy, trusted, and valued—

Not paying attention.

In the old days she'd have *felt* the presence of the watcher well before she heard the faint rustle of clothing, the intake of breath, and the sudden convulsive rush of footsteps.

Not this time.

The blow to her lower back was a complete shock, deep and cold. She gasped, breathless, as the knife went into her, then she instinctively twisted her body to narrow the target.

She never really saw the man, just a glaring pair of no-color eyes ringed with white, and a squared mouth like a mail slot through which spewed a jumbled litany of hate—*dirty terrorist God will strike you down you had this coming*—while his body leaned into hers with the closeness of a lover as he dragged the knife free to strike again.

She felt the hot pain flooding through her body, the wetness running down her side, and the blood welling into her mouth. She struggled for breath and knew she must act fast. She didn't have long—*You're going out, girl*—there was no time to wonder what had been done to her and whether she was dying. She ordered herself to stay on her feet, and to keep her mind focused on just one thing: survival.

Derelle ignored the knife—you never watched the blade, you watched the guy holding it, his eyes; you could tell what he'd do from his eyes. The hard-earned instincts clicked in from thirty years ago when she was a feral child on the streets of Oakland.

Why doesn't anyone come? Where is everybody? There should be people—someone to help

She dropped her chin to protect her throat and raised her knee, not to drive into his groin but to bring the edge of her boot sole hard, *hard* down the length of his shin. As he screamed and doubled over in pain, she flung her head upward to connect under the point of his jaw, and when his head flew back, she smashed first at his throat with the stiffened edge of her hand, then at the bridge of his nose, which flattened with a satisfying *crunch,* finally stabbing for his eyes with two fingers rigid as iron.

It took all of three seconds.

Derelle heard the knife clatter on the concrete floor, felt her attacker reel away, heard a thin, wailing scream—her last coherent thought was that she couldn't have crushed his larynx if he could make a noise like that. Then his screams were growing fainter as the garage darkened, while cars, pillars, walls, and ceiling slowly moved outward and away from her and faded while the pain faded, too, until she was only aware of intense cold, of arms too heavy to lift, then the floor was coming up toward her.

CHAPTER TWENTY-FIVE

They'd expanded the conference table so that, with extra chairs, it could comfortably accommodate the fifteen or so reporters from the California press.

Ellen sat at the far end, all business and armored for confrontation in a black suit over a crisply tailored white shirt. In front of her lay the material Rachel Adoni had handed to her not ten minutes before.

Rachel had been waiting for Ellen on her return from the Vietnam Memorial, a pale blue folder under her arm. She'd said formally, looking quietly pleased, "I have something for you, Senator—background info on the Aboud family. I'm sure it's what you wanted!"

Ellen ushered Rachel into the office, where David was already waiting, sat her down, and began to leaf through her findings. "Well done—this is more than I ever hoped for!"

"I had copies made for the press. As for that photo," Rachel said, "as you can see, the mystery is solved."

"I should have thought of that myself," David said.

Ellen had been thinking guiltily of the toll the last few days had taken on her communications director, who looked pallid and puffy-faced due to lack of sleep and hasty, irregular meals. Upon reading Rachel's report, however, he'd become immediately refreshed, greeting Ellen's decision to keep Derelle as her Chief of Staff with equanimity rather than the resigned shake of the head likely yesterday.

Thank you, Rachel!

Susana from the press office entered with fifteen individual press kits in pale blue folders, and an intern bustled in with two bakery boxes, one containing a mixed assortment of doughnuts, the other of bagels, which she unpacked on the side table beside the twenty-four-cup coffeemaker, just now gurgling into readiness.

A few minutes later, Celia Chen buzzed from Reception to report the arrival of the reporters, who moments later filed into the room with murmured morning greetings.

Norene Parker of the *San Francisco Chronicle* planted herself in the seat to Ellen's left, heavy shoulder bag in her lap, a jelly doughnut in one hand and a cup of black coffee in the other. Adam Hampshire of the *Los Angeles Times* took the chair on Ellen's right, with a bagel and cream cheese. With the exception of the *Oakland Tribune* and *Sacramento Bee,* whose reporters sat on the couch with laptops on their knees, all the other papers' reporters were soon seated around the table, which quickly assumed a lived-in appearance beneath a layer of notepads, tape recorders, Styrofoam cups, bagels, and napkins.

Ellen tried to gauge their mood, settled on cautious skepticism. They weren't very happy about a Saturday briefing, nor about venturing out in the heavy snow.

David, facing her at the other end of the table with his back to the door, opened the proceedings. "The Senator has a statement to make, after which she's happy to take your questions."

"Thanks, David." Ellen glanced around the assembly, knowing what they expected to hear, guessing they'd have a surprise.

"Recently," she began, "we met in the press gallery following a leak of the details of my family's blind trust. On Thursday, my husband, Ben Lind, flew to Phoenix, Arizona, to meet with our trustee and attempt to track down the source of that leak." With a martial glint in her eye, she said, "And off the record, despite everything you've heard, our marriage is in *great* shape!"

She did not allow herself to be sidetracked, however, and returned directly to the issue at hand. "Here we go again, another day, another story, this time involving serious allegations against Derelle Simba, my Chief of Staff."

The reporters watched as she opened the folder Rachel had given her, extracted two printed sheets and laid them on the table, then covered them with yesterday's *D.C. Times* with its inflammatory headline.

"You all know the basic situation, though I'll refresh your memory." Ellen led them quickly through the events of last November's New Delhi conference on global warming, from Derelle's first meeting with Salima Aboud to that predawn visit to the Taj Mahal in Agra. "Soon afterward," Ellen said, "a certain picture appeared in the *Straits Times,* an English-language newspaper in Singapore, with a circulation of four hundred thousand across southeast Asia. The caption read, 'East and West share a magical moment.' Two days ago, it appeared, with truly fortuitous timing, on the front page of the *D.C. Times.*"

Parker of the *Chronicle* interrupted her, "Senator, who took that picture?"

David reminded her, "The Senator will take questions at the end."

"No," Ellen said, "that's okay. I'm happy to clear this one up right now. The picture was taken, unknown to my Chief of Staff and Ms. Aboud, by a member of the Singapore delegation who ran into them in Agra."

The reporter from the *Mercury News* raised a hand: "So how did the *D.C. Times* get hold of it?"

"My researcher accessed the picture through Google Alert, simply by entering the name Derelle Simba. Anybody could have done this just as easily; she found it at once."

The *Sacramento Bee:* "So you're suggesting someone sent the photo to the *D.C. Times?*"

"It seems likely."

"Do you believe there was a conspiracy to damage you?"

"I don't want to use the word *conspiracy,* but it seems to me more than a coincidence that my Chief of Staff has been harassed and hounded and I've been discredited by association for the second time in a week."

The *San Jose Mercury News:* "Can you comment on who you believe might be behind this alleged conspiracy? Or let me put it this way: Who do you think is after you?"

"I'm making no accusations at this time."

The *Oakland Tribune* again: "Can you comment on the head scarf issue?"

"Certainly! As you well know, in some quarters a woman's head scarf is more than a fashion accessory, it's a religious statement. An attempt—and a pretty far-reaching one—has been made to incriminate me through association." Once again Ellen related the saga of the scarf, concluding with a wry grimace, "We've really fallen pretty far when we read so much into a purchase from a bazaar." Turning to Parker, she said, "For instance, Norene, I see you're wearing a very attractive scarf. Do you think you should tell us where it came from? Did you buy it yourself or was it a gift?"

During the ensuing muted, half-amused buzz, she glanced down the table at David and was rewarded by a tiny but definite nod of approval.

"And now," Ellen said, "I want to address that malicious accusation against my Chief of Staff and her friend. Please save further questions till I'm done."

In a calmly controlled voice, she went on, "We have made it our business to explore the background and the various associations and activities of Salima Aboud and her family, political and otherwise."

Silence.

"Unfortunately these days, for many people in the West, Islam and terrorism appear inextricably linked even though the vast majority of the world's Muslim population are not fanatical jihadists but as peace loving as you and I—as is Ms. Aboud, who does all in her power not merely to promote peace but the sustainable lifestyle necessary for nurturing it.

"Here are the results of my researcher's efforts. There're copies available for all of you. David? Would you please?"

As David passed around the press kits, Ellen covered the essentials of Salima Aboud's background, her immediate family, her education—"and current involvement with various humanitarian and environmental groups, which you'll find listed among the materials you've been given. Ms. Aboud also serves on a subcommittee of the Indian Department of the Interior on pollution issues in the major cities, which was why she happened to be at the conference in New Delhi last fall."

Ellen paused, listening to the soft whir of tape machines, the tap of fingers on laptop keys.

"So where does this accusation come from?" she asked. "Might Ms. Aboud indeed be a terrorist? Might any member of her family be linked with a terrorist group—or are we being fed a barrage of guilt by ethnicity?

"For example, Ms. Aboud, who is an Indian national, has been described several times in the media as a Pakistani—could this be intentionally to link her in people's minds with Al Qaeda?

"We are also told, in a blatant subversion of truth, that a distant relative of Ms. Aboud's, living in the Pakistani province of Sindh, is connected to local Islamic insurgents. Check in your folders and you'll find a map."

Ellen waited while her audience located the relevant sheet. "As you can see, Sindh province, which directly borders the Indian state of Gujarat—and let me remind you that until Partition in 1947 India and Pakistan were the same country—is the stronghold of the Bhutto family and the People's Party of Pakistan, and for some time has been actively agitating to secede from the nation of Pakistan. Hassan Aboud, a distant cousin of Salima Aboud's, is involved with the separatist movement, specifically"—Ellen scanned the page—"the Sindh Taraqi Passand Party, which does indeed advocate a local insurgency—but one with no global threat whatsoever, and no association with Islamic militancy.

"A serious grievance in the region, and one of the major issues in favor of secession, involves the government damming of the Indus, upriver in the state of Punjab—please check the map— which, downriver, depletes the irrigation of Sindhi crops in the Indus Delta."

Ellen laid her hands flat on the table, pushed herself back in her seat, and eyed the group around the table. Into an attentive silence, lacking even the click of a laptop, she said quietly, "Ladies and gentlemen, we're not talking about war and terror and suicide bombers. We're talking about the redress of a clearly perceived wrong. We're talking about *farmers,* about simple people whose irrigation canals are running dry, who cannot water their crops; whose banana and mango plantations, carefully cultivated over generations, must now be plowed under; whose whole livelihoods are at imminent risk.

"We're talking about once-fertile land that is steadily eroding into desert.

"We're talking about water rights, folks. *That's* the big issue for Hassan Aboud and his separatist group:

"Not the right to be a terrorist—the right to *water!*"

★ ★ ★

As the raised hands clamored for recognition, Ellen said, "One more point, and a vital one, and then we're done here.

"Earlier this morning, I met with Derelle Simba, who I've been under pressure to dismiss. She offered to resign of her own free will." With a kindling eye, she said, "I did not accept her resignation. Ms. Simba will continue, with my full confidence, in the job she does so well. I have no intention of letting her go—"

"Senator, excuse me!" Celia Chen stood in the doorway, her face ashen. With a gulp of distress, she said, "This can't wait!"

In one fluid movement, the faces of the reporters turned from Celia to Ellen and back again.

Clearly, something terrible had happened.

Ellen thought of Ben, still in the air. Of poor visibility and a crash landing on the runway. Then, inevitably, of weapons smuggled onto an aircraft and a fiery explosion. The blood drained from her face. She rose to her feet and gripped the table for support as the room swam before her.

"Excuse me," she said, and left without looking back, her arm around Celia's shoulder.

Outside in the hallway, her voice hushed, she asked, "Is it Ben?"

"Not Ben, it's Derelle." Celia wavered. "Oh my God, Ellen, she's been stabbed and they're not sure she'll make it."

CHAPTER TWENTY-SIX

The First Lady, nursing a cold, had elected to spend a lazy morning catching up with her reading.

The President, with the Vice President, the British Prime Minister, and the putative Director of Homeland Security, had retired for an informal debate on trans-Atlantic antiterrorism policy.

The Prime Minister's wife, up early and filled with energy upon sniffing the astringent, piney air, had declared herself eager for a nice morning walk around the grounds, so here they were, three women striding along the hiking trail under the trees, their booted feet crunching on the carpet of frozen pine needles, Grace Fulton in a thick navy pea jacket over trousers of Harris tweed, Cynthia Satcher in a belted camel-hair overcoat, and Frances Ewing trotting between them, wearing a puffy, brown ski parka over a Norwegian-style sweater with reindeer on the chest, and navy twill slacks tucked into borrowed moon boots.

Grace thought Frances Ewing looked like a bundle of old clothes.

The Prime Minister's wife, however, had already declared that she didn't give a hoot what she looked like so long as she stayed warm. "I'm glad they keep jackets and boots to lend to people! Imagine, Mr. Putin himself might have worn this jacket—that's a thought, isn't it?—though being from Russia, he'd have brought his own winter things along, wouldn't he!"

Her narrow face flushed by wind, cold, and exercise, Frances enthused about their visit to date: the helicopter ride, the scenery, the cozy fireplace in the great room, last night's dinner of London broil, ending with apple pie and ice cream—"real food, too, none of that airy-fairy nonsense"—and the after-dinner movie, *March of the Penguins,* a favorite of the First Lady.

"I'm glad you're enjoying yourself," Grace said.

Frances declared, "It's wonderful that there can be a place like this. So informal. And I like it that the guards don't wear uniforms but just sort of blend in." She gave a small skip so she could catch up with the longer strides of the American women. "There's just so much I can take of all the starchy ceremony, to say nothing of the press breathing down your neck morning, noon, and night. It's nice to be able to let your hair down, with everyone acting natural."

Grace agreed aloud that the sequestered privacy of Camp David, without the customary oppressive and constant scrutiny, was certainly a plus. Personally, however, she felt the studiedly informal atmosphere could, on occasion, impose a treacherous dimension upon the regular public persona one learned to assume like a well-worn overcoat, much as corporate "dress-down Fridays" could expose employees' flaws and foibles through wardrobe gaffes. We must always watch what we say and do, she thought—and if Frances believes we can let our guards down completely, she's either delusional or just plain stupid.

Which she knew was far from the truth.

Frances Ewing, particularly in her present getup, might look like someone's cleaning lady. However, beneath the ill-fitting, borrowed clothing, the cockney bounce, and the artless chatter lay a cool, keen brain, and Grace reminded herself that not only did the Prime Minister's wife possess a master's degree in psychology, and had a successful ongoing career in the field of adolescent mental health, but her husband, no slouch himself in the brains department, made no secret of tapping into her views on national policy.

"I love this country," Frances was saying now. "I hope we'll be over in the States a lot more."

"You must visit us at the ranch!" Cynthia told her. "We'll fly you out!" She described the beauty of the Satcher property. "It's close to the Pacific, with wonderful views of the mountains, and, of course, there're the horses—my husband's major hobby, you know. He was raised on a horse—he could ride before he could walk."

"Count me out there," Frances said at once. "I've only ever sat on a horse once, a kiddie ride on the beach, and I bounced up and down like a sack of potatoes and ended up falling off. I'd be dead scared to get up on one again. Johnny rides, though—he loves it. But, of course, he was brought up on it, too."

"The ranch is Carl's favorite getaway," Cynthia said. "It's a great place to unwind, and he holds meetings there when it's important to be really private with no distractions. We have our own airstrip, and it's a lot less of a hassle getting there than to L.A." She added with a smile, "He thinks of it as *his* Camp David!"

"We'll look forward to that," Frances said.

Grace had never yet been to the ranch; Craig had been just once.

They'd routinely visit Satcher's Bel Air mansion whenever Craig was in California, but the ranch was where the movers and shakers of Carl's far-reaching empire gathered to plot their strategies. It was the place where the private jets landed at night, and where the real deals were made.

It occurred to Grace that Carl Satcher didn't include Craig in his inner circle just as, today, she suspected Cynthia of trying to usurp her own position. It was an uncomfortable thought, and she set it aside for later.

"How do you like your cabin?" she asked Frances. Each of the guest couples had their own cabin.

"It's ever so comfy," Frances said with another skip. "It's called Dogwood. We've been put there specially because it was where Winston Churchill stayed during World War Two when he was planning strategy with Franklin Roosevelt. They thought we'd like that."

"I'll bet the decor hasn't changed since," Cynthia said drily.

"But that's just what makes it marvelous!" Frances said. "Just think, we watched the fire burn down just like Winston Churchill might have done, with the same rugs, bedcovers, and curtains. I can see him drinking brandy and smoking a cigar, sitting in the same chair I sat in last night! With the same seat covers!"

"We're in Rosebud," Grace said. "We watched the fire, too."

They'd sat up very late because Craig needed to think.

He thought best while exercising, preferably while running, but since pounding the trails of Camp David in the middle of winter in the dark was hardly a feasible option, he'd settled for brooding before the smoldering fireplace, his back to her, his legs braced and head bent as if listening to music only he could hear.

Grace, tucked beneath a quilt and leafing through an old issue of *Town and Country,* had longed to go to sleep, and eventually begged, "I wish you'd come to bed. You're not even undressed."

He seemed not to have heard her.

"Craig! I said come to bed."

"You go to sleep. I'm not tired. And I still have some reading to do."

"You know I can't sleep if you're still up and the light's on and you're wandering around."

"Wear your sleep mask. I'll be quiet."

"It makes no difference."

No response.

"I'm worried about you."

"Don't be. I'm fine."

"You don't look fine. There's something on your mind and it's eating at you. Craig, please. We've been married twenty-five years. What is it?"

"Nothing, really."

"I don't believe you."

"Grace. *Please!*"

Another section of log collapsed into ash with a faint hiss, and Grace returned in frustration to her magazine. A little while later, her eyes closing despite herself, she heard the rattle of ice cubes and was instantly fully alert again. She raised herself on one elbow in time to see Craig reach for the scotch bottle.

"For heaven's sake," she said, "you don't need another drink now. You don't even *like* to drink."

"Sometimes I do."

"You're going to have to tell me what's wrong! Please, Craig. I'm on your side. Remember?"

He said very softly, "Then you're one of the few."

She had seldom seen him so depressed and preoccupied, and it worried her. It made no sense, not now, and she said so.

He didn't respond for a long time. Then: "Time passes," he said, brooding, as if to himself. "And people. They don't realize— don't even *want* to realize—how hard I've worked, and what it's cost me, just so they can sleep safely at night."

Oh, thought Grace, if that's all . . . She said soothingly, "I know, and it's not fair."

"This business of impeachment . . ."

"It'll never come to that, and you know it." She closed her eyes again and pulled the blanket up to her chin. "Come to bed."

"In a minute."

"No, Craig. It's late. Come to bed *now.*"

He'd sighed, risen, set the fire screen safely in position though there was nothing much left in the grate to burn, undressed, and joined her under the covers. He'd slept badly. Grace hadn't slept well, either, and each time she dozed off, she'd had formless, tumbling dreams, which, on waking, left a residue of vague menace.

Cynthia was saying now, "Ours is Holly. It's my favorite. Such a grand view across the mountains."

"Of course," Frances said. "You've been here before."

"Not for a long time now. Not since Carl was in the Senate."

"You must be glad to be back," Frances said.

"Oh yes," Cynthia agreed.

Although she spoke quietly, something resonated in her voice, the certainty that she was returning to her rightful place. Grace threw Cynthia a quick but uneasy glance, recalling that unguarded expression on the White House lawn as Cynthia recalled past glories. Now Grace had the definite feeling that Cynthia was featured in last night's dreams—though for the life of her, Grace couldn't remember how or why.

The three women trudged further along the trail, the only sound the soft crunch of their boots. At one point Frances said, "Funny, it feels like it's getting darker by the minute—like late afternoon, not the middle of the morning."

It did seem darker, Grace thought, and the sky lower with a strange, brassy tinge. It was oppressively still. A lone snowflake drifted past Frances's face. Grace watched her catch it on her tongue and give a wide grin like a schoolgirl.

"I think we should turn around," Grace said. "There'll be more where that one came from."

"Anyone hear a weather forecast?" Cynthia asked.

"I hope it does snow!" Frances said. "We don't have snow in England the way we did when I was a girl—it must be global warming." With a note of almost wistful anticipation, she added, "Imagine getting snowed in up here, at Camp David!"

"At least we wouldn't run out of food," Cynthia said. "We'd last till spring easily. We're not exactly the Donner Party." She related to Frances the story of the ill-fated California pioneers, trapped by an early snowfall on the wrong side of the Sierra Nevada and reduced to cannibalism.

And the moment she finished, as if, far above, some mighty hand had ripped apart a cosmic-sized feather mattress and shaken it, the whole world turned white around them.

CHAPTER TWENTY-SEVEN

The small room outside the doors to the surgical suite was studiedly neutral in its beige-and-ivory decor, its fake leather furniture, and the table-load of tattered copies of *Sports Illustrated, Auto Mechanics,* and *People.* It was a private waiting room, and a security guard stood outside to protect Ellen from the ravenous press. She felt she'd been sitting here for years, crumpled coffee cup clasped between her hands, gazing at the door with its two narrow glass panels, waiting for the re-appearance of Dr. Sledd.

"Derelle has a chance," he'd told Ellen before surgery in much the same tone of voice as a mechanic might assess repairs to her car—but that was what you needed in a surgeon, wasn't it, a talented technician who could set aside emotions, and whose hands wouldn't shake. "She has a punctured lung and damage to the spleen, which I might have to remove entirely. I won't know until I get in there. There's extensive tissue damage. She was lucky she was wearing a heavy leather coat since the blade didn't penetrate as deeply as it might have. It was very cold, which was lucky, too, as the blood loss could have been greater. However, she wasn't found for at least five minutes, since not many people were going in and out of the garage. That was not so lucky."

Ellen thought how five minutes was far too long when your life was steadily leaking away onto the concrete floor, and then, once she'd been found and 911 called, the paramedics were delayed by the snow.

"Did she have much pain?" Ellen hadn't wanted to know that but felt she had to ask.

"Intense pain." Dr. Sledd was quite blunt. "Though not for long."

Ben's plane had been diverted to Richmond, Virginia, and he was on his way to D.C. in a rental car. He explained this in a phone message for Ellen, saying he was going directly to a meeting. Ellen had no idea what meeting that was or with whom. She wanted to talk to him but they still hadn't connected.

David called in regularly, however, both to keep her posted on what was going on outside the hospital and to attempt to raise her spirits.

"Listen," he'd told her, "Derelle's tough. Bad things have happened to her before and she's come through."

But never this bad.

Ellen tried to guess the number of times she'd crossed the room and peered through the glass panels in the door, waiting for the surgeon to reappear. She wondered if time passed more quickly in the general waiting room, where there'd be people and activity.

Seated at Ellen's side, Celia tried her best to reassure her. "Dr. Sledd said it would be at least two hours till they'd know anything definite."

"It's been three," Ellen said.

"No news is good news," Celia said without much conviction. She picked up their empty paper cups from the table. "Would you like more coffee? Or shall I get you something from the vending machine?'

Ellen shook her head. "I couldn't eat anything. And I'll jump right out of my own skin if I have any more coffee."

"Hot chocolate, then. Comfort food? I'll be right back."

Alone again, Ellen paced restlessly across the room to the window. It overlooked an air shaft, the opposite wall a mere ten feet away, and she could see only a vertical line of lit windows, reduced to undefined, glowing rectangles against which the snow fell in sliding skeins of black.

She envisioned the ambulance, its flashing lights and siren both half stifled by the tumbling snow, crawling, crawling toward the Watergate garage while Derelle lay bleeding and unconscious beneath a stranger's overcoat.

At least they'd got the man who'd done it.

"He didn't even make it to the exit," David had said. "She did quite a number on him!"

"Good," Ellen had said fiercely.

"A damaged larynx, busted nose and jaw, and a badly abraded shinbone, possibly cracked."

"How do you know all that?"

"I've been talking with the cops."

"Do they know who he is?"

"He claims he's Joan of Arc, doing God's work. They could barely shut him up, even with all that damage to his voice box, or get him to listen to his Miranda rights. He's a *Slaughterhouse* fan, though—that came up pretty quickly, too. In a better system, we could slap that bastard Slaughter with one hell of a lawsuit for inciting violence."

"In this system," Ellen said, "Sam Slaughter might sue Derelle for giving his listeners cause—to say nothing of the fan suing her for assault."

"They're already saying on *Bridger* how she must have had terrorist training to react so fast."

"I suppose we'll get to read that tomorrow in the *D.C. Times*," Ellen said wearily.

"Probably. But trust me," David said, "we're not taking this lying down. We're taking the fight right to *The Slaughterhouse*, with our own release—'The Harvest of Hate'—going out even as we speak. And the phones are all ringing, the e-mails are flooding in, most of them shocked and supportive. People are sending flowers—they're filling up Derelle's office."

"How did that man get into the garage in the first place?" Ellen asked. "Building security must have been asleep at the switch."

"You can't entirely blame them," David replied. "He said he was an elevator serviceman, responding to an emergency call from management."

"They didn't check his credentials?"

"There was a lot of confusion in the lobby due to the weather and not enough people on the desk—late coming in, stuck in traffic, sick, you name it—trying to deal with any number of problems. A malfunctioning elevator would have been a nightmare. So when a guy in a uniform showed up saying he was sent by management, they let him in without question."

"It makes me sick that he was able to find out so easily where she lived. To say nothing of what level she kept her car on, and which was her slot."

"It's not hard to find these things out. Derelle wasn't exactly under deep cover."

"Nothing would have happened to her at all if she didn't work for me."

"It doesn't do any good beating up on yourself like that."

"I can't help it. If she doesn't make it. I'll never forgive myself."

"She'll make it. Like I said, Derelle's tough."

★ ★ ★

"Okay, here you go," Celia said, returning with a steaming cup of hot chocolate. "This'll help. I put a whole lot of extra sugar in. Careful. It's really hot."

At the same moment, the door from the O.R. at last swung open on the angular frame of Dr. Sledd, still in scrubs, mask pulled down below his chin. He looked very tired.

"Well, Senator," he said, "it's been a long haul and she's not out of the woods by a long shot, but I think there's a margin of hope."

"That's surgeon-speak for 'She's going to make it!'" Celia Chen said with a beaming smile.

And then, suddenly, Ben was there, large and comforting, the snow melting on the shoulders of his coat. He grabbed Ellen up in his arms and pressed his frigid wet cheek to hers. "I came as soon as I could get away," he said.

CHAPTER TWENTY-EIGHT

The attack on Senator Ellen Fischer's Chief of Staff by a crazed *Slaughterhouse* fan, and the fact that she might not make it, had hit all the noon broadcasts. For those on the Eastern seaboard, however, the story was secondary to weather news.

The snow fell all the rest of that day, imposing a soft paralysis from northern Maine to Norfolk, Virginia. Traffic was next to impossible, and what there was of it was slow and muted save for the clanging roar of the snowplows out on the highways.

Power and phone lines collapsed under the accumulated weight; parked cars were reduced to softly shaped white mounds.

The District of Columbia was more or less shut down. Non-essential social services were canceled across the board, and any but the most vital business was put on hold.

A bunker mentality set in: Stay home, stay warm, keep those candles and batteries handy, eat what you find on your kitchen shelves, and hold off on anything not of life-and-death importance—it can wait until this is over.

★ ★ ★

At Camp David, the kitchen staff served a lunch of hot vegetable soup and a choice of deli sandwiches or pepperoni pizza, followed by German chocolate cake, and fruit and cheese. The First Lady then retired, sneezing, to the floral needlepoint chair cover she was making to enliven her mother's room at the rest home, and the remainder of the party split into two main groups: as the President, the Ewings, and Grace Fulton headed outside to enjoy a brief but animated snowball fight on the terrace, returning flushed and rosy with exertion, clapping their gloved hands together and stamping packed snow from their boots, the Vice President and the Satchers retired to a corner of the great room near the fireplace where they conferred in low tones.

For the rest of the afternoon, the President and Prime Minister had a private discussion of state matters; the First Lady, Grace Fulton, and Frances Ewing worked on a giant and very difficult jigsaw puzzle of an English country village, featuring thatched cottages, hollyhocks, and a pub called the King's Head; Cynthia Satcher got a manicure and massage; and the Vice President and Carl Satcher met in Satcher's cabin, where they made various cell phone calls over an encrypted line.

To round out the afternoon's activities, the President organized a bowling match, which he, the First Lady, and the Satchers narrowly won over the Fultons and the Ewings—the First Lady's less-than-stellar performance being more than compensated for by Carl Satcher's intense determination to win at all costs.

★ ★ ★

In the cabin called Holly, carefully making up her face before dressing for dinner, Cynthia Satcher asked, "Did Freddie Sobel get back to you?"

"Sure he did," her husband said. "He's getting the sleazy bastard off the air as of tomorrow—quote, pending an inquiry, unquote."

"That crazy fan of his didn't do us any favors," Cynthia said as she fluffed blush onto her cheekbones.

"It couldn't have come at a worse time," Satcher agreed, "though this weather will take people's minds off it for a day or so longer. Which, of course, will be time enough."

"Sam Slaughter's useful, but I'd say he's played his part, wouldn't you?"

"Overplayed it," Satcher said. "Maybe right into Ellen Fischer's hands."

"But that'll soon be irrelevant—just water under the bridge," Cynthia said.

Satcher looked at his watch. "I'd say in about four hours from now," he said.

Cocktails beside the fireplace were followed by an early supper of lamb chops or poached Atlantic salmon and, afterward, a screening of the President's current favorite movie, *Castaway*, with Tom Hanks surviving four years on a tropical island alone with a volleyball. Toward the end of the movie, while the deranged and suffering Hanks tosses on a raft in the ocean, still unrescued, the Vice President's cell phone rang and he excused himself to take the call.

The President, who earlier had humorously though definitively requested all cell phones to be switched off, gave a snort of exasperation, but Craig Fulton was already on his way out the door.

Five minutes later, Craig returned in a state of controlled agitation, leaned over the President's shoulder, and whispered urgently, the top of his pale head and the slope of his back bathed by the projector in ripples of oceanic blue.

The President looked up with an expression of shock, glanced about the room, and quickly nodded at Craig, who stepped back, raised both hands, and called on the projectionist to stop the film and turn the lights back on. He announced to the gathering that they faced an emergency situation, and told them to follow him back to the great room.

Once they were all assembled there, Craig stood solemnly before the fireplace.

"I much regret to inform you," he said in a voice that was calm but tinged with urgency, "that moments ago I received a call from the Office of Strategic Operations—who have been monitoring all known terrorist cells in this area—to report suspected violent and imminent activity against Camp David."

The President placed his arm protectively around the shoulders of the First Lady and the Ewings moved closer together. Craig's blue eyes sought Grace's; in them she read both deep regret and controlled fury.

"The nature of this attack is unclear," he went on, "but some form of missile appears the most likely. I at once informed the Director of the FBI and we are taking preemptive action. Nevertheless, the danger is very real and Camp David must be evacuated at once. Please return to your cabins and prepare for immediate departure. Dress warmly and bring only essentials. Leave your luggage; it will be packed and delivered to you." Turning to Johnathon Ewing, he added gravely, "I much regret this, Prime Minister."

★ ★ ★

How quickly and fluidly Craig took charge, Grace thought.

He was a tower of strength, forgetting no detail as he organized the evacuation.

Within moments, it seemed, the snowplows were mobilized, Marines were everywhere in full weapons gear, three armored SUVs were in front of the main entrance, and emergency boxes of food were being put together. Never had her husband appeared so commanding, or more presidential. Never before had she appreciated him so much. With one stroke he had justified her belief in him, and any doubts she may have harbored during the past difficult years dissipated like smoke.

"You were wonderful in there," she told him back in their cabin as she hurriedly changed into wool pants and her thickest sweater. "You knew exactly what should be done, and you did it. And you were so calm."

"Some people would say I was just doing my job," the Vice President replied, thrusting his laptop, documents, and other essentials into his briefcase, his cell phone and BlackBerry into the inner pockets of his Goretex ski jacket.

"Now I understand why you couldn't sleep last night," Grace said, gazing at him with new appreciation. "You must have sensed something like this would happen!"

"I've learned to fear the worst," her husband said. "And right now we're the answer to a terrorist's prayer. We're all in one spot, we're sitting ducks—the President of the United States and the Prime Minister of England, leaders of the free world, to say nothing of you and me, and the Satchers, and everybody else who happens to be here who'd be collateral damage. *That's* why I always take every precaution. *That's* the reason we keep tabs on certain people, no matter how unpopular that might be. Unfortunately, these days, unpopularity is the price of vigilance." With a thin smile, he added, "I've been paying that price for quite a while now."

"And you were right all along," Grace said, sinking back on the bed.

"I'm afraid so. The worst could really have happened. Without those wiretaps and surveillance I insisted on, we could all have gone to sleep without a care in the world—and never woken up."

"We'd have burned. Oh God, Craig. Brianna—"

"Yes, think of Brianna."

"I was horrible last night," Grace admitted almost tearfully. "I know what you have to cope with, day after day. So much responsibility. I feel ashamed. I'm sorry."

"Don't think about it again," he said. "But for God's sake, Grace dear, don't just sit there. Get your coat on, and warm boots. The snowplow will be going out in five minutes, and we'll start pulling out right after it. The Marines and Secret Service first in the Hummer, our group in two cars, and more Marines following us."

Grace rose and gathered up boots, coat, and gloves. "We won't have people sitting in the car with us with loaded guns?" she asked. "I hate that."

"No."

"Who do you think should ride in which car?"

"The Secret Service will decide."

"Do you seriously think someone could somehow be watching us? That they'd actually *know* where we sat?"

"Of course not," he said firmly.

But she wasn't sure he meant it. "I don't know what's safe anymore," Grace sighed, "or who to trust."

"You can trust me," her husband said stoutly. "Everything's under control and we're going to be safe."

"That makes me feel a lot better," she said.

He pulled her close and kissed her forehead. "I'm glad," he said.

★ ★ ★

Cynthia Satcher was folding the last of her clothes into her bag.

"Leave all that," Carl Satcher told his wife. "They'll pack for you."

"I'm not having some ham-fisted Marine touching my clothes!" Cynthia declared as she zipped up her suitcase.

"Cyn, the point is you don't want to look as if you were prepared," Satcher explained with patience. "This exit is supposed to look spontaneous, not fully packed and ready. Take some stuff out again—the sweater and bathrobe, that blouse you just took off. Toss them around."

"Oh, come on, Carl. Nobody's going to notice or remember."

"Just do it!" he ordered.

"*Okay!*" Cynthia opened her suitcase again and tipped her clothes back onto the bed. "There! Satisfied?"

"That'll do."

"I only hope my bags make it down in time for tomorrow night."

"What the hell does it matter?" Satcher demanded. "If they don't, you can buy something new. There're plenty of boutiques in the lobby."

★ ★ ★

They assembled outside the main cabin, eight bundled figures almost indistinguishable one from the other, the snow squeaking under their boots and already coating their heads and shoulders while an icy wind whipped their faces.

We look like a party of bears, Grace thought. Then, seeing the men surrounding her, tall men in camouflage with weapons ready, she changed the image: bears *and hunters.*

A shivering young Marine appeared from the kitchen with the hastily assembled sandwiches and thermoses of hot drinks.

The vehicles drew up, quietly and without lights. The security detail divided the party into two groups, the President and the First Lady with the Satchers in the first car, the Fultons and Ewings in the second.

Their drivers were large, taciturn young men, appearing even larger, Grace surmised, because of the bulletproof vests they would be wearing beneath their jackets.

Their SUV was bulletproof, too—but, of course, there'd be no chance it could withstand a missile.

The snowplow, yellow beacon rotating atop its roof, clanged and roared away down the hill, flinging a powdery bow wave to either side and spreading a layer of salt and ash on the roadbed. Moments later the Hummer pulled out behind it.

Who was in the Hummer? They couldn't see through the tinted windows, but Grace envisioned a group of hard-faced Marines armed to the teeth.

The President's car was next in line, then Craig Fulton's, with a third SUV filled with armed men bringing up the rear.

They drove with slow deliberation down the long driveway and through the gates.

The windshield wipers struggled and squeaked against the hard-driving onslaught of snow, and they could see little but the occasional flash of brake lights from the vehicle in front.

They could have been at the bottom of the sea or far out in space.

Nobody spoke, though Frances Ewing was humming an old folk tune Grace recognized from childhood—*She'll be coming round the mountain when she comes*—while she placidly explored the contents of her snack bag, finding a sourdough roll stuffed with cheese and a slice of ham, a small container of orange juice with a straw, and a banana.

Half a mile further, obeying some previous and unspoken directive, their convoy pulled into a turnout and the President's and Vice President's cars changed places so that the Fultons and the Ewings were now next in line behind the Hummer.

Grace's mouth was dry. She opened her own bag, needing the juice, so welcome and deliciously sweet, but how could Frances actually *eat* anything? Grace found her entire body waiting in taut anticipation for the explosion, the shock wave and rolling fire, the rush of meltwater, mud, and rocks that would hurl them off the road, over the barrier, and into the dark abyss hundreds of feet below.

The minutes ticked by, and she prayed they'd gotten out in time.

She thought about those nice young Marines passing out the food packages and thermoses, the cooks and waitstaff and projectionist, and prayed they'd get away in time, too. If they didn't, she'd never forgive herself.

She thought of Brianna, safely asleep in her chaotically untidy bedroom at the residence, wondered whether she would ever again hold her child in her arms and how, if she did, it would be all due to Craig's foresight.

Impulsively, she sought his hand in the dark.

His fingers clasped hers, warm and reassuring.

"Don't be afraid," he whispered. "There's really no need."

CHAPTER TWENTY-NINE

Late Saturday night, Ellen still sat beside Derelle's bed in the ICU, where she lay flat and motionless beneath the smooth bed linen, arms at her sides, palms facing upward, fingers lightly curled. Ellen stroked Derelle's flaccid fingers, then reached for the paper cup of ice and touched some to her dry, crusted lips, but whether Derelle felt any relief, Ellen had no idea.

Where was her mind? Where did one go in a state like this? Was there any awareness? Any sense of touch, of sound, of light?

Did Derelle have any idea Ellen was here?

So many questions; no answers.

The nurse had asked, "Has the family been notified?"

"There is no family."

"A close friend? A boyfriend?"

"I don't know. I don't think so."

"Poor dear." The nurse surveyed Derelle, so still, so barely alive, one side of her face abraded and swollen from the fall to the garage floor, gauze shrouding her from the chest to the hips, tubes running into her wrist, her nose and mouth, the drip releasing a cocktail of antibiotics, narcotics, and nutrients into her veins, and the monitoring equipment ticking along behind the bed.

"She's certainly lucky to have you, Senator," the nurse said, then having rechecked Derelle's vital signs and passage of fluids, moved away to the next curtained bed.

Ellen listened to the diminishing squeak of orthopedic shoes and took Derelle's hand again. That nurse is wrong, she thought, Derelle's not so lucky having me, and she whispered aloud, "I'm so sorry. This is all my fault and I'm not leaving you."

"It was touch-and-go for a while," Dr. Sledd had told Ellen, "but she's a strong young woman, and if there're no complications or infections, she'll be okay."

But Derelle certainly didn't look okay.

There was a dab of blood at the corner of her mouth and Ellen wiped it gently away with moistened gauze. "Hang on," she said aloud. "Please, please hang on. I need you. I can't lose you. Can you hear me?"

Derelle's breath wheezed on through her endotracheal tube, her chest rising and falling gently with the induced air, and she made no sign.

Before he left the hospital earlier, Ben had told Ellen that he and the judge had found the source of the leak of information about the trust, that they had confronted the person responsible, and Ben had flown with him from Arizona.

"He's still a little squirrelly," Ben said, "but I think we convinced him to cooperate with law enforcement. It's out of my hands now, but I don't think there will be any more leaks—or photos, either, since he was involved in that, too."

Ellen wanted to know more, but Ben said they could talk at home later.

"It's too public here, and you're exhausted," Ben said.

"I don't want to leave her."

"Isn't there anybody else to sit with her?"

"I don't want her to be alone or with some stranger when she wakes up."

He hadn't liked that, but hadn't fought Ellen over it. "When she does," Ben said, "give her a message from me. Tell her I'm flying that Indian woman over here for her. Her friend Salima."

It was a wonderful, generous idea, and Ellen wished she had thought of it herself. "You're really doing that?"

"She's already on her way to London, so consider it done!"

The moment he left, Ellen had called David at his home to tell him the news.

He'd been skeptical. "Salima Aboud's coming to the U.S.? How's that going to happen?"

"Ben's making it happen," Ellen told him. "If anyone can do it, he can. That terrorist rumor was exactly that—rumor. Salima has never been on any undesirable watch list, and I don't foresee a problem."

"She'd be quite an asset," David agreed, "if she's presentable."

"She's presentable," Ellen said. "I've met her. She's beautiful and bright, and she must be an experienced speaker if she's on all those committees. "

"There's the human-interest angle, too," David said, gaining enthusiasm. "How this woman flew halfway across the world to be at her friend's hospital bedside after a brutal stabbing. It would be heartwarming. Exactly the kind of story to counter any lingering negative gossip. Ben's right. You're right!" After several more minutes, he hung up sounding energized and positive for the first time in days, already planning to be in touch with Diane Sawyer, Larry King, and Barbara Walters first thing in the morning to arrange interviews.

Ellen sat down again at Derelle's bedside, where she remained far into the night.

Sometimes she held Derelle's hand, sometimes she stroked her fingers, mostly she just sat and watched the almost imperceptible rise and fall of Derelle's chest and listened to her breath go in and out. Occasionally the rhythm was broken by a sigh or a small snort, and Ellen would think Derelle was regaining consciousness, but she never did.

The drugs continued to inch down the tubes into her arm and the vital signs continued to crawl unchanging across the screens.

Ellen had once read of the healing power of white light when transmitted by concentrated thought. With this in mind, she imagined a pillar of warm radiance descending from the ceiling and pouring into Derelle's chest. She concentrated so hard that she lost track both of the passage of time and of her surroundings, and may even have fallen asleep. When a heavy hand fell upon her shoulder and, abruptly opening her eyes, she saw a massive, huge-headed shadow cast on the opposite wall, her heart leapt in panic.

It was Ben in his bulky overcoat.

"You listen to me now," he was saying with severity. "Enough's enough, and you're not staying here one minute longer. You won't help Derelle by making yourself sick. And what about me? I'd like a chance to spend some time with my wife. Even if you're asleep," he added, "at least you'd be under the same roof!"

Ellen was about to argue, but found that between the thought and the words there lay a murky ravine where nothing quite connected. Ben was right; she was doing no good here. She'd go home and return stronger in the morning.

She rose, his arm tightly around her, finding she'd sat so still for so long in the same position that her muscles were locked in place.

As she headed for the door on Ben's powerful arm, Ellen told Derelle, in case she could hear, "I'll be back first thing tomorrow." She was half sure she heard a rusty whisper in reply—"Okay. See ya!"—but when she swung around in shocked delight, Derelle was lying quiet and still as before.

For the first time, however, Ellen allowed herself the real hope that the healing process had begun, and conscious thought was struggling to break through. That Derelle *had* heard her and answered from inside her head, and that she, Ellen, had picked up on it.

"Come on," Ben said. "We're going home."

CHAPTER THIRTY

January 6

SUNDAY

At the residence, while the Vice President and Carl Satcher sat down with Fulton's press officer to hammer out the statement for the nine P.M. national broadcast from the Old Executive Office Building, Grace Fulton and Cynthia Satcher shared a light lunch of chicken bouillon followed by avocado-and-watercress salad.

"We pulled that off rather well, didn't we," Cynthia said.

Grace wasn't sure what Cynthia meant by that, but after years in politics, she knew that to appear in any way out of the loop was always a bad idea. She took a sip of mineral water and agreed, "Didn't we!"

Cynthia glanced around the room as if to make sure they weren't being overheard. Satisfied that the Navy steward had closed the door properly after leaving the dining room with their soup bowls, she said, "Between you and me, I'm rather proud of myself. I know it was Craig's idea originally, but the planning was all mine!"

"Really?" Grace said.

"Of course, I don't think Craig took us seriously at first. He never believed we could actually make it work. Well, he knows better now. We're a good team!" Cynthia regarded Grace across a forkful of lettuce. "Has anyone told you you're a terrific actor? You looked so scared last night."

"Thank you."

"You had me fooled. For a while I actually thought Craig hadn't told you."

"He didn't tell me everything," Grace said ambiguously, wanting to keep the conversation going.

"It all worked like clockwork, and it proves you really can fool all of the people some of the time!" Cynthia laid her fork down and took a sip of Chardonnay. "By tonight your husband will be a hero again!"

Don't be afraid, Craig had whispered last night in the car. *There's really no need.*

An alarming, surely impossible suspicion crept into Grace's mind. However, drawing on years of practice, and excercising rigid control, she was at once able to marshal her face into a neutral expression. She could do it, she was a good actress.

"A hero," Grace repeated. "And they say the people behind the plot have been caught. *What* people?"

"Who cares?" Cynthia shrugged. "I guess they'll have rounded up the usual suspects."

The suspicion deepened. Carefully, Grace said, "But they'll be accused of something they didn't do."

With a narrow-eyed glance, Cynthia said, "You're not worried about *them,* are you? They were on the FBI wanted lists. They're bad guys, Grace. We want them gone. And if they didn't do this, they did something else, or would do it."

"What'll happen to them?"

Again she shrugged. "I guess they'll be jailed, deported, or taken care of one way or the other—and good riddance. Don't worry—it'll all be quite tidy."

Grace felt a sickening tilt inside her head as everything she'd previously believed rearranged itself into new and horrifying patterns.

Last night's "terrorist attack" had been a hoax. And Cynthia had assumed that she, Grace, had known all about it.

A lie in which Cynthia had been a willing participant, as had Carl Satcher—and Grace's own husband, whom she loved and admired, had orchestrated it.

She wasn't sure how she got through the rest of the lunch, but she managed. She'd had too many years of presenting a calm face to the world, sometimes at great cost; of course she managed.

At last Cynthia returned to the Willard Hotel and Grace climbed the stairs on leaden feet to her bedroom, where she sat on the bed, stared at her still-packed suitcase, which the Marines had delivered as promised, and thought about Craig being declared once again a hero, as he would be after tonight's press conference.

Grace wanted to weep, but she felt too frozen inside. At that moment, Brianna burst in, still wearing the camera-appropriate skirt-and-sweater set in which she'd greeted her parents on their triumphant return from Camp David.

"Have Mr. and Mrs. Satcher gone?" she demanded.

Grace nodded.

Brianna looked at her searchingly. "Mom? Are you *okay?*"

"Of course I'm okay." Grace fixed her eyes on Brianna's pretty pink sweater, finding herself wishing that, instead, her daughter had changed back into her customary black crocheted cardigan, which she fastened across her chest with an old-fashioned diaper pin.

"You look upset. All shook up," Brianna said.

"I'm just tired," Grace said, and summoned a smile.

"Though I don't see how you could be anything else but shook up. My God," Brianna said bluntly, "I nearly barfed when they told me what happened."

"Oh my dear—but nothing did happen."

"But it *might've.*" Abruptly, Brianna's face crumpled. "I love you, Mom! You and Dad! I couldn't bear it if anything had—if you'd—I mean—" She hurled herself into her mother's arms, as if she were eight years old and not a woman of almost twenty. "It must have been so *horrible!* Were you terrified out of your *mind?*"

"We were all scared."

"Even Dad?"

"He didn't show it," Grace said, and thought, He didn't even need to act.

"What about Mr. and Mrs. Ewing?"

"They were brave. Mrs. Ewing sang songs all the way down to cheer us up."

"What songs?"

"'She'll Be Coming Round the Mountain.' 'Oh My Darling, Clementine.' She ate all her snack and most of mine."

"I don't know what I'd do if anything happened to you and Dad," Brianna said.

Which was when Grace lost it. She buried her face against her daughter's bony young shoulder and howled.

Brianna held her tight and stroked her hair. In a gentle, strangely mature voice, she said, "It's all right, Mom. Have a good cry. It'll make you feel a lot better."

CHAPTER THIRTY-ONE

By early afternoon, Derelle was fully conscious and in a private room on Surgical 5A. Ellen sat on her bed holding her hand while Ben admired the cards arrayed on the windowsill, as well as the display of flowers, which included Ellen's basket of gold-and-olive-colored cymbidiums, and a vase of yellow roses, bound with a gigantic and symbolic yellow ribbon, from the staffers in her office: *We miss you. Come back soon!*

The cocktail of nutrients, narcotics, and antibiotics still dripped into Derelle's veins, but she had stabilized. Dr. Sledd said that her recovery had been remarkably quick, though it would be a couple of days before the tubes would come out and she could talk.

Derelle was certainly awake and aware, though her eyes still wore an expression of medicated haziness. She had a notepad and pencil on the bed beside her on which she'd written, for Ellen, *Heard you last night. Did you hear me?*

"Clear as anything!" Ellen said.

Ben said, "They tell me you're doing just fine, that you're way too tough to kill!"

Derelle's lips twitched in what was almost a smile.

"You'll be back at work in no time at all." He reached down to the briefcase at his feet and removed a small package wrapped in dark blue tissue. "In the meantime, I have something for you. I'll open it, okay?"

Derelle's eyes shifted to his hands as they unwrapped the gift box and lifted the lid. Inside, on a bed of cotton, lay a pendant of silver and heavy-cut rough turquoise on a silver chain. He held it up so she could see.

"Turquoise is the sacred stone of the Navajo," Ben told her. "A turquoise bead worn in the hair protects against lightning strikes. Warriors wear it to ensure victory and a safe return from battle. You're a brave warrior, Derelle. Wear turquoise in good health."

Her swollen, chapped lips stretched in a real smile. She reached for her pad and wrote, *Thanks Mr Lind.*

Ellen watched a tear leak from the corner of each eye and trickle down her cheek. Ben wiped her face gently with a tissue.

He said, "Tomorrow something even better will be coming, but it's a long way from Bombay to Washington, D.C."

Derelle's eyes opened wide. Hurriedly, jaggedly, she wrote, *Salima?* just as Ellen's cell phone rang in her purse. Ellen almost didn't answer—it seemed such an intrusion at this time—but she ducked outside the door to take the call. A moment later, she returned to watch Derelle's pencil scratch out another thank you with lots of exclamation points.

"If it's not a great deal to ask," Ben said to Derelle, "could you manage to change that to 'Thank you, Ben'?"

Her smile was radiant as she wrote: *Ben!!!!*

He smiled back. "Go to sleep now," he said, but Derelle's eyes were already closed.

Ellen whispered urgently, "I have to meet with Douglas Brewer. He just called and said it's urgent."

"Good," Ben said. "With any luck, all the pieces are coming together."

CHAPTER THIRTY-TWO

Ellen swiveled herself back and forth in her chair, gazing at the coffee table on which she'd arranged a pair of black stoneware mugs, a coffeepot, and a small platter of oatmeal cookies. From time to time she'd look across the room to the sturdy, closed door.

She was waiting for FBI Director Brewer in her hideaway in the Capitol, her own private space in which she could conduct meetings or hold a small conference without needing to return to her office in the Hart Senate Building.

Ellen had always respected and trusted Brewer. Though they'd had their differences—she recalled the times during the past few years when he stood before the Judiciary Committee so staunchly defending Craig Fulton's position and policies on surveillance— she knew Brewer to be honest and direct.

What did he want with her? What was so urgent it could not wait?

Punctual to the second, he rapped softly on the door at two P.M. and she rose to let him in.

"Good afternoon, Director."

"Senator."

Brewer sat on the green leather sofa, placing his fat black briefcase on his knees.

Ellen positioned herself adjacent to him on a matching armchair and poured coffee for them both.

She hadn't seen Douglas Brewer at close quarters for many weeks and was shocked by his appearance. Always lean, he had clearly lost weight, and his face was haggard, the skin almost translucent with fatigue, so she could see the dark beard pressing up beneath.

"First," Brewer said, "I want to tell you in person how concerned and sorry I am about the attack on Ms. Simba. I'm glad they're expecting a full recovery."

"Thank you," Ellen replied. "It's a huge relief."

"And I apologize for imposing on you at such a time. I wouldn't do so if there was any choice." The Director picked up his mug and nursed it as if his hands were chilled. "But certain matters have come to light in the past forty-eight hours and it's imperative you know about them before Carl Satcher's hearings tomorrow morning."

He paused as if gathering his thoughts.

"I've talked several times with an individual named Alan Sharpe. I don't believe you've heard this name before?"

"No, I haven't," Ellen said.

"I first met with him and Congressman Lind yesterday while you were with Ms. Simba in the hospital. Because our discussion involved an ongoing criminal investigation as well as matters pertaining to the operations of OSO, I specifically directed Congressman Lind not to reveal the details to anyone, including you, Senator."

"He told me nothing," Ellen said.

"Sharpe is the man, identified by an investigator hired by Judge Ray, who leaked the details of your husband's blind trust. He was acting under the direction of Carl Satcher, with whom he's been associated for quite some time."

"It always seemed clear to us who was behind the leak," Ellen said.

"Mr. Sharpe's actions, and the publicity they generated, were designed to discredit you. The affair must have been extremely personally distressing."

"That's an understatement."

"He was also responsible for the dissemination of the photograph of Ms. Simba and her friend to the media—also at Mr. Satcher's instigation."

"No surprise there, either. We've always known they'll stop at nothing."

Brewer took a sip of coffee and set his mug carefully down on the cork coaster. "On Friday, in Judge Ray's office in Phoenix, your husband and Judge Ray met and confronted Alan Sharpe with evidence of his illegal activities. They pointed out, in no uncertain terms, that Sharpe faced considerable legal and professional difficulties as a result of his actions. They suggested a solution, however, appealing to his sincere patriotism—"

Ellen drew breath in vehement objection.

"They *did* believe him to be sincere, and now, having met him, I believe I do, too. They also appealed to his sense of self-preservation, and that it was in his best interests to travel to D.C. to meet with me."

Ellen nodded. It seemed to her that Brewer was struggling to get the story out.

"During their meeting in Phoenix, Sharpe revealed that he had on occasion worked as an independent contractor for OSO, which I have verified. He has a good reputation and is quite competent. He also revealed his knowledge of plans regarding a terrorist attack." Brewer paused. "Senator, have you been briefed on the reported plan to attack Camp David last night?"

"First thing this morning, by Homeland Security," Ellen said. "Thank goodness it was discovered. It could have been a disaster. Is that the plot Sharpe was referring to?"

"When Sharpe mentioned 'terrorist attack,' Congressman Lind immediately called me and I talked to Sharpe directly. He was adamant that no details or names be discussed over the telephone. He would only say that in a face-to-face meeting in my office he could provide more information about 'a false report of an imminent attack involving high elected officials.'"

"False?" Ellen interrupted. "You're saying that attempt on Camp David was false? There wasn't a plot after all?"

"There was certainly a plot," Brewer said, "but not the kind we were led to believe."

"Why would anyone——" Ellen began, her mind racing.

What she was thinking seemed too horrible, too sad to be true.

"It seems to have been a final desperate attempt to restore the Vice President's standing and popularity," Brewer said. "He would be perceived as a hero, and the obvious success of the surveillance policies he favors would, despite whatever else came out at the hearing, likely ensure Carl Satcher's confirmation."

"I don't want to believe this," Ellen said, shaking her head.

Brewer waited as the information sank in. He took one more sip of coffee, then pushed the mug away. "I'm sorry, but these days coffee isn't sitting so well in my stomach."

"There's herbal tea if you'd prefer," Ellen said.

"Just water, if you have it."

It was a relief to perform such a simple, unambiguous action. Ellen rose, opened the refrigerator, and poured a glass of mineral water, which Brewer drank as if parched.

"What little Sharpe revealed to me on the phone dovetailed with very real concerns that I'd been having about the Vice President."

Brewer gazed at Ellen, his expression bleak. She leaned forward and waited.

"I've worked with Craig Fulton for many years," the Director said. "He's a man I've always respected. Lately, however, I've sensed a change. He's grown secretive and evasive. Last week he made an unusual—and borderline improper—request for specific information on potential terrorists. Although Fulton is head of OSO and the de facto Secretary of Homeland Security, that type of information would ordinarily be developed and analyzed by other agencies before it reached him. I felt he was being less than frank, and had the strong impression that he was sidestepping regular channels. However, with only suspicions and no concrete information or basis on which to act, my hands were tied."

"You were in a delicate situation," Ellen said. "But then you had that conversation with Sharpe."

"Immediately following that call on Friday, I had listening devices put in place in selected common areas and private cabins at Camp David, where the Vice President and Satcher were going to be staying. The President and Prime Minister were there, too, but I did not monitor their quarters."

"You bugged Camp David?!" Ellen exclaimed.

"It was unprecedented, but I felt I had to act, and there was no time to get more evidence. As it was, there was only the narrowest window of opportunity."

"What did you find out? Were your suspicions confirmed?"

"Not until a few hours ago, when all the pieces came together. After our phone conversation, Sharpe and Congressman Lind returned to D.C., as I said, and we met yesterday afternoon in my office. Sharpe would not provide any further details or information without a grant of immunity from prosecution. I needed a more specific demonstration of the value of the information he would provide before I could convince the Deputy A.G.—on a Saturday—to offer immunity. Sharpe kept saying time was critical, but at the end of the day, we were at an impasse. We agreed to meet again early this morning."

"Did you have him in protective custody or witness protection?" Ellen asked.

"He made it clear that he didn't trust the government to keep his whereabouts secret, and he would not cooperate at all unless he was able to guarantee his own safety and stay in a place of his own choosing. He called in every three hours."

"You were able to get him immunity, though?"

"There was some grumbling, but yes, this morning. And then Sharpe told us the full story."

Brewer raised his water glass, but put it down before taking a sip.

"This hasn't been easy for me," Brewer said. "I've thought long and hard about how to proceed. I've spoken to the President personally, and he agreed I should talk with you." The Director paused. "Sharpe was at the center of the false-terrorist-attack operation. He was the person who called the Vice President at Camp David last night to announce the terrorist activity and threat."

"Just another dirty trick, like the blind trust leak and photograph of Derelle, but this time it involved national security and the Vice President," Ellen said.

"Sharpe never dealt directly with the Vice President until the phone call," Brewer said. "The call was the verifiable trigger for the Vice President's actions—instructing me to arrest suspected terrorists, deciding to evacuate Camp David, and scheduling a press conference for this evening—on the eve of the hearing. But the whole operation had been worked out between Satcher and Sharpe."

"And Sharpe will testify to this at the hearing tomorrow?"

"He will, now that he has immunity. His other condition was that he get to tell his side of the story, his reasons, at the hearing."

"Why do you think he made the call last night if he was thinking of testifying?" Elln asked.

"He probably felt that he needed to stay with the program and not burn his old bridge to Satcher until he had his new friends firmly in place."

"Did the bugs at Camp David confirm Sharpe's story?"

"There were several relevant conversations between Carl Satcher and Cynthia Satcher, and one particular conversation between Carl Satcher and the Vice President. It's that conversation that most directly ties the Vice President to the plot. I have the transcripts of the conversations here."

Brewer removed a manilla envelope from his briefcase and handed it to Ellen.

"I'd like to call you as the first witness at the hearing," Ellen said.

"Yes, of course."

"Your testimony should be more than enough, along with Sharpe's and the tapes. Although," she said, raising her eyes in sudden doubt, "can we expose all this at a public hearing?"

"Public disclosure of any surveillance—in this case, electronic eavesdropping pertaining to terrorist activity—is definitely prohibited by amendments to the Patriot Act."

"But you're not worried?"

"In his signing statement, the President specified that this prohibition doesn't pertain to an event or activity already made public by himself, the Vice President, or the Secretary of Homeland Security."

"In other words," Ellen said carefully, "after Fulton's press conference tonight, the door will be open."

Brewer nodded. "However," he said, "we need Sharpe to testify, because it would be impermissible hearsay if I tried to tell the committee—or a court—much of what he told me."

"Then we'd better be sure Sharpe shows up," Ellen said.

"He'll be there."

"What happened to the suspects, the people who were supposed to be terrorists?"

"They're in custody. They're being well treated. Their residences are in the process of being searched, but so far there's no evidence of any plot against the President of the United States, the Prime Minister of Great Britain, or of any plan to attack Camp David. No missiles. Nothing of any particular significance beyond religious fliers, tracts, and propaganda, which are currently being translated, and some small-caliber handguns."

"I still find it hard—if not impossible—to believe Fulton would agree to this," Ellen said. "Satcher, yes—I'd believe anything of that man. But not Fulton."

"I didn't want to believe it, either," Brewer said, his face set in harsh planes. "You know, this has been one of the most depressing weeks of my life."

"I certainly understand," Ellen said. "I thank you beyond words for coming forward."

"Senator, it was my job to tell you. You have oversight responsibility—you need to know."

She held out her hand and he shook it.

"Until tomorrow," he said.

CHAPTER THIRTY-THREE

Dressing for dinner at the White House, to be followed by the press conference she dreaded, Grace Fulton decided she had never before felt so tired, depleted, or unhappy. She was seated at her vanity, clipping on her diamond stud earrings, when Craig emerged from the bathroom, his sandy hair flattened and damp from the shower.

He paused behind her, lifted her hair, and kissed the nape of her neck. He smelled good, of clean, warm skin and aftershave. But at that moment she despised him.

"It'll be good to sleep in our own bed tonight," he said.

"We need to talk," Grace said.

"Of course, we'll talk," he said.

"Seriously."

"Can't it wait till morning?" he said, his eyes suddenly guarded.

"I'd prefer not."

"What, then?"

Grace couldn't quite bring herself to look at him. "Cynthia and I were talking at lunch. She finally brought me into the loop."

Craig said nothing. In the mirror, she watched him watching her.

Grace said, "I was afraid last night. I suppose I should at least thank you for telling me there wasn't any need to worry—I was grateful to you, at the time. Now, though, I hear there was no danger at all."

"I thought it best you didn't know."

"Because you didn't trust me?"

"Of course not. I'd trust you with my life."

"Cynthia knew."

"You musn't be jealous—that's a different situation altogether. Cynthia plays an active role in Carl's business."

Grace managed to keep her voice steady. "So, being a mere appendage, I was allowed my moment of terror?"

"But you didn't show it. I was proud of you. You're a courageous person, Grace."

She felt him playing with a lock of her hair, coiling it around and around his index finger, and pulled away from him. "Don't," she said.

"Of course, we should have taken you into our confidence. It wasn't right to exclude you."

"There's a lot that wasn't right," Grace said. After a pause, she added, "Such as arresting those men as terrorists when they've done nothing wrong."

"Be realistic, Grace. Maybe not this time, but you can bet they've done something else wrong. They're not innocent people. They were problems waiting to happen, all of them."

"And what about misleading—lying to—the American people?"

"Listen, *please*. It's for the benefit of the people. When I go on TV tonight, the whole country will recognize us again as winners. We'll have the country at our backs, in full support, instead of sniping at us, nipping at our heels, and destroying everything we've accomplished. When I'm President, with Carl heading Homeland Security, we have a *real* chance to put the country back on top, to be more powerful, richer, and, finally, secure! The last few years, the country's gone to hell in a handbasket. The people need us!"

"Do you seriously believe that?"

"Of course I believe it."

"Was this plan yours or Carl Satcher's?"

"I raised the idea hypothetically. Carl picked up on it and put it into operation."

"How could you have *done* this? It was a *terrible* mistake!"

"If you need more justification, look close to home, right here and now—and see how Brianna has changed. She's back to her old self. Didn't you see her face earlier, when we finally made it back safely? Daddy's top gun with her again!"

"That's important, of course, being top gun with Brianna." Grace rested her elbows on her vanity table, leaned into her hands, and rubbed her knuckles in her eyes as if to erase the image of Craig's triumphant face.

"She was afraid for us," he said. "She'd been crying. You'll see, she'll be a different girl from now on."

"She was crying for all the wrong reasons—because she believed in a *lie*!" Grace felt her husband's hand on her shoulder and said again, wearily, "Please don't touch me."

His hand fell away and he stood behind her, silent. "You're not going to tell her, are you?" he asked anxiously.

"I won't have to. The truth has a way of coming out, whether you like it or not."

"I never expected you to react like this."

"What did you expect?" Grace asked curiously.

"Your support. Or was that too much to ask?"

"I won't be the one to sell you out," Grace sighed. "At least I promise you that—I have some pride. But this isn't something you can keep the wraps on indefinitely. Sooner or later, *everybody* will know. And when they do, I'm warning you, I'm not going to stand at your side like your supportive, smiling *appendage*."

"Then what will you do?"

"Do?" She raised her head from her hands and gave him a long, measured look. "I don't know. But to be honest, Craig, I don't hold out any great hopes for you and me."

CHAPTER THIRTY-FOUR

By nine P.M. Ben and Ellen were seated in their living room, in front of the TV awaiting the press conference, eyes fixed on the image of the massive granite exterior of the Old Executive Office Building next to the White House on 17th Street and Pennsylvania Avenue.

There were more than two miles of corridors inside that building, and more than five hundred rooms, several of which comprised the official quarters of the Vice President, with the offices of the OSO located conveniently down the corridor.

The cameras were rolling through the pillared entryway now, along the glorious Minton-tiled hallway, and up and around a curving staircase. They held briefly on the doorway into the auditorium: on the multiple rows of theater seating, entirely filled; on the stage banked with American flags; on the crystal chandeliers and the tall drapery-swagged windows, and, in a prominent niche, a marble bust of George Washington—the President, Ellen reflected, who never told a lie.

A sweeping pan of the auditorium showed the press lined up to either side, then the camera closed in on the audience, on Grace Fulton front and center, pale and composed in pearl gray;

Cynthia Satcher to Grace's right, her fall of blond hair contrasting dramatically with her severely cut black suit; an effervescent Brianna to Grace's left wearing a pink turtleneck sweater over a plaid skirt, then Frances Ewing in a heather tweed outfit that looked too warm for the room.

The Vice President appeared to much applause, accompanied by Carl Satcher and the British Prime Minister. All three men wore dark suits and had every hair in place, but to Ellen it seemed that Fulton's smile was strained, and she noted deeper-than-usual grooves running from nostril to chin. She decided that nobody would now describe him as boyish, and that it was Carl Satcher who appeared the man of the hour.

The Vice President's voice, however, was strong and confident as usual.

"Yesterday could have been one of the darkest in this nation's history," he declared, "a day of horror and tragedy. We could have lost our President and our First Lady, the Prime Minister of our close ally Great Britain, our next Homeland Security Secretary, Carl Satcher, and their wives. My wife and I"—the cameras instantly fixed on Grace's weary, unsmiling face—"would also have been included among the victims. In one fiery moment we would all, including the entire personnel at Camp David, have been annihilated."

Unconfirmed stories of a foiled terrorist attack had been running widely in the media since early that morning. Craig Fulton now told the world of the escape from Camp David during the blizzard. He embellished the dramatic details, and modestly but clearly emphasized his role in averting disaster.

"By the grace of God, and through the use of the surveillance protocols I established, and which remain in place, this conspiracy was intercepted, and the diabolical attack against this country's leadership and our British allies safely averted.

"The terrorists have all now been apprehended, and those involved will be swiftly brought to justice. . . ."

Ellen wished she could tell the committee and her staff, particularly David, the facts behind the story, but that must wait until tomorrow, as she and Brewer had decided. There could be no inadvertent leak—no wrong response or expression, attention called, question asked, or inference drawn. Sharpe would never show up if there was any public hint of what was coming at the hearing.

David called minutes after the press conference ended, as Ellen had guessed he would. "This seriously changes the complexion of tomorrow's hearing, " he said bluntly. "Satcher and Fulton could have been killed in the line of duty. It's going to be tough now to get folks to think of those two as anything but heroes."

We'll see, Ellen thought.

★ ★ ★

Late that night, the Vice President entered the bedroom to find his wife packing a suitcase.

"What's going on?" he asked. "What do you think you're doing?"

Grace Fulton replied, very calmly, that she planned to leave for California first thing in the morning, with Brianna, and that they would not be watching Carl Satcher's hearing tomorrow.

"I ordered the car for seven-thirty," she said.

Perplexed, Craig Fulton stared at her. "But you can't do that."

"Certainly I can."

"And what do you mean, you're taking Brianna? We're watching the hearing together. It'll be a great experience for her, seeing Carl confirmed."

"No," Grace said.

"What's come over you?" Fulton demanded.

"Nothing," Grace said. "Except that I've had time to think."

"But Brianna—"

"I want to get her away from here." Grace's voice hardened. "Don't you understand anything, Craig? I'm *ashamed*."

Fulton stared at her and then, defeated, sat down heavily on the bed.

★ ★ ★

Ben switched off the light just before midnight. "Are you ready for tomorrow?" he asked Ellen in the darkness.

"I am," she said. "Thanks to what you made happen."

"It was the judge who convinced our friend to cooperate," Ben said. "I just backed him up. My only real achievement was in getting through to Brewer and arranging the meeting."

"That was some achievement," Ellen said.

Ben said with satisfaction, "I might be out of office, but my connections are still solid—at least for now."

"And thank goodness," Ellen said. "His testimony, together with the tapes, will be just like the tapes at the Watergate hearings—explosive."

"No qualms about facing down Carl Satcher?" Ben asked.

"None. There's nothing personal about this, not on my side. Not anymore."

"No," Ben agreed. "You're past all that. And I'll be rooting you on every step of the way!"

"Not too loudly, I hope," Ellen said just as her cell phone chimed from the night table. "Damn!"

"I hope this won't go on all night," Ben said. "You need your sleep. Can't you switch it off?"

"Better not." Ellen reached for the phone. "Yes," she said, flipping it open. "Of course I want to know. . . ."

She struggled onto her elbow and switched on the light. "Keep me posted," she said, staring at Ben with stricken eyes. "No, it doesn't matter. Any time."

She clicked the phone shut. "That was Director Brewer. Alan Sharpe's missing. He was supposed to call in every three hours, but he's missed two check-ins. We might have lost him."

She added with despair, "I was afraid this would happen."

CHAPTER THIRTY-FIVE

Monday

JANUARY 8

Virgin Atlantic flight 404 from Heathrow, London, landed at Dulles Airport at 9:17 A.M., fifteen minutes early, and approached the terminal.

At the same time, Virgin America flight 12, running fifteen minutes late, pushed back from the gate and trundled along the taxiway to the takeoff apron to begin its flight to San Francisco. For a moment the two aircraft were within a hundred yards of each other.

"I don't understand you, Mom!" Brianna Fulton cried yet again in frustration. "For years and years you keep on at me like I'm a horrible daughter with all the mean things I'd say about Dad—how he was a fascist and how I was ashamed of him—but now he's done something great and saved all those people and I'm realizing maybe I made a mistake and want to sit with him to watch Uncle Carl's hearings, and you're taking me away. I don't want to go. You're spoiling it all. I *hate* you!"

Brianna had fought and argued far into the night and begun again at five A.M. She wouldn't be here now if, in the end, Craig hadn't told her, sounding sad and weary, "Bry, darling, do as your mother says."

"No! Why should I?"

"Because I'm asking you."

Brianna had gazed from one parent to the other. "What's going on? What's happened? *Are you two getting a divorce?"*

"Absolutely not!" her father had said.

"Are you *sure?* You never tell me anything!" Brianna said.

"Your mother and I will never divorce. I promise you." He looked at Grace, who said nothing.

Brianna wasn't sure whether she would trust either parent to tell her the truth ever again.

She had felt confused and miserable. She'd been close to tears, hugging her father good-bye. She thought he might have cried a little, too—she could feel his body trembling somewhere deep inside as he held it all in. Then the Secret Service man was loading the hastily packed luggage into the trunk, she and Mom were climbing into the car, and he was still standing in the doorway, sad and lonely, one hand raised.

She'd looked back as they drove away, and he was still there.

Then they were at Dulles and delivered to the VIP lounge, brought cups of coffee, orange juice, pastries, and newspapers, and finally escorted into the first-class cabin to be pampered across the country by the flight attendants. Brianna slumped into her seat beside the window, fastened her seat belt with a defiant snap, swiped the tired, angry tears with the back of her hand, and turned her face away.

"I'll explain everything later," Grace said.

"It won't make any difference," Brianna muttered mutinously. "I'll still hate you."

★ ★ ★

While their flight took off into the blazingly beautiful blue sky, Flight 404 pulled up to the terminal and the jetway reached out toward the cabin door. Salima Aboud, tired-eyed and anxious, clutched the long black wool coat which she hadn't worn since her London School of Economics days across her blue-and-purple sari. Climbing to her feet, she gazed impatiently at the long line of passengers ahead of her waiting to disembark after the long journey. She wondered how soon she could see Derelle and how she was recovering. She also wondered about Ben Lind, Senator Fischer's husband, the man Derelle didn't like but who had arranged this trip. Salima had never been to the United States before and she wasn't sure what to expect, but she felt ready for anything.

★ ★ ★

In the Senate dining room, pausing beside the corner table where Ellen, Ben, and David were catching a hurried breakfast of coffee and toast, Tom Treadwell asked Ellen, "Do you still think you have a chance of making a case against Satcher, given his latest heroics?"

"I'll give it my best shot," Ellen said with a determined smile, trying to sound more confident than she felt. God, how they needed Sharpe. Without Sharpe, the outcome was far from certain. Where was he? Postponing the hearing was not an option, in light of recent events and the focus on national security.

"We're counting on you," Treadwell told her.

"Mr. Leader," Ellen said, "something big is happening. You're just going to have to trust me."

"I do—and I know you won't let me down." Then the Iowan asked, "How's Derelle Simba? I hope she received our flowers."

"They're beautiful," said Ellen, who could not have told which, among the many floral offerings, had been sent by the Senate Majority Leader.

"That was a terrible thing, what happened to her." And, lowering his voice: "I'm glad you chose not to take my advice about dismissing her."

"I didn't think you'd really want me to do that," Ellen said, her voice equally soft.

"There are many ways to test toughness," he said. "I surely know what you're made of."

★ ★ ★

In a jacket the color of autumn leaves, Ellen strode through the gauntlet of flashbulbs, passed the Calder sculpture without even noticing it, and rode the elevator up one floor, carrying herself straight as a soldier and radiating a confidence she didn't feel.

Then she was inside the hearing room, taking her chair in the center of the raised, U-shaped table, offering a courteous good-morning greeting to Senator Kenneth Stearns, Democrat of Michigan, seated to her left, and to Senator Samuel Latham, ranking Republican from Texas, on her right.

While the remainder of the committee entered and seated themselves according to seniority, Ellen's eyes scanned the huge room, where more than three hundred people shifted and murmured in their seats. The TV reporters occupied risers on each side, the print reporters, at least fifty of them, sat with their laptops at two rectangular tables out front, and the photographers clustered in front of the committee table, their camera flashes a constant barrage—like the Fourth of July, thought Ellen.

Just minutes to go.

Let Alan Sharpe have thought it over, she prayed. Let him walk in at any minute. Let him *not* have gone back to Satcher, believing that that man would be able to fix things for him.

Douglas Brewer approached her and leaned across the table. "The fault is mine," he said quietly, "and I'm deeply sorry. We'll have to go with what we have and hope for the best."

At the center of the thirty-foot-long witness table sat Carl Satcher, immaculate in navy pin-striped worsted and gray silk tie, his thick white hair brushed tidily back behind his ears. He watched Ellen with an expression of sardonic amusement. *No, little girl,* that expression seemed to be saying, *your best will certainly not be good enough. Not now!*

And then it was time.

Ellen banged her gavel, giving no hint of the turmoil inside her. "The subcommittee will come to order," she declared to the newly silent room. "We are here today for the confirmation hearing of Carl Alexander Satcher for the position of Secretary of the

Department of Homeland Security," and she launched into her opening remarks while the cameras rolled.

"This position requires a person of the utmost integrity," Ellen continued. "It requires a person of the utmost intelligence. It requires a person who not only loves this country more than he loves himself, but also someone who loves the Constitution and realizes that if we lose the rights that make America a shining example of freedom, then we have lost everything."

She watched Satcher fold his arms across his chest and give a small, supercilious smile.

"I have no more to say at this point in the proceedings," Ellen concluded. "I will turn to our ranking member, Senator Latham of Texas, for his remarks."

Latham, a Satcher clone in build, manner, mane of white hair, and ice-blue eyes, pulled his microphone closer and softly cleared his throat. He offered a warm smile to his friend at the witness table and spoke out with robust sincerity:

"I'm happy to say that Mr. Satcher and I have been acquainted for a long time and have been colleagues in the Senate, too," Latham boomed. "Although, I grant you, Carl Satcher lacks a background in law enforcement, in my view there's no one more qualified to hold the post of Secretary of Homeland Security. He has served as a U.S. Senator for the state of California and knows his way around Washington. He's closely acquainted with state governors and big-city mayors. His major business and management experience will serve him well when he heads a large government department with global outreach and thousands of employees. It's my personal feeling that Carl Satcher will do an excellent job, bring in the right people to move the department forward, and in these times of crisis, he is definitely the right person to win the war on terror. He's not merely a patriot but a tough man for tough times . . ."

Senator Latham rumbled through a few more fulsome remarks before lapsing to silence, his job well done.

"Thank you, Senator," Ellen said.

She glanced at Senator Stearns, who, in the past few days, had acquired new and noticeable luster as well as a better-fitting wardrobe. With an expression of complacence Stearns was gathering himself to address the subcommittee.

But he would not be given the opportunity.

"At this time, I am digressing from the usual form of these hearings," Ellen said, "to accommodate a special witness, Mr. Douglas Brewer, Director of the Federal Bureau of Investigation. Accordingly, I shall ask members of the committee to yield their time."

Senator Stearns instantly objected. "Madam Chairman, this is highly unusual!"

"I agree," Ellen said, "but these are unusual times."

A buzz of conjecture filled the room and Ellen banged her gavel once again for silence. "If the committee would like to take a vote on this request, I will accommodate that, but"—in a voice that brooked no refusal—This request is not made lightly.

This was the moment she had been eagerly anticipating before that late-night phone call, and which now she dreaded.

For one long moment an electric silence hung in the air. Ellen waited to be challenged; she was not.

"Director Brewer," she said evenly, "I would like to swear you in at this time. Do you swear to tell the truth, the whole truth, and nothing but the truth?"

★ ★ ★

In the hospital, Derelle watched the hearings on the small TV set suspended in the corner of her room. She wished she could be there with Ellen, to help and offer her support. Now that she was getting stronger, she felt lonely and was frustrated to be out of the loop.

There was Ellen, gesturing with her hands as she spoke. There was Mr. Lind, seated in the front row of the audience, Director Brewer at the witness table, and that evil man Carl Satcher at another table.

Derelle rubbed the turquoise pendant between her hands in case it could impart warrior vibrations by remote control. She wanted to get up, to move, to leave. "You're too impatient," the nurses had said earlier, "but that's good, it means you're getting well. Just give your body a chance to heal. You'll be out of here soon!"

Derelle thought how it couldn't be soon enough. But where was Salima? Mr. Lind—Ben—had said she was on her way. When would she get here? Her body ached with the whole new pain of longing.

Director Brewer was speaking now, his face a granite mask. "Madame Chairman, ladies, gentlemen, I have to inform you that I appear here to testify with the greatest reluctance. I am compelled to report on a chain of events that pertain to the confirmation of Mr. Carl Satcher. Five days ago—"

But his words were lost in the sudden activity outside her door, a familiar voice, and someone else—a nurse—saying, "In here ... she's looking so much better!" Then the door was opening and there she was, Salima, carrying flowers and a suitcase, looking exhausted and strange in her dark coat with the bright, gauzy sari showing beneath, but so beautiful.

"Oh my goodness, my dear, just look at you!" Salima was saying in that lovely lilting accent. "I'm so very sorry! But we'll get you well in no time at all!"

It was a reunion that Derelle had dreamed of for so long, and had never really believed would happen. Now, through a miracle wrought by Ben, here was Salima, come to her from halfway across the world.

Derelle couldn't remember crying since she was a very small child, but for one of the few times in her life, her eyes filled with weak tears. Wordlessly, she reached out the hand that didn't have all the needles and tubes in it. Salima dropped her bag and tossed the flowers onto the foot of the bed. She clasped Derelle's hand and kissed it, then gently touched her face.

The door closed softly behind the nurse. Neither Derelle nor Salima noticed her leave, nor did they notice that the TV was on and that the FBI Director was still speaking.

★ ★ ★

In his office at the Vice President's residence, Craig Fulton sat alone watching his flat-screen TV as Douglas Brewer addressed the committee: ". . . Vice President Craig Fulton approached me directly, requesting a list of individuals with suspected terrorist ties in the Washington, D.C., area."

Senator Fischer asked, "Director Brewer, can you describe what terrorist action the Vice President imagined might take place?"

"He did not say."

"Did you have any knowledge of an attack or believe there was any indication that an attack was imminent?"

"Not insofar as there had been any reports or increase in chatter or suspicious activity. However, when the Vice President voiced his concern, I carried out his instructions."

"Did you subsequently receive information from any other source regarding a possible attack?" Fischer asked.

"I did," Brewer replied. "I received a telephone call last Friday morning from an individual who has carried out surveillance work for the Office of Strategic Operations in the past, and who is recognized as a reliable source of information."

"And on the basis of this information, what did you do?"

"Under the authority of OSO, I authorized that certain areas of Camp David, with the exception of the quarters of the President and the Prime Minister, be immediately wired for sound recording."

There was a collective gasp, then a moment of dead silence in the hearing room, which gave way to the intensified soft clatter of laptop keyboards.

"Was anybody else aware of this surveillance?" Fischer asked.

"The agents of the Bureau who installed the devices and the Marines who run and operate Camp David."

"And can you describe the results of this surveillance?"

Brewer replied, "Recordings, which include a series of conversations between Vice President Fulton and Mr. and Mrs. Carl Satcher."

"Do any of these conversations relate specifically to the matters pending before this committee?"

"Several, Madame Chairman."

"Do you have the original recordings in your possession, and do you have transcripts that can be made available to the members of the committee?"

"I do."

"Please hand those transcripts to the clerk, who will distribute them."

The Vice President grasped the armrests of his winged chair. What was going on here? What did Brewer think he was doing, and saying? How could he *dare* . . .

Fulton felt the walls of his cozy office recede around him until the room seemed huge and dim as an aircraft hangar. He was aware of the motes of dust hanging in a sudden intrusive ray of cold sunlight. The spaces inside his head grew hazy and airy, the sounds around him diminished, and his insides gave a sickening lurch. He sank back into his chair, gripping the arms for support, wondering for one terrifying moment whether he was having a heart attack.

The clerk approached the FBI Director. Fulton watched with helpless dread. Then to his great relief Carl Satcher rose precipitately to his feet. *Thank God, Carl would take charge now, like he always did.*

"Madame Chairperson!" Satcher thundered. "I must object both to this procedure and to the introduction of any recordings made in the privacy of the Presidential retreat."

The room erupted in conversation and Senator Fischer pounded the gavel with increasing force.

"Mr. Satcher, you are out of order!" she said. "While the committee has before it the matter of your confirmation, you are not running this meeting. I must ask you to kindly take your seat and let the committee proceed."

Satcher did not sit down. "Illegally recorded conversations pertaining to national security cannot be considered by this committee! I demand a recess to allow my legal counsel to be heard on this point."

"I must ask you again to sit down, or I must call on the guard!"

Fischer said. To Fulton's dismay, Satcher sat, glaring and slightly purple, his arms crossed belligerently across his chest.

The hearing continued.

"Director Brewer," Fischer asked, "can you explain to the committee the legal basis for the recordings?"

"I can." Brewer looked calmly into the eyes of each committee member as he explained that the Patriot Act did indeed allow warrantless surveillance in connection with suspected terrorist activity, and since the Vice President had made a public statement concerning this particular incident, the recordings could also legally be made public.

Fulton sank his head into his hands and closed his eyes.

★ ★ ★

Ben, seated in the audience, felt a lawyer's frustration that Brewer would not now be able to go all the way and introduce Sharpe's testimony. All the pieces of the puzzle would have then fit together so neatly and damningly, and the country would know, without a doubt, how Fulton and Satcher had conspired to mislead the American people.

Without Sharpe, Ben feared that the recorded Camp David conversations, suggestive though they might be, would not conclusively prove the deception, and that Satcher, Fulton, and their lawyers would have some wiggle room.

He watched despondently as Ellen turned to Brewer.

"I see you've brought a portable sound system for playing the surveillance recordings of the conversation between Mr. Satcher and the Vice President at Camp David," she said. "Will you please tell the committee when and where each conversation takes place."

As the room fell into another deep hush, Brewer complied. "The tape of the following conversation was made on Saturday, January 5, at six fifty-five P.M. in the great room at Camp David, Maryland," he said. "The exchange is between Carl Satcher and Vice President Craig Fulton."

The click of the Play button was clearly audible.

FULTON: You're certain your man understands what he's supposed to do? Timing is critical here.

SATCHER: It will be fine, not to worry. He's reliable.

FULTON: And he's calling my cell?

SATCHER: Toward the end of the movie. All you have to do is make sure you leave the damn thing on.

FULTON: This is when I wish I still drank martinis.

From his seat in the hearing room, Carl Satcher called out angrily, "This is an inconsequential personal conversation and I have to object once again to——"

Senator Stearns spoke up: "Madame Chair, I must agree with Mr. Satcher that——"

Senator Latham, ranking Republican, cried, "This charade has gone on long enough, Madame Chairman, and I must request that we clear the hearing room while the committee decides in closed session how to proceed."

During the commotion, because their attention was riveted on the witness table, few saw the doors open and two uniformed members of the Capitol Police escort a small, disheveled man into the hearing room. Having been deposited at the witness table in the empty seat beside Director Brewer, he glanced apprehensively about the room before lowering his head, removing a ballpoint pen from his pocket, and restlessly twirling it between his fingers.

Ellen recognized him from Ben's description.

When the room had finally quieted once more, Ellen calmly said, "Good morning, Mr. Sharpe. I'm glad you were able to be here, and I think we can now conclude this matter without further ado."

CHAPTER THIRTY-SIX

Ben Lind sat in his living room at six P.M. that evening watching CNN with irresistible but appalled fascination as, outside the Vice President's residence, the Navy struggled to keep the mob of reporters under control.

He wondered if Craig Fulton was watching from inside the house, and how he was feeling right now. How high he had soared, Ben thought, and how disgraceful this final plummet to earth.

The broadcast returned to a press conference, where the FBI Director was again explaining the legality of the Camp David surveillance and providing details of the role Alan Sharpe had played in the disclosure of Congressman Lind's blind trust, the false accusation against Senator Fischer's Chief of Staff, and the phony terrorist threat.

"The amendments to the Patriot Act specify that false reporting of terrorist activity, or the spreading of knowingly false information regarding such activity, is a felony," Brewer declared. "The Justice Department has granted immunity to Mr. Sharpe in exchange for his complete cooperation, although other persons—"

The phone rang. Ben startled, then reached for the receiver.

James was calling from the car. The Senator was on her way up.

Ben hurried to the front door to let Ellen in while behind him on the TV screen Brewer was saying that the investigation into the alleged terrorist attack was continuing but that the President was not a target and there was no indication that he had been involved.

Ellen emerged from the elevator, exhausted but smiling. "I don't need a day like that any time soon," she said. "Or another night like last night!"

As she sank gratefully into the sofa, Alan Sharpe's face filled the screen, his eyes blinking into the lights as he related how he had always been a patriot, how much he loved and tried to help his country, how badly he'd been led astray, and how grateful he was for a second chance.

"The little weasel," Ellen said. "How could he pull a disappearing act on us like that!"

"He probably didn't trust Brewer, or anybody else, and we totally underestimated his fear of Satcher. He must have convinced himself Satcher could trace his calls if he kept phoning in."

"I heard he was playing tourist," Ellen said, "wandering around the city." Ferociously, she added, "I could have throttled him for what he put us through!"

"Your restraint was admirable," Ben said, smiling. "Actually, Sharpe was doing a clever thing, hiding in plain sight. Can you imagine, he had never been to Washington, D.C., before? After the snow stopped, he had a wonderful time riding around in tour buses. He visited the Smithsonian and all the monuments. If he wasn't a real patriot before, he certainly is now. He admits he cried at Lincoln's feet!"

"*Mr. Sharpe Goes to Washington,*" Ellen said. "Though he's definitely no Jimmy Stewart!"

"He refused to ride in taxis in case Satcher tracked him down through the cab company dispatchers. He was late this morning because he got lost in the Metro."

On TV the commentators were discussing the current national turbulence, the vacuum at the head of Homeland Security, and who, in light of Craig Fulton's inevitable resignation, would be named Vice President.

"What happens to Carl Satcher?" Ellen asked Ben. "And to his wife."

"There'll be an investigation," Ben said. "Satcher will fling his best legal brains into the mix, who'll make sure it lasts a long time and the public gets thoroughly bored. Any future political career is, of course, out of the question for him, but I'd guess he'll continue as a behind-the-scenes power broker. At the very least he can go on breeding racehorses."

"And Craig Fulton?"

"*His* career's over, that's for damn sure—and no fallback position with horses."

"I feel almost sorry for Fulton," Ellen said. "He really believes in this country."

"But he undermined the country he believes in," Ben said.

Ellen recalled the Senate Majority Leader voicing the same opinion.

"Fulton deserves all he gets, and we're well rid of him," Ben said.

"He was capable of great things," Ellen said. "I can still see the good in him, even after all this. Now, Satcher—"

"Now let's think about dinner instead. I've ordered in from Hunan Dynasty," Ben said. "All your favorite MSG products are waiting for you on the kitchen counter."

"That sounds wonderful!" Ellen said. "I haven't eaten since breakfast."

"Did you get a chance to see Derelle today?" Ben asked.

"I did!" Ellen smiled with pleasure. "I stopped at the hospital on the way home. Her tubes are out now and she's so happy. She can't talk properly yet, but at least she can whisper. She's doing really well, expects to go home in a day or two, and she looks radiant, especially now that Salima's there. And, of course, she's delighted for us. She—" Ellen broke off abruptly and stared at the TV. *"Ben!* They're talking about you now! *Turn up the sound!"*

And to his astonishment Ben looked into his own face, vibrant with satisfaction, superbly confident, as he left the Hart Building earlier in the day. And below his picture, two words:

POSSIBLE VEEP?

"My God," Ellen exclaimed.

Ben's face was replaced by pundits seated around a table in the studio, two men and two women.

"Some observers are suggesting," said the representative of *The New York Times,* "that given his contribution in exposing the false terrorist conspiracy and his ability to get along with both Republicans and Democrats, former Congressman Ben Lind may be a good choice as Vice President for the remainder of the current term."

"Ben!" Ellen whispered. "Did you have *any* idea?"

Ben mutely shook his head.

"A distinct possibility," agreed an editor from the *Washington Post.* "The President will want to get as far away from his disgraced Vice President as possible, and who better than Benjamin Lind, a liberal Republican who was run out of Congress by a challenge from the far right. The selection of Lind would be seen not only as a healing gesture, but also a message that the Republican Party is done with the manipulations and politics of fear that they unleashed on this country, and recently—and personally—upon Congressman Lind and his wife, Senator Ellen Fischer."

"The President could go even further and pick a Democrat, even Senator Fischer," suggested the reporter from the *Los Angeles Times.* "She took control of an explosive situation with commendable ability."

Ben and Ellen exchanged glances.

"You'd make a great Vice President," Ben said.

Ellen looked at him with mock anger. "If you really love me, you'll never say that again," she said just as every phone in the apartment began to ring.

ACKNOWLEDGEMENTS

Many thanks to my partner, Mary-Rose Hayes, who is a wonderful writer and the best of collaborators. Our characters take on a life of their own in both our minds, which is definitely something that has been a bonding experience.

Both of us feel strongly that our story editor, Jay Schaefer, was invaluable in keeping us on course. Also, without our agent, Fred Hill, we wouldn't have had the drive to write this second book together.

Finally, I would like to thank the people of California who have given me the opportunity to serve them these many years in work that I love so much and that hasn't dimmed my imagination one bit.